Dear Reader,

The Ark of Crystals is rea[...] nation has such an ark. C[...] ceremonial objects for ea[...] comprise this nation.

The three crystal clan totems in my story are fiction. To divulge the true contents wouldn't be honoring the Eastern Cherokee nation. Secret is sacred. Sacred is secret.

While the Eastern Cherokee nation does have a Paint Clan, to my knowledge, a quartz-crystal mask roughly the size of a woman's hand does not exist. I created this mask to symbolize the power of this particular clan.

The seven-pointed star is, again, a figment of my imagination. The seven points on the star represent the seven clans of the Eastern Cherokee nation and, more importantly, the Pleiades, which is the seven-starred constellation you can see in our winter skies.

The Wolf's Head crystal, also fictional, symbolizes the Wolf Clan of the Eastern Cherokee nation. It is from this clan that leaders, both men and women chiefs and counselors, originate and are molded. Without good leaders, a nation becomes disorganized and confused.

Without the return of these three crystal totems, there is loss, disharmony and imbalance on the reservation, which people feel keenly. With their return come healing, abundance and balance.

Enjoy!

Lindsay McKenna

Dear Reader,

Welcome to Silhouette Bombshell, the hottest new line to hit the bookshelves this summer. Who is the Silhouette Bombshell woman? She's the bombshell of the new millennium; she's savvy, sexy and strong. She's just as comfortable in a cocktail dress as she is brandishing blue steel! Now she's being featured in the four thrilling reads we'll be bringing you each month.

What can you expect in a Silhouette Bombshell novel? A high-stakes situation in which the heroine saves the day. She's the kind of woman who always gets her man—and we're not just talking about the bad guy. Take a look at this month's lineup....

From *USA TODAY* bestselling author Lindsay McKenna, we have *Daughter of Destiny,* an action-packed adventure featuring a Native American military pilot on a quest to find the lost ark of her people. Her partner on this dangerous trek? The one man she never thought she'd see again, much less risk her life with!

This month also kicks off ATHENA FORCE, a brand-new twelve-book continuity series featuring friends bonded during their elite training and reunited when one of them is murdered. In *Proof,* by award-winning author Justine Davis, you'll meet a forensic investigator on a mission, and the sexy stranger who may have deadly intentions toward her.

Veteran author Carla Cassidy brings us a babe with an attitude—and a sense of humor. Everyone wants to *Get Blondie* in this story of a smart-mouthed cop and the man she just can't say no to when it comes to dealing out justice.

Finally, be the first to read hot new novelist Judith Leon's *Code Name: Dove,* featuring Nova Blair, the CIA's secret weapon. Nova's mission this time? Seduction.

We hope you enjoy this killer lineup!

Sincerely,

Natashya Wilson
Associate Senior Editor, Silhouette Bombshell

Please address questions and book requests to:
Silhouette Reader Service
U.S.: 3010 Walden Ave., P.O. Box 1325, Buffalo, NY 14269
Canadian: P.O. Box 609, Fort Erie, Ont. L2A 5X3

LINDSAY McKENNA

DAUGHTER OF DESTINY

Silhouette®

BOMBSHELL™

Published by Silhouette Books

America's Publisher of Contemporary Romance

If you purchased this book without a cover you should be aware
that this book is stolen property. It was reported as "unsold and
destroyed" to the publisher, and neither the author nor the
publisher has received any payment for this "stripped book."

 SILHOUETTE BOOKS

ISBN 0-373-51315-1

DAUGHTER OF DESTINY

Copyright © 2004 by Lindsay McKenna

All rights reserved. Except for use in any review, the reproduction
or utilization of this work in whole or in part in any form by any
electronic, mechanical or other means, now known or hereafter
invented, including xerography, photocopying and recording, or in
any information storage or retrieval system, is forbidden without
the written permission of the editorial office, Silhouette Books,
233 Broadway, New York, NY 10279 U.S.A.

All characters in this book have no existence outside the imagination of
the author and have no relation whatsoever to anyone bearing the same
name or names. They are not even distantly inspired by any individual
known or unknown to the author, and all incidents are pure invention.

This edition published by arrangement with Harlequin Books S.A.

® and TM are trademarks of Harlequin Books S.A., used under license.
Trademarks indicated with ® are registered in the United States Patent
and Trademark Office, the Canadian Trade Marks Office and in other
countries.

Visit Silhouette Books at www.eHarlequin.com

Printed in U.S.A.

LINDSAY McKENNA

served in the U.S. Navy as an aerographer's mate 3rd class, a weather forecaster. She's no stranger to flying and got her student pilot license at age seventeen! The military is in her family and in her blood. Her family has a U.S. Naval history, and she was proud to serve her country. She has ridden in a T-38 "chase plane" during an actual test flight at Edwards Air Force Base and flown in a B-52 on a day and night mission. She goes where the action is to get the sights, sounds and experiences to put into her books. Known as "The Top Gun of Military Romance," Lindsay created the first military romance in 1983 as a Silhouette Special Edition title. She's pioneered the field in many ways and continues to be a leader, just like her heroines.

To the one and only Lynda Curnyn, editor and now writer. Friend from beginning to end. She started this new line and I was thrilled to be a part of it to support her dream. And what a great dream it is. Thank you, Lynda, for all your help, guidance, encouragement and belief in me as a writer. You are the GREATEST!

Chapter 1

The lurid, churning blackness swirled around Kai Alseoun. She moaned, turning over in the narrow bed and shoving the sheet off with her legs. *No. No...this can't be happening again!* Since receiving her bad conduct discharge from the U.S. Navy, she'd found her life tumbling like an out-of-control F-14 Tomcat. Not even sleep brought her peace; nightmares stalked her every time she closed her eyes.

Breathing hard, Kai twisted her head from side to side. It was October and she was staying in her grandmother's old log cabin in North Carolina. But not even her return to the reservation could protect her from the darkness that plagued her in earnest now. It called to her in a hissing voice. Fear vomited through her. Kai hadn't known fear until the last few months. When Lieutenant Commander Ryan Thorval had accused her of assaulting him and breaking his nose—trumped-up charges—her hotshot combat-aviator existence had come to a shocking halt.

The reason she'd broken his nose in the Ready Room aboard the carrier was because he'd groped her. Thorval had come up behind her and slid his hand across her hip, angling down toward the apex of her thighs. Without thinking, Kai, who was a former national kick-boxing champion of North America, had lifted her elbow and shoved it backward into his face, fracturing his nose. Unfortunately, there had been no witnesses to his assault, so Thorval had pressed charges against her for striking a superior officer. He was a lieutenant commander and she a lowly lieutenant, and Thorval had made the charges stick. The board had a tendency to believe the superior officer, and Kai was below him in rank. With shame, she had come back to where she'd been born—the Quallah Eastern Cherokee Reservation near Cherokee, North Carolina—to salve her wounds. Her grandmother, Ivy Sanderson, the Elder Medicine woman on the reservation, took her into her humble log cabin in the Great Smoky mountains to recover.

Kai came from an honored and respected medicine family, her mother once renown for her healing abilities. She desperately wanted to erase the humiliating black mark on her family's name.

She turned on her side, pressing her face into the old feather pillow. Days after her return to the res, Grams had sent her up the mountain to ask the Great Spirit what she should do with her life. And this…this nightmare had haunted her nightly since she'd come back down. For four days and nights she'd been without water and food while she prayed for a dream that would help her sort out her life. Well, the dream that had come to her up on the mountain was a nightmare, as far as Kai was concerned.

Moaning, Kai felt the roiling darkness begin to enfold

her. *No! Oh, no!* Perspiration soaked the hair at her temples. Sweat covered her face. She turned over again, fists clenching and unclenching. The storm clouds were palpable. Heart slamming into her ribs, she couldn't see her way out of the suffocating darkness. She felt fear so vivid that she could taste it like burning acid in her mouth. Never had she felt terror like this!

The sensation of being spun around, as if in a tornado, began. It always started this way. What to do? How to escape it? Kai heard the shrieking of the wind as it tugged violently at her body. She felt the howling gale grasp at her like greedy hands. Where was it taking her? Where?

Groaning, Kai pulled the pillow over her head and flopped onto her stomach. If only she could escape this dream! But she couldn't. Out of the thick, cloying darkness, she saw a white glow in the distance. And just as before, it came closer and closer, racing toward her at what seemed to be the speed of light. She saw three hand-carved crystal totems. One looked similar to a mask that she'd seen worn by Cherokee medicine people, members of the Paint Clan. The mask was transparent, with slits for eyes and shaped to cover the upper half of a person's face. A lightning bolt had been painstakingly carved diagonally across it. Another carved crystal formed the head of the wolf. Kai knew that this totem belonged to the Wolf Clan, where all leaders and chiefs came from. The last crystal that hovered before her, sparkling and nearly blinding with its light, was a seven-pointed star that represented the Yam Clan. That was the clan that cared for the sacred Ark of Crystals—seven quartz crystals that had been a part of the Cherokee nation since it had been cre-ated in millennia. The Yam Clan was responsible for the ark's protection.

In her dream the three objects, all transparent quartz crystals, turned slowly in front of her. Then she saw the first crystal, the Paint Clan mask, arc across Mother Earth and land in the center of Australia. The second crystal, the wolf's head, flew to South America. The last one, the seven-pointed crystal star, arced skyward and disappeared onto the island of Hong Kong.

A voice kept whispering, "Seek out and find the Paint Clan mask...." over and over again. She knew she had to find it and make it her own. But fear stopped her.

In the midst of her nightmare, Kai screamed out for her grandmother. Grams was the most revered medicine wom-an on the reservation. She was the one of the few people in Kai's life who had ever loved her and protected her. Now Kai cried out for her help.

The slowly moving thunderheads in her vision were like the wall of a hurricane moving threateningly toward her. Lightning forked between the gray and menacing clouds. The sound created by the huge Thunder Beings caromed against her, vibrating like the roll of kettle drums through every pore in her body until she felt as if she were going to shake apart and burst into a million pieces.

"Seek and find the Paint Clan mask...." Kai heard the soft voice whispering in her ear again.

Yes, grab it!

She reached out to the mask hovering over Australia. Her fingers stretched to touch the glowing crystal. Groaning, she strained forward, but no matter how she tried to capture it, the mask hovered in space, just inches away from her fingertips. *Impossible!* Frightened, Kai felt the energy of the crystal throbbing. It was as if a stone had been thrown in a clear, quiet pool of water, and she could feel each wave as it reached her, sharp and clear. She felt battered by the powerful energy.

Then the second crystal, the seven-pointed star, came out of the malevolent clouds and appeared to her once more. Again a voice whispered, "Send the snake woman after it. She will find it in Peru…." Moaning, Kai turned over on her back. Finally the third crystal, the wolf's head, reappeared. The whispering voice said, "Send the wild woman after it. She will find it on an island where the Yellow People live…." The clear quartz wolf shone with a blinding white-gold light as Kai watched it slowly rotate in front of her. Each of the crystals floated across the face of Mother Earth and disappeared as before. And then the real terror began.

Kai saw a monster with a man's face stalking Mother Earth. Men had made her life miserable of late and caused her such deep, wounding pain. But this face hovering before her scared the hell out of her. The man appeared to be in his eighties, balding on top with white hair encircling his skull and green eyes that were slitted like a cougar's on the hunt. He seemed to be heading purposefully toward her. Kai felt helpless, but she knew she must battle this man to help save those crystal totems. But how was she going to do that? She stood in the midst of the growling, rumbling storm without a weapon. Completely unarmed, Kai moved into one of her kick-boxing positions, her hands raised, feet spread for balance, her body poised to do battle with this powerful man.

The man's face was gruesome, his flesh sagging, his eyes like sockets in a skull. He smelled of death, a rotten scent that made her gag. He wanted *her* death. And he wanted the power of the three crystals she'd seen. Kai knew with certainty that he would kill her if she tried to take one of those crystal totems from him.

Her body damp with perspiration, Kai suddenly sat up, a scream on her lips. Shaking, she pulled her knees to her chest and buried her face in her hands. Breathing hard, she tried to reorient herself. The chill of the room felt good against her hot flesh.

I'm safe…I'm safe. I'm here in Grams's cabin…I'm okay. It's just a nightmare. Just a nightmare…

Kai sat there for a long time, trying to steady her wildly beating heart. She was still sweaty and hot. It was October in the Great Smoky Mountains and the small window in her bedroom was covered with a lacy coating of frost. Outside, she could hear the nearby stream's gurgle, which soothed her ragged state somewhat. Moonlight filtered through the frosty window and spread lacy patterns across the narrow pine bed where she slept.

Lifting her head, Kai ran her fingers through her straight hair, which shifted like a dark cloak about her shoulders and breasts. She wore a gray cotton T-shirt and gray sweatpants, her normal bed attire. They were soaked with sweat. Wrinkling her nose, she reached over and turned on the small lamp next to the bed. The light made her wince. Kai had to get up, take a shower and wash off the fear. Every night for the last week the nightmare had occurred. Grams had said that if Kai would act upon the vision the Great Spirit had given her, the nightmare would stop stalking her. She needed to take action. But what kind? She was used to the hard physical reality of combat jets and in-your-face danger, not the mystical world that Grams lived in. Still, Kai couldn't dismiss the ominous nightmare that returned to her now every time she tried to sleep.

Slowly getting up, her feet meeting the cool, smooth surface of the polished pine floor, Kai looked forlornly around the tiny room. The log cabin was over a hundred years old. Grams had been born here, and so had Kai's mother. And so had Kai. The cabin was filled with family memories. Shaking her head, she felt her life was like a tumbleweed in comparison to her family, all of whom had lived and died on the res.

Her mind gyrated back to solving her problem. Who could she go to for help with this vision that haunted her nightly? As she padded down the hall toward the bathroom, Kai remember a man who had come aboard their carrier one time, Major Mike Houston. He was retired from the U.S. Army, they'd said, but everyone called him Major Houston out of deference. He'd been with Perseus, a Q-Secret organization under the canopy of the CIA. That meant very few people in the government knew of Perseus. She remembered him because he was of South American Indian blood, and she'd boldly introduced herself to him in the squadron conference room after the mission debriefing and asked him what Indian nation he'd come from.

Kai would never forget the Special Force's A team officer smiling back at her. He'd told her he was a Quechua, from Peru, and that his ancestors had been shamans in the Inca Empire. His skin was not copper-colored like hers, and she'd found out that his father had been an Anglo from the USA, an officer in the Army. He'd followed in his father's footsteps by joining the military.

When Kai found out Houston had been called the Jaguar God down in Peru while on a mission there, she'd felt oddly safe with him. She knew part of the reason was because he was an Indian like herself, but that wasn't the only thing. Her medicine man father, a drunken alcoholic, had been Indian, too, and he certainly hadn't inspired any sense of security in Kai. No, there was something about Major Houston that had urged Kai to trust him.

Reaching the bathroom, Kai quietly shut the creaking door behind her. Then she turned on the shower faucets and adjusted the temperature of the water. Shedding her T-shirt and sweatpants, she dropped them on the floor and stepped into the shower stall. As the warm water hit her skin, she groaned in gratitude and closed her eyes. Lifting her face to the spray, she shut her eyes and allowed it to wash away the sweat clinging to her skin.

As she stood there, Kai remembered Mike Houston handing her a business card and saying, "If you ever decide to stop flying F-14s around the sky and raising hell with the Iraqis, come see me. Perseus is always looking for women warriors. We can put your talents and your intelligence to work, and help save this world of ours…."

She knew now that he might be able to help her with

her quest. As the warming water pummeled her flesh and cleansed the fear stench that surrounded her, Kai felt oddly better this time. There was an answer, a way out of this. Yes, she would pack what few clothes she had, mount her Harley Hawg and motorcycle across the U.S. to Mike's headquarters in Montana. At least it would be a nice, easy ride, especially in the fall weather. If Mike could help her follow up on her vision quest and end her nightmares, it would be worth the trip. Somehow, Kai knew that when she told Grams what she was going to do, the old medicine woman would smile and nod her head. Yes, it felt like the right thing to do....

After emerging from the shower and drying off, Kai changed into clean clothes. She put on a bright red, ribbed cotton turtleneck, black corduroy slacks and warm black socks. Pushing her feet into a pair of wool-lined slippers, she headed out to the kitchen. She hesitated at the door when she saw Grams sitting at the table, wearing a faded cotton print dress that fell to below her knees, and a warm pink wool shawl that she'd crocheted half a century before. She had on an old pair of black tennis shoes and purple socks. There were two cups of tea on the table and Grams was gazing at her with that wise look that made Kai certain everything was going to be all right once more.

"I heard you scream, child," Ivy murmured. She patted the wooden chair next to where she sat. "Come, sit. It's time to talk of this vision you saw up on the mountain, which stalks you nightly."

Relief poured through Kai. "Sounds good to me, Grams." She sat down and wrapped her fingers around the chipped white mug. The cabin was cool because it was heated only by a wood stove, the embers dying down throughout the night. Kai could hear the snap and crackle of new logs that Grams had placed in the living room stove. Already the chill was beginning to recede as she picked up a cup and sipped the honey-laced, white sage tea.

"Tell me what you see in your dream," Ivy urged.

Kai sat there and told her everything. She knew that a vision quest dream was more important than any other dream a Native American could have. It was a guide for that person, a way of showing her what needed to be done to make her life right. Shrugging wearily after she'd divulged the entire vision, Kai muttered, "I don't know *what* I'm seeing, Grams. What are these three pieces of carved crystal? Totems? Power objects?"

Ivy smiled briefly and sat up, resting her thick, callused elbows on the rough-hewn oak table. "Child, you turned away from becoming a medicine woman when you were very little. Originally, the firstborn child of a medicine family is trained, but you refused." She gave Kai a kindly look. "I understand why you didn't follow the path. Your own mother did and she spent her life being beaten by your drunken father. You saw medicine women as being helpless and passive. You also saw that being a medicine woman or man did not necessarily make you a better person. And by all rights, it should. To walk the path of a healer means learning about compassion and helping others." Nodding, she reached out and patted Kai's hand. "But the fact that you refused the path does not mean you were denied the vision quest for your people. What you saw in your dream has to do with something that happened here a little over a year ago. Something our nation is in mourning about."

Tilting her head, Kai studied Grams's hooded expression. She saw the way the tiny vertical wrinkles across her upper lip deepened with displeasure. "What are you talking about? Do the star, wolf's head and mask totems exist? Are they real?" Her heartbeat sped up a little. Kai had never gone on a vision quest before. Oh, she'd had ample opportunity, but she'd refused to join her people's spiritual path. She'd turned away from it entirely, so her knowledge of her heritage was sketchy.

"We have seven clans in the Eastern Cherokee nation," Grams told her quietly, turning the cup slowly around in her work-worn hands. "What you do not know is that in the Ark of Crystals, which is kept by the Yam Clan, is charged with keeping them safe. There are seven totems along with the seven single terminated quartz crystals. Each totem is a symbol for one clan. A year ago, three men broke into Elmer Black Raven's house. Elmer was the current caretaker of the ark. When he came home he discovered that three of the totems were stolen. One was the quartz crystal wolf's head, the symbol for our Wolf Clan. The second was the seven-pointed star, representing the Yam Clan. The third was the crystal mask, which belongs to the Paint Clan."

Kai sat up, her eyes widening with surprise. "Oh…"

"Yes, indeed. Oh." Grams shook her head. "When our people lost these three of our seven very sacred and powerful items, the clans were left without their totems." She opened her hands. "You were in the U.S. military, were trained in its beliefs. The loss of these three totems is akin to the United States having the original Declaration of Independence stolen by thieves, child."

"I see…." Kai murmured, beginning to understand.

"So the Great Spirit has come to you and is asking for your help. You've seen where all three of the stolen totems are presently located. This is great news for our nation. I will share it with the medicine society later today. Our people will be filled with hope. Since the theft of the crystals, we've been bleeding, spiritually speaking. These objects, which are thousands of years old, are sacred to us."

"I didn't realize all of this." How could she? Yes, she sent letters regularly to Grams, but her grandmother didn't write English too well and didn't own a telephone, so news from her was sparse.

Ivy studied Kai's shadowed face. "The Great Spirit is asking you to find the first totem, the one in Australia. You were also shown that two other women will retrieve the second and third ones for us. To find the crystals and return them to us will give our nation back its spiritual lifeblood. Without the totems, the three clans and the thousands of people who belong to them are suffering badly. It is a blow to our spirit, a terrible tragedy to our nation."

Clenching her hands in frustration, Kai muttered, "But *how* do I do this, Grams?"

"Follow your instincts, child. You come from a long line of medicine people. On both sides of your family. I know you don't like to acknowledge this, but it will take your inner knowing to find this first crystal, the Paint Clan mask totem."

"I refused training from Mom, Grams. You know that. I'm absolutely *worthless* when it comes to the metaphysical aspects of the medicine way."

"You refused training because you didn't want to be a passive victim like your mom. That is why you walked away from your legacy. Well, you must have faith that the Great Spirit will provide you help through others who will be drawn to assist you in your quest."

Kai stared at Grams doubtfully. "Listen, I left that stuff behind when I was nine years old, Grams—when my parents died. I never wanted to be like them. All I wanted to do was become a buzzard and fly on thermals in the air. I accomplished that when I became a fighter pilot." Her shame at being kicked out of the Navy washed over her once more. "I feel as if you're throwing me to the wolves, Grams. I don't know what I'm doing. This is like having my squadron leader tell me to get into a combat jet and go fly, when I haven't had flight training yet."

"I believe that part of your vision quest is about learning to have faith in our people and their ways, child. I also believe that you must learn to trust that inner voice of knowing." Ivy touched her heart with her hand. "We cannot live without our natural instincts. Everyone has an inner voice that counsels us, guides us and keeps us safe and out of harm's way." She smiled gently at Kai, who looked absolutely dismayed over where her life was suddenly going. "You mentioned that you already know a person who can help you. Why not go to see this man? Our people say that you must take the first step and go through the door of opportunity. Only then does the Great Spirit aid you."

Lifting her head, Kai thought about Mike Houston. Going to him felt like the right choice. Not only was he formerly military, he was Indian and would understand the nature of this quest. Giving Grams a warm look, Kai whispered, "Okay, I think I see what you mean. Maybe Mike Houston can give me the next bit of guidance I need to bring the Paint Clan mask back home to your people."

"*Our* people," Ivy whispered. "Stop separating yourself from us, Kai. You are a full-blood Eastern Cherokee. You can no more disavow what runs through your veins than Mother Sun could deny her light to Mother Earth and all her relations."

Shrugging restlessly, Kai sipped her tea. "I'll try, Grams. I promise I'll try…." But that was all she could promise. Kai had never gone out on a limb as she'd have to on this quest, had never trusted the teachings of the Cherokee people. The fact that she had to now scared her.

"Hey! You can't go in there! Wait! Stop!"

Kai paused before the door that said Mike Houston, Assistant Director. Then, easily avoiding the blond woman's grasping hand, she opened the door and stepped into the spacious office. Mike Houston sat behind a cherry-wood desk in the center, dressed in a blue polo shirt and tan trousers. He lifted his head, his dark brows bunched.

Mike watched as his assistant, Jenny Wright, tried to grab the arm of the tall woman who stood before him. His visitor was dressed in a black leather jacket studded with silver conches, the long, thick leather fringes on each arm swinging as she avoided his assistant's grasp. Jenny's efforts were useless. She was short in comparison to this woman, who stepped forward confidently, a black helmet with a white wolf's head painted on it beneath her arm. She moved with the grace of a jaguar, her long, firm legs encased in black leather pants studded with silver conches from hip to knee, and a pair of knee-high black leather boots. Her hair was the same color as the leather and swung freely around her shoulders, nearly touching her waist.

Mike rose. "Jenny? It's all right…." He held up his hand to the assistant he shared with his boss, Morgan Trayhern. He saw the frustration and fear in Jenny's wide eyes. She thought this unannounced stranger was here to do them harm. But as Mike glanced at the intruder once more, he recognized her as a U.S. Navy aviator he'd met a year ago.

Halting, Jenny sighed. "I'm sorry, Mike. This…this woman has no appointment scheduled with you. I thought she might be…well, you know—a terrorist…."

Kai swung gracefully toward the petulant blond woman in a gray pantsuit, whose balled fists were resting on her hips. Kai's lips barely twitched. "Trust me, if I was a terrorist, Ms. Wright, you wouldn't be standing here trying to stop me from getting into Major Houston's office."

Jenny looked at her challengingly. "You're right, but your manners need some polishing. Making an appointment would be a good start."

Kai's mouth curved a little more and she gazed back with respect. "You might be small, but you're mighty." She looked toward Mike Houston, who was standing there grinning at them. "I don't have an appointment because Major Houston gave me his business card and told me that if I ever wanted to see him, I could just show up on his doorstep. And I'm taking him at his word." Kai glanced into Houston's laughing eyes. "If that offer still stands Major Houston, you can get this blond guard dog off my six." That was a fighter jet term. The six was the rear of the plane where the pilot could not see the enemy coming up behind and had the advantage of surprise.

"I never break a promise. Welcome, Lieutenant Alseoun." Mike held out his hand to her. As he did, he lifted his gaze to his assistant. "She's right, Jenny. It's my fault." He saw her visibly relax.

Kai felt a tingle of relief as the major offered his large, square hand to her. The smile on his mouth had reached his eyes, and she knew his welcome was genuine. "Thanks, Major." She gripped his hand firmly in return.

"Take a seat, Lieutenant. Can Jenny get you coffee? Tea?"

Kai released his hand and looked toward the still frowning assistant. "No…thank you. I ate lunch in Phillipsburg just before I came over here. I'm fine."

"Jenny? Do me a favor? Call Miles Danforth and reschedule him for tomorrow? I'll need an hour here with Lieutenant Alseoun."

She raised her chin and nodded. "Of course, Mike."

"Thank you, Jenny.…"

Kai set her motorcycle helmet on a chair in front of the desk, then opened the snaps on her black leather jacket, took it off and hung it across the back. She tugged at the neck of the purple mock turtleneck she wore as she sat down in the next chair. Houston sat behind his desk once more.

"Thanks for seeing me," Kai told him.

"Not a problem. I remember you well."

"You remember what you told me?"

"Of course I do. I told you that Perseus, our company, is always looking for warrior women like yourself. We never get enough of them."

Feeling nervous, although she wasn't going to show it, Kai threaded her fingers through her hair, spreading it across her shoulders. "I'm not here to join Perseus, Major Houston. I'm here to ask for your help and support on something that has happened…. I have nowhere else to go, nowhere else to turn…." She frowned and bit her lower lip. Looking over at his square face, she saw his eyes flicker. Even though she had refused to become a medicine woman, the tradition in her family, Kai had strong intuition. She could feel Houston's interest. It was a good feeling, so she went on.

"First of all, you need to know some things about me. When you met me on the carrier a year ago, I was flying F-14s. I had the world by the tail. I was the only woman in my combat squadron. I'd flown in Afghanistan, and later, I patrolled the No Fly Zone over Iraq, where I downed two Iraqi MiGs."

"That's impressive. You have two kills to your credit." Mike leaned back in his chair.

"Yeah, well, it doesn't seem to mean much to the Navy," Kai told him, her voice husky with barely concealed anger. "I just received a bad conduct discharge three weeks ago, Major Houston. You need to know that."

Frowning, Mike sat up. "What?" He couldn't keep the disbelief out of his voice. Kai Alseoun was the first Native

American woman combat F-14 fighter pilot in the U.S. military. There had been a lot of press about that fact. His eyes narrowed as he studied her eyes. Despite her Native American parentage, Kai had eyes the spectacular blue of the glacial lakes in northern Alaska. It was the mysterious quality in them that had drawn him to her in their first meeting. They were large and intelligent-looking, with huge black pupils. What made them so arresting to Mike was that her irises were ringed in black, giving her the intense, focused look of an eagle. Kai Alseoun was a hunter of the first order. Mike had sensed that from the start with his own powerful intuition, just as he did now. She was a force to be reckoned with and not a person to mess with. He sat up. "A BCD? Impossible!"

"Yeah, you'd better believe it. A lieutenant commander in my squadron attacked me from behind in the Ready Room right after I got off a flight. I had just finished writing my report, when I stood up to leave. I didn't hear him come in. The next thing I knew, he was grabbing my ass and telling me in no uncertain terms just what he wanted to do with me."

Mike stared at her. Kai's eyes were slits of fury and her full mouth was pursed as she sat tensely in her chair. "You've got to be kidding me!" he exclaimed. This was one woman Mike would never tangle with. He had sensed the power of her Indian heritage swirling around her like a storm just waiting to break, though he also saw now she closeted that power, whether to protect herself or others, he wasn't sure. He had also been as keenly aware of her anger then as he was now. Mike had learned that she'd come from a long line of medicine people, and that explained the turbulent power that swirled around her. The anger he felt her carrying…well, he figured that had come from her past, from her childhood, but he didn't know her well enough to be sure.

"Lieutenant Commander Thorval paid for the attack," Kai told him. "My kick-boxing skills come in handy from time to time." She flexed her fingers. "I broke his nose."

"He's lucky you only did that."

"I was going to do more, but the commanding officer of our squadron appeared unexpectedly at the door. Thorval was screaming that I'd hit him for no reason at all, Major Houston. I had no witnesses who could tell the wing commander that Thorval was lying."

"My God," Mike breathed, "don't tell me…they court-martialed you?"

"That's exactly what they did," Kai told him grimly. "But that's not why I'm here, Major. I got busted out of the Navy and came home to where I was born—the Quallah Reservation in North Carolina. My Grams, Ivy Shining Star Sanderson, sent me out on a vision quest, to pray to the Great Spirit to give me new direction in my life. I wanted to save my honor. I wanted to salvage my family's name. Right now the gossip on the res is that I've given the entire nation a black eye. People don't understand what happened and they blame me. The newspapers painted me as an outcast. A rebel. Someone who would strike a superior officer…."

Shaking his head, Mike got up and came around his desk. He leaned against the front of it and faced Kai.

"You've come to the right place, Kai. Do you want to vin-
dicate your good name? We can help. We can start an in-
vestigation—"

"No," she whispered, "that's not why I'm here, Major.
I'm not here for me. I'm here as a representative of my nation, the Eastern Cherokee people…."

Chapter 2

Mike studied the determination in Kai's eyes. "What can I do to help?"

"Aboard the carrier I made a connection with you," she answered. "I believe you're someone I can trust and I need to talk with you." She looked around the office, which held a pair of crossed cavalry sabers on one wall, an American flag in the corner, with the flag of Montana nearby. One wall was devoted to photos of Mike Houston with various Peruvian Army personnel. There was no doubt he was a warrior of the first order. Clearing her throat, she said, "I don't know much about your people's culture down in Peru. Are you familiar with vision quests? With Native American protocols?"

Shrugging, Mike said, "We have similar things in our culture, beliefs and practices in common with our cousins to the north. Why?"

Kai sat back and held his gaze. "I need to share my vision quest dream with you. I know that's not normally done, but you have to hear it to understand why I'm here…." Taking a deep breath, Kai launched into the nightmare that had dogged her heels nightly since she'd come off that mountain in the Great Smokies. When she was done, she added, "Here's what you don't know, Major, and it's key to my dream. Cherokee storytellers say that our clans each have their own totem, hand-carved by a medicine person with prayer and ceremony, over a period of many years. To outsiders, these are nothing more than art objects." She shrugged. "But to us, they are alive, real, and exude an energy that helps the clan and, in turn, all the people of our nation. Without the three stolen totems, our people are suffering badly in a spiritual sense." She halted to see if he understood. His dark blue eyes were narrowed and thoughtful. Kai sensed he did.

"Among the Quechua, my people, we also have totems," Mike affirmed. "For example, I have a jaguar spirit guide." He smiled slightly as he fished a small black figure out of his pocket and showed it to her. It was a jaguar carved out of obsidian. "This is a fetish—an archetypal symbol of the energy of the animal, insect, bird, fish or whoever we work with, spiritwise."

"Yes, I'm familiar with them," Kai said. She knew better than to reach for it. One never touched a sacred item unless it was directly offered. To do so was to put one's energy upon it and alter it. That was taboo. She saw that the jaguar was beautifully carved from the shining black stone. Watching as Houston slid the object back into his left pocket, she murmured, "Fetishes are usually personal totems. The three clan totems of the seven we own are a hundred times more powerful and valuable, spiritually speaking, from what my grandmother told me."

Nodding, Mike said, "No question there. I understand your concern over them being stolen. A nation can disintegrate without sacred items such as these being kept where they belong. I know they need special care. I'm sure there is a moon ceremony for them each month to keep their power aligned with the clan."

Kai sighed, knitting her fingers in her lap and staring down at them. "That's correct, although Grams, who is one of the oldest and most revered medicine people on the res, didn't say much about them in that regard." Kai looked up at him. "As you know, that kind of information is kept secret and sacred as it's passed down from generation to generation. One family, and one member of that family at a time, is educated and charged with the care and protection of each clan totem. Only they know what must be done to look after them."

"I understand perfectly," Mike said. "Some things, especially totems that have come down through thousands of years in a clan's lineage, are very, very powerful and need special care, cleansing and honoring to maintain their energy."

"Major, finding the missing crystal totems and bringing them home to the Quallah Reservation will help to save my nation's honor and help my people find their balance and harmony again. Grams was telling me that since these totems have been stolen, some of the young people on the res have gotten into drugs. She believes that many of these young people are simply trying to get in touch with the Great Spirit. Before the totems were stolen, there were ceremonies in which they could have wonderful, heart-centered experiences that fed their spirit and gave them a sense of bonding and balance within the clan. Without the totems there are fewer ceremonies to attend, and they don't have the same impact. As a result, some of the young people have turned to drugs to try and find that same special feeling of oneness that you get from attending this very special ceremony."

"I grasp the importance of finding these treasures. And yes, a nation can be sent reeling without its totems being present."

"It appears I need to find the first totem, the crystal mask. The other two will be found by different women later."

"You sound hesitant about going after it."

Kai snorted. "I'm hardly a saint! I'm not even a medicine woman, which is what has me worried about this. My grandmother told me that even though I don't have metaphysical training, I have been chosen by the Great Spirit for this venture."

A slight smile tipped the corners of Houston's mouth. "We know that the Great Spirit moves in mysterious ways, Kai. And that none of us are perfect down here in human form. We all have our flaws." Smiling more widely, he added, "And if we weren't flawed, we wouldn't be in human form. It sounds to me like the Great Spirit is more than ready to work through you to find the first crystal totem for your clan. By getting it back, you will help restore balance among your people. A totem works similarly to the rudder on a ship, which holds the vessel on course.

Without its totem, the people of the clan are without direction. This mission is worthy of you."

Kai tilted her head and scanned Houston with her senses—an ability she had had since childhood. In the right conditions, Kai could send out energy like a radar signal. She would bounce it off the person in question and receive an accurate reading back on them, giving her an indication of their character and what they were thinking. Of course, she could only do it when she was relaxed. If she had honed the skill instead of turning her back on her Native heritage, she'd have known Commander Thorval was stalking her. Instead she had been completely blind, deaf and dumb to his intent toward her.

Now Kai was very sorry she hadn't accepted her spiritual training. Spreading her fingers, she admitted, "Major Houston, I have to tell you that I think they've got the wrong person for this task. I have absolutely no metaphysical training. I walked away from all of that when I was nine years old after…well, after my parents were killed. I was forced into an Anglo foster family shortly after that and I left the res. I wanted nothing to do with anyone except Grams. She eventually got the state of North Carolina to let me come live with her. But I was so angry—and still am—about my father, who was an alcoholic. He was driving drunk with my mother in the car and plowed into a tree, killing them both. I just haven't forgiven him. I doubt I ever will…."

Hearing the pain in her voice, Mike unfolded his hands and stood up. "I'm so sorry, Kai. I had no idea. That must have been a terrible loss to you, especially at such a young age."

Anguish filled Kai's heart. She could defend herself better than nearly anyone physically, but she had no defense against the pain she felt over her mother's loss. She had idolized Janet Alseoun and held close those cherished memories she had of her.

"Th-thanks, Major. I appreciate your words…."

"Call me Mike, Kai. You look like you really need a cup of coffee." He pointed to a sideboard behind his desk, where a coffeepot sat on a warmer.

Nodding, Kai smiled thinly and said, "Yeah, I think I'd like a cup of coffee now. Thanks…"

Mike ambled over and poured two cups. "Cream? Sugar?"

"Straight and black."

He smiled wryly. "Spoken like a true Navy aviator." He handed her one cup and then leaned against the desk again. She sipped the steaming coffee and he saw her tense features relax a little. "So, what you're wanting is monetary and logistical support from Perseus to locate these three crystal totems, right?" Perseus was the organization founded by Mike's boss, Morgan Trayhern. It was a covert team of military trained men and women who came to the aid of others when government intervention wasn't possible.

"Yes, exactly." Kai studied his dark features and saw him thinking as he sipped from his own mug. "I haven't a clue as to how the other two women are going to be found." She rubbed her wrinkled brow. "Maybe they'll appear to me in a vision later, after I find the first totem. I really don't know how this works…."

Mike smiled benignly. "In my experience, whoever is

supposed to go after it will get the message, just as you have. And come forward when called to do so. But let's not worry about that right now. Let's take this one step at a time, shall we? Let's get you on the trail of the Paint Clan crystal mask."

"I don't have any money. What little I'd saved went for a civilian attorney to defend me against the charges, but I lost the case…. Lost everything—my good name, my family's honor. I've shamed them—shamed my nation—and I can hardly live with it. All because of Thorval. Looking back on it, I think he was jealous of me. When I bagged those two MiGs, he went after me. He couldn't stand the fact that a woman combat aviator had two kills to her credit when he had none."

Nodding, Mike said, "Unfortunately, there're men like that everywhere in the world, not just in the service."

"I know. So I was more or less forced into this mission, Mike. I don't really think I'm the best one to handle it, but I keep getting a dream every night about the crystal mask. It's over in Australia. I recognize the continent. In the vision, I can see the land and the face of a very old Aboriginal woman. I know she's a medicine woman for her people. And I know she knows where the crystal mask is hidden."

"You need bankrolling, Kai."

She searched his face. "Could you do that for me? I have no way of paying you back. I don't want to work for Perseus, I want to fly. That's what I really want to do…but with a BCD, I'm not going to be hired by any commercial airline company."

"I know," Mike murmured. He saw the ravages of pain in her eyes—eyes as blue as a mountain lake. "Look, let me talk to Morgan about the possibility of such a mission. This sort of request is a little out of the ordinary for us. We generally help people in foreign countries who can't be helped through regular ambassadorial channels or through the political process. We handle a lot of undercover missions, but this one is different. We're not going after people, we're going after a special object, a crystal totem. My boss is not exactly educated about Native American spirituality, nor does he necessarily believe in it."

Mike smiled slightly and drummed his fingers on his desk. "However, his son, Jason Trayhern, just married a full-blood Apache woman, Annie Dazen, and she comes from a family of medicine women. And Jason was healed by that medicine, not via conventional means. So I think Morgan may be a little more open toward this mission than he would be normally. Let me write up a mission brief for him, Kai. He needs to read it, we need to talk, and that's when I'll try to persuade him to support your request. Okay?"

Kai didn't know whether to be relieved or not. "I still don't think I'm the person for this, Mike. I'm so unskilled when it comes to anything spiritual…."

"I know you feel that way, Kai. But the Great Spirit is behind this one, and who am I to question it? I believe you. I believe in your vision. And yes, this world is a locker-ful of trouble. The darkness is out there. As a shaman, I can vouch for that. I see it all the time. Perseus is on the front lines—warriors of the light, if you will, combating it and the people who employ the power of darkness for their own selfish end. So you have someone on your side who understands you and your mission." He set his cup down on the desk. "Let's see if I can persuade Morgan to run with this."

"Just what the hell kind of mission *is* this, Mike?" Morgan muttered as he held up the assessment report and then dropped it on the bird's-eye maple desk in front of him.

Mike smiled briefly and sat down in front of Morgan's huge desk. It had taken a week to get the report written up, after several more sessions with Kai discussing the particulars. Mike was having her stay at one of the company condos in Phillipsburg while he waited to see if Morgan would go for the plan.

"This falls under our 'unusual' category," he told Morgan with a grin.

"That's putting it mildly," the older man said as he stared down at the mission brief. He adjusted the pink silk tie at his throat. "This reads like science fiction, Mike. If I didn't know you, I'd say someone was playing a prank on us just to see if we'd knee-jerk on it or not."

Nodding, Mike watched as Morgan, who was dressed in a charcoal gray suit with a white silk shirt, scowled at him across the desk. "You know, for a long time I've been wanting to create a department within Perseus for just this type of mission." He pointed to the brief.

"Really?" Morgan sat up, eyeing Mike curiously.

"Hasn't what happened to your son Jason convinced you that there's more to this world than what we see, Morgan?"

Sitting back, he picked up his coffee cup. Jenny Wright, their assistant, had left two Krispy Kreme doughnuts on a plate on his desk. Not that he needed them, but he did enjoy them. "Well, yes…"

"Annie's mother is a medicine woman for the Apache nation. Annie's now training to become one herself. That's how this knowledge is passed down from one generation to the next."

"Ah, yes. I remember Annie showing me the rainbow medicine necklace that was passed on to her," Morgan said.

"Exactly. That necklace is hundreds of years old and possesses magical qualities, if you will, that help others. Annie's family are caretakers of it. Jason was helped by it. You saw it with your own two eyes."

"If I hadn't, I wouldn't have believed it," Morgan growled, tapping his fingers on the brief. "I *still* have a tough time believe it, Mike, but Jason *is* better. He's nearly fully recovered…."

"We've never really sat down and talked about this aspect of life, Morgan, but you know I'm Quechua Indian and come from a medicine family myself."

Nodding, Morgan said, "Yeah…I guess I just overlook that part of you."

"And I understand why," Mike told him, his voice low and earnest. "I live in a world of magic, Morgan. I don't go around talking about it, but I live it daily. Metaphysics is just as real as you and me sitting here talking to one another right now. You're used to dealing with the third-dimensional world. My mother, who was a medicine woman, taught me about the *other* dimensions. We live in a complex universe, Morgan. Most people aren't aware of the other dimensions, but those who are sensitive or psychic often tap into them." He spread his hands. "Without years of training, though, people don't know how to access these other dimensions. I've learned to turn on my psychic equipment when I need it, and turn it off when I don't."

Houston smiled dryly. "I still have to live the bulk of my life here—" he pointed to the floor "—in what we call the here and now. My abilities don't hinder me, they only enhance who and what I am, for the benefit of all who live here in the third-dimensional world. Real time, in military terms."

Morgan shook his head. "It all sounds so crazy, Mike, so far-fetched."

"I know. Anyone who connects with the other dimensions without proper training can get into a lot of trouble with it, too. People in mental hospitals who hear voices and see things we don't—they fall into that category. Psychosis can occur. What they're seeing and hearing is in other dimensions—the good, the bad and the ugly all mixed into one. The problem with the mentally ill is that they don't know how to screen it out or shut it down. I was trained to do so. Open it up and shut it down, and stay sane in the process."

Morgan grinned at him. "You're one of the sanest people I've ever encountered, Mike, and you know it."

"Sure I do. But this is another side of me, Morgan, one I've purposely cloaked so you aren't aware of it—you and most people. I know other individuals who are trained like myself, and none of us go around advertising the fact. Usually, we work behind the scenes, quietly doing what we do. The universe is made up of energy. You might say we've been instructed in how to utilize and work with this energy. Metaphysics means seeing into the unseen. Seeing that which isn't physical. That's all."

"Well," Morgan muttered, "if Annie's necklace hadn't been a crucial part of Jason's return to health I'd have already told you that this mission was dead in the water."

"Understandable, boss."

Sighing, Morgan picked up the brief and frowned. "This woman, Kai Alseoun, has a BCD from the Navy, and we're going to fund her trek across the globe to find a quartz crystal mask and bring it back to the Quallah Reservation in North Carolina?"

"That's it in a nutshell, yes."

"I like your idea of forming a department in Perseus for this." Morgan stared at him. "I have a gut feeling this isn't going to be the only mission requiring metaphysical skills that we'll fund. I see there are two more totems to find for the Cherokee people."

Mike gave him a sour grin. "With your permission, I'd like to call our new branch Medusa. You know, the woman with snakes in her hair who is pictured on the hero Perseus's shield? According to some interpretations of Greek mythology, Medusa's skill was described as being able to freeze men who looked into her face. The real truth was that Medusa was an enlightened being, a woman of immense power and a healer of incredible repute. I would like to name our new department in her honor, recognizing that women are powerful, and supporting them in this way."

Shrugging, Morgan said, "Fine with me. And you're running this bureau, Mike. Not me. I really don't understand your secret world of metaphysics, but with Jason's recovery, I'm not going to say it doesn't exist. I *do* believe in miracles."

"Well," Mike murmured, "you may think of metaphysics like that. It can be miraculous in the right hands. But if the prana—the energy that the universe is made up of—falls into the wrong hands, it can be turned on us and harm us just as much as it can do us good in the hands of the right people."

Morgan signed the brief, which would give Mike authorization to put the mission into action. Handing it over, he said, "Keep me out of the loop on Medusa, okay? I have my hands full dealing with third-dimensional things." And he grinned.

Smiling, Mike said, "Yes, sir, not a problem. Let me work up a template for Medusa, a yearly budget and so on, and I'll get it back to you within a month. In the meantime, we'll fund Kai's mission out of Perseus."

"Sounds good to me. Oh, and one thing I insist on, Mike, is that you send out teams of two on each mission. One man, one woman. That's what we do at Perseus, and it works well. So no deviation from that procedure, okay?"

"Not a problem," Mike assured him, standing. "In fact, I have just the man for this mission with Kai."

"Excellent. Okay, you've got your work cut out for you. I really don't want the CIA to know about Medusa. This is *our* secret."

"Fine, but you know the CIA has its own psychic department?"

"Oh, I've heard rumors…."

"Yeah, it's true. They use remote viewing, a psychic skill some people possess. But for now, I have no problem keeping Medusa a secret."

"Fine, I'll let you handle this entirely. I'm sure Kai Alseoun will be very happy to hear her quest funds have been granted."

Kai could barely believe her ears as she sat in front of Mike Houston's desk that afternoon. Not only had Medusa been created as a new bureau of Perseus, but her mission to Australia was a go and would become the template for the newly created department. Pride filled her for a moment. Something good had already come from her fall from grace.

As Mike finished telling her about the bottom lines, he added, "Perseus has a standing S.O.P.—standard operating procedure—Kai. For any mission that originates through us, we put one man and one woman on each team. Morgan wants it done with anything coming out of Medusa as well. That means you'll have a male partner."

"Hey, no way!" She jumped to her feet. "What makes you think I need a man on this mission? I don't! This is unacceptable!"

Mike held her blazing blue eyes. "This isn't up for discussion, Kai. You either agree to have a male partner or this mission will never get off the ground."

Trying to temper her reaction, Kai rasped, "Where in the *world* are you going to find a man besides you who knows anything about Native Americans or metaphysics on such short notice?"

Mike saw Kai clench her fists at her sides as she leaned forward, probably to try and intimidate him. Sinking back in his chair, he refused to be drawn into her emotional drama over this point. He knew she had a lot of ugly emotions to sort out about men in light of her recent experience with Thorval and, Mike sensed, even more because of her relationship with her alcoholic father. The emotional wounds he had inflicted were clearly still raw and bleeding. But not all men were like her father, and at twenty-four years old, Kai was still too young to fully comprehend these weighty issues in order to make distinctions among men. Mike didn't take her reactions personally.

"You know, Kai, the first thing you have to do is *trust* me," he murmured. He watched as she took a step back, her eyes flaring. Softening his voice further, he said, "From what you've shared with me earlier, I know your father wounded you. He hurt you deeply. You're of medicine lineage and one thing you must know is that all medicine people must heal their wounded side, whether it's their female half, the left side of the body, or their male half, the right side. They must make the effort to heal and then integrate. Otherwise, none of the skills and knowledge that have been passed down to them will surface. Without integration, it just doesn't happen. You're angry with your father. As a result, you're projecting that most men aren't worth much." He held her stare. "They aren't all bad, Kai. Not every man in your life has been unkind or negative toward you." Mike opened his hands. "Look at me. I'm a positive male in your life. So is Morgan Trayhern. He approved this mission for you. And I'm sure there were men in your squadron who respected you, too."

"You won't ever find a man that could help me on this special mission! I'm better off going alone!" Kai declared. She was wrestling with emotions that writhed like a tangle of angry snakes within her.

"I've located just such a man, Kai."

Disbelief made her voice raw. "That's impossible."

"There's one," Mike told her mildly. Sitting up, he opened another folder on his desk and drew out a colored photo. "Chief Warrant Officer 2 Jake Stands Alone Carter. You know him. You grew up with him. When you left the res at nine years old, you two parted. You might not know that, a decade later, he went on to join the U.S. Army, and now he's an Apache helicopter combat pilot who was recently stationed in Afghanistan. His mother was a medicine person. He trained with her father for a while before he made the decision to go out into the world, join the military. Jake knows a lot more than you do about energy and Cherokee spirituality. That is why he'll be your partner, Kai. He can educate you, help you deal with what you don't know. He should be a great asset to this mission."

Stunned, Kai took the photo. With her heart pounding in her chest, she stared down at the picture. It was of Jake…but how he'd changed from the ten-year-old she'd known on the res! His face was square, copper-colored with high cheekbones, and those golden-brown eyes of his seemed to look into her heart. Jake was in his official class A green uniform, his beret on his head, a look of pride on his unsmiling features.

Oh! Kai uttered a sound and sat down before her knees buckled beneath her. Her head was suddenly swimming with hundreds of questions and snippets of memories spent with Jake when she was growing up, and she had to take several deep breaths. He had been one of her protectors besides her Grams that lived fifteen miles away. She could run to him when she needed a safe haven, and he'd always been there for her. Somehow, he would instinctively know when she was hurting, and they would meet at their secret place, at a huge old beech tree high up on the mountain. Kai never understood how Jake knew when she needed to see him. Occasionally he didn't show up, but most of the time he'd be there waiting, and she came to rely on him.

Kai would run up to the beech tree, tears threatening to come, but she'd never shed them. No, she'd gulp them back down until she reached that five-hundred-year-old tree. And Jake would be standing there in his ragged jeans and faded cotton T-shirt, his eyes huge and filled with concern. How many times had she burst into tears when she saw him there? Jake would open his spindly arms and she would throw herself into them, pressing her face against his thin shoulder as she sobbed—sometimes so hard she couldn't talk for minutes at a time.

Bitterness swam through Kai as she grappled with the demons of her past. Gripping the photo of Jake in her trembling hand, she felt her heart open side. A wave of warmth, like a ribbon of peach-colored light along the horizon at dawn, flowed gently through her. The feeling scared her, yet didn't really surprise her. She had tried to explain away her "puppy love" of Jake for all these years. Kai had told herself that the feelings she'd had for the young boy with golden eyes that shone with pure adoration for her was simply a childhood love that would never go anywhere or amount to anything. "You can't do this to me!" she cried. "You can't...."

Mike sat very still. Kai was struggling with a mountain of grief, rage, hurt and need, he knew. "I had no choice, Kai. Morgan isn't going to clear this mission unless you have a male partner. I did a little investigating and came up with Carter. He's the right person to be at your side. He was someone you trusted."

"*Then!* Not *now!*" She threw the photo down on the desk. "This sucks! I don't even know if I can do this alone, much less with *him!*"

Mike gave her a gentle smile. "Kai, Jake was someone you trusted growing up there on the res."

"I don't trust him any longer. I haven't been in touch with him since I was a little kid."

Mike saw the anguish in her eyes. He used his other senses to ferret out where Kai was coming from with her stubborn refusal. "After getting burned by Lieutenant Commander Thorval as you have, I can understand your initial reaction about men right now. But Jake is not Thorval, and you've got to separate the two of them. Part of a medicine person's walk toward harmony and wholeness is to work through weaknesses. You need to feel your way through this, Kai. You're the one who had the vision about the crystal totems. The Great Spirit has called you to go find the first one and bring it home. The real test here is are you able to transcend your own personal wounds, look beyond them and respond positively to the bigger picture? The more important one? Light instead of darkness for Mother

Earth and all her relations... Are you big enough to look beyond your own pain, grief and anger to help all of us?"

Miserably, Kai looked down at Jake's picture. Mike Houston was correct—on all counts. "You're right," she whispered. "And that's what I have to do." Just looking at Jake's photo gave her some reassurance. How handsome he was now! He'd grown into a very good looking man. And it was true: Jake came from the Paint Clan, as most Cherokee medicine people did. She knew he had been in training with his mother to walk the path of a medicine man. When she'd left the res as a girl, Kai had figured he'd continue on and take his parent's place someday.

"I have faith in you," Mike told her quietly. "Even if you don't have it in yourself at the moment. I think teaming up with Jake will be the right thing, Kai. For you. For your nation. And for us."

Touching the photo briefly with her fingertips, Kai wondered why Jake had not followed the medicine path. He was in the military, like her. Life was throwing her more curves than she could adjust to.

Houston was right and she knew it. Jake had a lot more training than she did; she had next to none in comparison. Closing her eyes, Kai admitted that once more she was going to have to rise above her own selfish reactions and look at the larger picture. This mission was for the wellness of her people, the Cherokee Nation. She couldn't just walk away from it, no matter who was involved.

But *how* was she going to handle her wildly beating heart, which now yearned to see Jake once again?

Chapter 3

Kai was in the garage of the condo where she was staying when a black Toyota Tundra pickup slowed and came to a halt at the curb. It was a perfect autumn day—barely above freezing at dawn, with a lacy coat of frost on the Douglas firs surrounding the two-story building. By now, at noon, the temperature was in the low fifties and the fragrant scent of newly fallen leaves filled the crisp Montana air. Kai had spread out a canvas tarp beneath her Harley and had been in the process of changing the oil on her mechanical steed when the truck arrived. A prickle of warning hit her, then her heart opened automatically. It was Jake Stands Alone Carter, she knew, thrilled with the knowledge. Mike Houston had called her earlier and said he'd be arriving today.

Kai forcibly shut down those warm feelings in her chest. Frowning, she replaced the plug in the engine so that she could pour fresh oil into it. Four days had gone by since her initial meeting with Mike Houston and she was slowly going crazy in this quiet little Rocky Mountain tourist town, which was a haven for hunters in the fall and trout fishermen during the summer season.

The midday sunlight lanced down through the firs that grew all around the condos, painted gray with dark red trim. The sky was a pale blue, cleansed from the snow and rain that had passed through two days earlier. Dressed in olive-colored, Rail Rider nylon pants, a pair of hardy brown leather Ecco boots and a white fisherman knit sweater to keep her warm against the chill, Kai was careful not to get grease all over her. Wiping her fingers on a nearby rag, she set her used oil aside. The breeze blew languidly, lifting a few tendrils along her right temple. Pushing them back with her wrist, Kai narrowed her gaze on the truck that had parked in front of her condo. Jake was here. Oh, Great Spirit, what was she going to do?

The windows of the truck were tinted and dark, so Kai couldn't see his face. Compressing her lips, she waited, her heart beating in dread. How she wanted her ugly past to stay buried! Having to face Jake again was like having salt poured into the raw, unhealed wounds from her childhood. He reminded her of the past she wanted to forget. Oh, Kai thought about him often enough and warmly—but that was the past. He'd been her safe harbor growing up, his presence in her life crucial for her emotional survival at that time. But she didn't necessarily want to admit that now. Jake had his own life and she wished the best for him— but that was it. Having him show up only brought memories of suffering, misery, pain and heartache.

The truck door opened.

Kai raised her head, her gaze riveted there. Heartbeat

speeding, she tried to protect herself emotionally, but it was impossible.

A tall, lean figure emerged from the truck. Instantly, Kai froze. It *was* Jake Carter. As he turned to look at her, Kai felt a sharp pain stab through her heart, clear to her soul. Oh! How Jake had changed! He stood there looking across the yard at her, one hand on the door of the truck, an expression of yearning clearly written on his broad face.

Gone was the tall, skinny ten-year-old she'd known. He was half Anglo and half Eastern Cherokee through his medicine woman mother's blood. His skin was golden, not quite as coppery as hers, but his black hair glinted with blue highlights. Kai studied him hungrily, looking for what was the same about him and what had changed. No longer gangly, he was at least six foot one and medium boned, built like a boxer in his prime. He wore a light green wool sweater with the sleeves pushed up to his elbows, and his wide, capable shoulders were thrown back with typical military grace. His gold-brown eyes had always reminded Kai of a cougar's, for they were large, inquisitive and set far apart. More than anything, Kai remembered the compassion that had radiated from Jake's eyes as a child. She had absorbed it hungrily like the emotionally starved child she'd been.

He'd been so sensitive and caring toward her. He had held her when she'd wept, rocking her with those thin arms that were now darkly haired and well-muscled. His face was broad, his cheekbones high, again shouting of his proud heritage. Maybe it was his full mouth, the corners turning slightly upward, that made Kai feel safer for just an instant. Jake had always been a jokester, making her laugh when she'd wanted to cry. He'd given her the gift of laughter, of fun. He'd loved to explore, and his hand had closed around hers often as they went off together on adventures into the woods and meadows.

The truck door shut, and Kai's stomach clenched. Her heart was now pounding like a runaway train. What should she do? What should she say? She wanted to tell Jake a thousand things, among them thanks for just being there when she'd needed someone who loved her. *Loved?* Well, maybe that was the wrong word. They'd been kids. What did kids know about love?

Frowning, Kai slowly unwound from her position on the canvas tarp near her Harley. Jake's gaze never left hers as he slowly walked around the front of his truck and headed toward her. She saw worry in his expression, his broad brow slightly furrowed, a strand of black hair dipping across it. Perhaps out of nervousness of his own, he reached up with his long, square fingers and pushed the errant strands back into place. He wore a pair of jeans that fit his body beautifully, his thighs long, hard and firm. It was clear to Kai that Jake worked out regularly. He wasn't a muscle-bound man, just solid and in good shape. And he walked like the cougar she'd always imagined as his spirit guide, with a kind of boneless male grace that belied his innate power.

Kai felt a wave of euphoria at seeing him once more, but struggled to contain it. Fear mixed with joy in her as Jake halted six feet from her, on the pad of concrete where the Harley sat. She stood there, gripping the oil rag in her hand. His golden eyes were shadowed, and he was remembering their past, Kai was sure. Words tumbled forward and then jammed in her throat. She wasn't the most sociable person in the world, and not one to stand on social etiquette. But though she wanted to greet him, she didn't know what to say. It was one of the few times in her adult life she was left speechless.

"*Osiyo*. Hello, Kai…"

That softly spoken Cherokee word shattered something in her, and Kai closed her eyes momentarily, reeling from the whispered greeting. Even though Jake was only half Cherokee, she remembered that his mother had raised him to speak Cherokee, a beautiful, rhythmic language that touched her soul. Opening her eyes, she stared at him, vaguely aware of a pair of blue jays screaming at one another in a nearby fir.

"*Osiyo…*" she whispered.

Jake stood easily, a lopsided smile dawning on his face. "How long has it been?" He rested his hands on his hips as he gazed at her. How Kai had grown! No longer the skinny little girl too tall for her age, she had turned into a breathtakingly beautiful and statuesque woman. Jake wondered why he had never gotten in touch with Kai once she'd gone. Why hadn't he tried harder? His father had taken them off the res weeks after Kai had left, and Jake had had no way to track her down. Great Spirit knew, he'd tried, but all his boyish efforts had met with heartbreaking failure. Jake had cried himself to sleep many nights after Kai had been ripped from his life. She'd been taken into protective custody by the state of North Carolina child care services after her parents' tragic death in a car crash. He'd loved her with a boy's fervor and he'd had a hard time adjusting to life without her fierce, passionate spirit at his side.

"You might as well know, Jake, I didn't want you on this mission."

He winced inwardly. Her voice was low and guarded. Kai's gaze was narrowed, but he couldn't help drowning in her incredible aqua eyes, which had always filled with warmth and gladness when she saw him. Even now he saw a glimmer of joy in them and it gave him hope. Maybe Kai really didn't mean those words. Maybe she was just scared. He was scared, too.

Kai's eyes had always had a haunted look, and they'd touched his soul. She was so different from all the other girls he'd gone through school with. He could never put his finger on why she was unique, she just was. And it made her special to him. Jake had always felt that she was a gift in his life—one he didn't deserve, but somehow he'd gotten lucky. And there she'd been…in his arms, her head resting on his shoulder, her tears wetting the T-shirt he wore as he rocked her and tried to comfort her.

Jake cleared his throat. "Yeah…Major Houston said you wanted to go alone on this mission." Shifting his stance, he added, "I was briefed about it before I took the mission, Kai."

She glanced at him defiantly, then looked down at the rag she gripped in her hand. "I suppose you got *ordered* on this mission?"

"My C.O. called me in. He said I was getting TDY, temporary duty, to a supersecret CIA agency for a special mission." He hooked a thumb over his shoulder. "I was briefed on the mission by Major Houston. It was my decision to accept." He gave her a soft, searching look. "He gave me your address and told me to take the condo across the hall from where you're staying. I'm glad to be working with you."

Kai turned and tossed the rag down on the canvas sheet. "I'm being forced to take you along, Jake."

"I can see that." Her statement seared his heart. He tried to recover, but had a tough time doing so. When they were kids she had trusted him with her life. Now she didn't seem to need him at all. What had happened in her life to turn her away from him like this? The question hovered on his lips and he struggled mightily to keep mute.

Kai heard the irony in Jake's husky tone. Turning back, she scowled warningly at him. "I don't need a partner on this mission."

Nodding, Jake murmured, "Major Houston told me what happened to you in the Navy. I'm sorry, Kai. I really am. They've lost one of their best combat pilots."

His words were gentle, soothing some of her ire. Going back to her Harley, she sat down on the tarp and opened up a can of oil. "Getting the crystal mask back, if that's possible, is more important than me. Or you."

He ambled over to the open garage and watched as Kai carefully poured fresh oil into the engine. Her face was set but beautiful. His ugly little duckling had grown into a lovely swan. In school, the other children had teased her mercilessly. As a child, her lips had seemed too large for her oval face. Though her body had been as thin and supple as a willow, she was big boned and had looked disproportionate as a result. Plus Kai had had legs that seemed to go on forever. Now she stood six foot tall and clearly had grown into a very shapely woman. Jake averted his eyes from the sweater she wore, and the lush curves of her breasts beneath.

"I guess we'll have to call a truce of some kind, okay? I've been ordered to take this mission. I'm in the Army and can't refuse it even if I wanted to. If I did that, they'd court-martial me and I'd be out of a career." Jake smiled wryly as he watched her complete the oil change. Her fingers were long and lean, her nails blunt cut, he noted. Afterward, she took a clean cloth and gently wiped the metal down until it shone like silver. He liked the wolf painted on the side of the gas tank. The Wolf Clan was where chiefs and leaders came from. The Paint Clan was the one Kai had been born into, just as he had—the clan of the medicine people. Shaking his head a little, Jake smiled to himself. They'd both come from medicine families and neither had chosen to walk the old way. Both had created a life made from the fabric of the white man's world, instead.

Why wouldn't her heart settle down? Kai frowned and compressed her lips as she got done wiping down her Harley. Looking up, she locked gazes with Jake. She had heard the wry humor in his voice and it stirred long-ago memories. Memories she wanted to forget once and for all. "This is *my* mission, Jake. You're just comin' along for the ride, as far as I'm concerned. I'm the boss. You do what I ask, stay out of my way, and we'll get along."

"Major Houston said you were in charge. I don't have a problem with that." Jake saw surprise flare in her vivid blue eyes, and he curved his mouth ruefully. "What's the matter? Don't you think I can take directions from a woman? We were raised on a matriarchal reservation. I've always honored women and their strength." *I've always honored you.*

Brows dipping, Kai got to her feet and rolled her Harley off the canvas. Putting down the kickstand with the toe of her boot, she turned to see Jake neatly folding up her canvas drop cloth. Why did he have to be so helpful? He walked over and handed it to her.

"Thanks," she muttered, taking the tarp out of his hand and tucking it up on a wooden shelf along the garage wall. She punched a button and the garage door groaned and then began to slowly descend.

"Do you have time to sit down and talk to me about your vision? Major Houston suggested that we go over it in detail together. He felt it should come from you, not him."

Nostrils flaring, Kai said, "Sure…come on in." She opened the door that led to the hall of the two-story condo.

"I could use a cup of coffee. It's been a long trip flying from Afghanistan and then driving from Fort Rucker, Alabama. You got some?" Jake followed her inside and shut the door. "I'll make it."

"Fine. I'll show you where the stuff is. Follow me…."

Jake tried not to take Kai's stiffness toward him personally. After all, fifteen years had passed, and a lot could happen in that time. As he followed her down the beige carpeted hall to a mauve-painted living room, he spied the kitchen to the right. The condo was decorated in Japanese style, the furniture black lacquered, the fabrics in muted colors. A tall, healthy-looking ficus tree graced one corner near a picture window framed with soft white curtains. He heard Cherokee music in the background and smiled. The singing was familiar. The corn dance, he surmised, as he followed her into the modern kitchen.

"Over there," Kai said, pointing toward the counter. "Coffee's in the fridge. Help yourself. I'm going to get changed and grab a shower. I stink."

Turning, he saw her leave the kitchen and heard her footsteps on the carpeted stairs. Smiling to himself, he quickly found everything to make a good, strong cup of black coffee. Of course, he made enough in case Kai wanted some. Did she even drink coffee? Jake didn't know. So many years had gone by. It felt like a lifetime in some ways. He wanted to ask her a million questions about her personal life, but realized it would do no good to pry. Kai had been like a willful wild horse when she was young, defying authority at every turn. He could see by the set of her clean jaw and the blaze of rebellion in her eyes that she wasn't going to allow him entrance into her life as she had when she was a child. Something deep within him grieved at the realization.

"So, that's the story," Kai told him, sitting opposite him at the kitchen table, a cup of coffee between her hands. It was well past noon and she was hungry. Rising from the table, she went over to the refrigerator and pulled out some tuna and a loaf of bread.

Jake sat back, digesting what she'd told him about her vision quest dream. "That's really something…. I remember my mom telling me about the crystal totems when I was a kid. I never saw any of them except for our Paint Clan one. Each totem was brought out for specific ceremonies for its clan at different times of the year."

"Yeah," Kai replied, pulling a knife from the drawer, "my mother told me about them, too. I thought it was just a fairy tale. I didn't want to hear anything she had to say…."

He watched as she slapped together a tuna sandwich, and wondered if she would ask if he wanted one. Jake had decided to expect nothing of Kai, for to do so under the present circumstances would be pure folly. But his stomach growled.

"Hungry?"

"Yeah," he said ruefully, sliding his hand across his flat stomach, "I guess I am."

"It's tuna."

"That's okay by me."

"One or two sandwiches?"

"Two, please. Thanks." He saw her glance briefly at him across her shoulder. Jake couldn't get over how deliciously curved she was, and obviously in top physical form. She was eye candy, and he found himself secretly salivating. If Kai could read his mind, she'd deck him, no question. His reactions to her were no longer a little boy's, but a man's.

"You always did eat enough for two people," she stated, setting out four more slices of whole wheat bread on the counter.

"I guess I'm still a growing boy…."

"Nice try. What are you now? Twenty-five years old?"

"Yeah. And you're twenty-four."

"Feelin' like I'm goin' on eighty, believe me."

"You seem bothered by this vision. Your Gram said the Great Spirit had chosen you for this quest. Why are you upset about it?" Jake got up and moved to the cabinet, pulling out two white china plates. Kai placed the sandwiches on them and he took them to the table.

Snorting, Kai sat down and tossed him a paper napkin. "Because I'm the *least* qualified person to do this, don't you agree? I was a hellion growing up. I defied authority, defied my drunken lout of a father, defied my mother's wishes that I learn the medicine ways…. I refused to learn to be a medicine person. Why would I want to end up like her?" Kai took a bite out of her sandwich, studying Jake with an intense look.

Jake wiped his mouth on the napkin and balanced a sandwich in his other hand. "You had your reasons for being a rebel, Kai. We both know that. Besides—" he held her tumultuous gaze "—my mother taught me enough that maybe I can be of some help to you on this mission. Between us, we should be able to find that mask. I don't think it's any accident that we're both from the Paint Clan. Who better to get the vision than you? Who better than us to find it? Seems right to me."

Kai knew Jake's mother was a well-respected medicine person. She was dead now, according to Grams. One thing Kai and Jake shared was that they had both walked away from their heritage. She was wondering if that decision was going to haunt them on this quest to locate the crystal mask. "Well, at least you got some training," she muttered grudgingly. "And maybe it will come in handy. I don't really know…." She was certain it would, but, out of stubborn pride, she didn't want to admit that to Jake.

Why was she fighting him so hard? Every time he gave her that gentle smile, her heart melted all over again and warmth passed through her like an invisible caress. It was fear that kept her fighting. Fear of men like her father, or Thorval. She knew it wasn't rational. But she also knew that just because she'd trusted Jake as a young boy didn't mean she could trust him now. No, he'd have to prove himself all over again before she'd let down her guard.

Kai didn't want to look too closely at the reasons for her distrust. She had too much rage toward Thorval. Jake was coming back into her life at a bad time.

"Well," she growled, "I don't know what's going on. I guess I believe Grams, but I'm having a tough time accepting it all. I have absolutely no metaphysical training under my belt. All I get are dreams, and I possess a strong intuition. But that's it. My mother was completely clairvoyant. She could see people's auras, see the spirit guides around a person and talk to spirits who passed through our house. Next to her, I can't even be considered a neophyte."

"I understand," Jake murmured. "I remember a lot of what my mother did, but my dad, as you know, didn't want me learning about this stuff." Jake's father had been a military pilot who had only believed in what he saw in the physical realm. He was never happy about Jake's spiritual training, or "hocus-pocus," as he'd termed it. There had always been verbal fights between his parents over whether Jake should be taught his heritage or not. His mother had been adamant that he should experience his Cherokee culture, and she'd always won that argument with his dad.

"I feel like the blind leading the blind," Kai grumped

unhappily. She opened her hands, frustration in her tone. "I mean, I keep getting this same dream every night. I see Australia. I see a cave situated at the end of a canyon that reminds me of the Grand Canyon, only it's a lot smaller. The canyon's out in the middle of a red desert. I went to the Internet and finally found a place to start, I think, but I didn't find any reference to the canyon or the cave. But the nearest landmark is Ayers Rock, which is sacred to the Aboriginal people. And then, in my nightly dreams, I keep seeing this old woman with milky-looking eyes, dark skin and curly gray hair calling to me."

"Does she call you by name?"

"Yes, she does. And she keeps repeating 'Kalduke.'"

"Did you find out if that's a real word or not?" He grinned at her.

"Yeah, it's an Aboriginal village about two days away from Ayers Rock, from what I can make out."

"Sounds like what you're dreaming can be verified by outer sources," Jake said, "so that means you're on the right track."

"Humph, whatever the hell track that is."

"Do you know this woman's name? Where she lives?"

Shrugging, Kai finished her tuna sandwich, then wiped her fingers on her napkin. "I keep getting 'Ooranye.' And then I see these two shaggy camels out in the middle of the red desert. And I see a very small village. She's standing there at the edge of it, waiting for me. I see her raising her hand and gesturing for me to come to her." Staring at Jake, Kai said, "Damned if I know what this is all about."

"It's about the crystal mask, I bet," Jake murmured. "Did Grams tell you anything else about the crystal totems?"

Kai shared with him what her grandmother had told her. "Do you know anything more about them? Did your mother instruct you about them? Did she tell you anything specific about the Paint Clan mask?"

"Not much. Mom said that each crystal totem was associated with the energy of that clan, as we discussed. It was like the heart of our clan and fed us energy. Each totem helps its clan to maintain balance and a peaceful state of harmony for all the people in it." Jake rubbed his brow, trying to recall more. "I remember when I was nine and undergoing my passage ceremony from childhood to becoming an adult. That day the crystal mask was brought out of the leather pouch where it was kept. It was held over my head as I was given my new, adult name, Stands Alone, by the medicine man."

Kai said, "So you've seen what it looks like?"

"Yes. But that was a long time ago, Kai. And I only saw it that one time." He gave her a rueful look. "But I do remember that when the crystal mask was held over me and the medicine man was chanting in our language, I felt so light-headed and woozy from the energy pouring off it that I wobbled a little. My mom, who was standing next to me, grabbed my arm and made sure I stood there and didn't fall." He gave Kai an amused look. "That crystal mask is powerful, Kai. I'll never forget the energy or what it did to me. It wasn't bad. I felt really good—empowered and almost giddy afterward. Like someone had shot me full of adrenaline or something."

Nodding, Kai muttered, "That's helpful. I remember my mother saying something about the mask, trying to teach me about it, but I ran out the door. I didn't want to have anything to do with it."

"So much for rebellion." Jake smiled briefly. He saw some of the tension thaw from Kai's face. Taking the napkin, he pulled a pen from his pocket and drew a rough sketch of a human being on it. Turning it around, he said, "Maybe this will be helpful to you. If you've seen this before, stop me, okay?"

"Okay." Kai looked down at what he was drawing.

"This is our energy system, from what I can recall. My mother taught me that there is a series of chakras or energy stations located in the first field out from our physical body. It's called the etheric field, and it reaches three to six inches beyond our physical form, like a glove that fits tightly around our body. People who can see it say it's light gray, and almost transparent. Embedded in this field are the energy stations, or what Hindu people refer to as chakras. Being vortices of energy, they're circular and are often represented by a lotus or other flowers. Think of a fan or a propeller whirling around in the center of each." Jake quickly drew seven circles on the human figure he'd sketched. "Now, each chakra is related to a different color. The color red pertains to the root chakra, located in the area of our tailbone."

Studying the napkin, Kai hungrily absorbed what Jake showed her. Maybe he wasn't going to be such a pain in the ass, after all. She needed this kind of information to try and put together what she was receiving in her dream state. Pointing at the circle at the bottom of the figure's spine, she said, "Well, what does all this mean? How does the crystal Paint Clan mask fit?"

"I don't know, Kai. I wish I did. I just know that the mask made me dizzy—" he tapped the head of the figure he'd drawn "—so that tells me it had something to do with my crown chakra. My dad, who was a fighter pilot, really tried to stop my mom from telling me this stuff. So she'd slip me the information when he wasn't around." He grinned. "She didn't take no for an answer."

"I'm glad she didn't. She was much more of a fighter than my mother was."

Jake gave her a tender look. "Under the circumstances, Kai, there was no way you could really live in that house with your father like he was. You had to run every chance you got in order to survive, and even then he still got his hands on you. And your mother…well, she took his beatings and I'm sorry about that…sorry about what he did to both of you…." Jake didn't want to get into how much seeing Kai battered had torn him up. He'd been a child himself, unable to do anything but hold her after the fact.

Pain flashed through her heart. If Jake had mentioned her past in any other tone she'd have lashed out at him. Instead, she whispered, "Look, let's just stick to what you know, okay? I feel like we're two halves of something. Maybe… just maybe…with my dreams and your knowledge of our medicine ways, we'll know what to do with this and where to go. Together, we make a circle. We're complete…."

"I think we'll make a good team, Kai," Jake said sincerely. "So we're heading for Australia, to Ayers Rock, to find this Aboriginal village?"

Kai lifted her chin and raised a brow. "That's what I told Mike. They're preparing our travel documents. But I'm really not sure, Jake. I've never put any stock in dreams before."

Jake saw her fighting with herself, questioning the vision she'd received. "Isn't it logical, with your dream? You've already checked it out on the Net. Let's just use the dream as a starting point. We'll use our wolf noses once we get there to snoop around, and hope the Great Spirit will give us another piece of information to follow. We have to have faith in this process. My mother always said being a medicine person was running a hundred percent on faith all the time. I'm now beginning to understand what she meant by that." He wanted to reach out and touch Kai's hand, but stopped himself. Seeing the uneasiness in her expression, her eyes fraught with questions, Jake sat quietly.

"I suppose you're right. I feel like an utter fool, Jake. I've never had a dream download into me like this, in pieces or parts. What if I'm wrong?" She touched her forehead. "Or just plain crazy? I'm sure Major Houston isn't going to be happy about spending all that money for nothing, if this turns out to be a wild-goose chase to Australia. There may be no Ooranye when we reach Kalduke...."

Jake murmured, "Instead of worrying, let's use this time to try and put together what we know for Major Houston. He's Indian. He understands how people get useful information through dreams. When we land at Yulara, near Ayers Rock, we might have a clue as to where to find this woman, and this place."

Chapter 4

"Damn, it's hotter than hell here," Kai said as she stepped out of the Yulara Airport at Ayers Rock. It was three in the afternoon and she saw wavering curtains of heat shimmering everywhere she looked. Jake had their luggage and he set it down nearby. As part of the undercover nature of their mission, Major Houston had issued passports, driver's licenses and credit cards created for them under the name Davis. As in Mr. and Mrs. Kai didn't like the fact that they were pretending to be married, but Houston told her they were dealing with thieves who had brazenly stolen from the ark to get the crystal totems. He wasn't going to take chances with their lives under the circumstances. Kai felt Houston was over-reacting, but she couldn't talk him out of the phony identification.

Kai squirmed over the fact she'd have to share a bedroom with Jake. That was something she didn't want to do at all and had adamantly said so. Jake had smoothly suggested they rent two hotel rooms next to each other and they could have separate quarters while appearing to be married. That made Kai a lot more comfortable.

"The temperature must be about a hundred and thirty degrees," Jake said. "October Down Under is the beginning of their summertime." Kai had placed her hands on her hips, scowling as she surveyed the surrounding landscape. Jake had spent his time on the unending flight reading up on the area, which was called the Amadeus Basin. Nine hundred million years ago, this place had been a shallow sea that had spread across most of central Australia. Nowadays, it was nothing but desert—the continent's famous Red Center.

The sea had been replaced with red sand, eroding in dunes that resembled ocean waves frozen in time. Wherever he looked, Jake saw clumps of prickly, spinifex grass and ghostly desert oaks. What drew him most were the vast, undulating sand ridges covered with tough vegetation that somehow endured this inhuman heat.

"Dude, this sucks. I like hot weather, but not this hot." Kai watched as crowds of tourists from around the world left the small air-conditioned airport for their destination hotels. Yulara Tourist Village was situated fifteen miles from the famous Uluru, or Ayers Rock. The red sandstone mountain would be most people's destination, but not theirs.

"At least it's dry heat," Jake said, smiling slightly. He was reeling with exhaustion. The twenty-hour flight from Montana, through Seattle, Washington, and then across "the Pond"—the Pacific Ocean—to Sydney had been a helluva long haul. Of course, first class seats made it bearable, and he'd slept off and on, but not well.

Settling his gaze back on Kai, which was always a pleasure for Jake, he saw she had plaited her hair into two thick braids shortly before they landed. She wore what she called her field gear—the Rail Rider tough-as-nails olive-green nylon pants, her brown leather Ecco boots, a dark red T-shirt with capped sleeves and a boat neck that revealed her beautiful collarbones and emphasized her slender neck.

Kai was the embodiment of power melded with beauty, as far as Jake was concerned. And she'd shut him out just as if she'd shut a door in his face. Sighing inwardly, he tried again to not take it personally. The flight over had been mostly silent.

They'd received their weapons, briefing, money and other information from the Perseus Sydney officer, Lionel Smythe, before coming to Yulara. Jake had wished for a helicopter flight from Sydney, but that was impossible due to the distance. It was nearly twenty-five hundred miles from the east coast to the interior, where Yulara sat in the middle of some of the most important Aboriginal sacred sites on the huge continent.

Jake had seen two rented helos at the Yulara airport, small commercial types, although one was a 1970s-era Huey painted blue and yellow, which had been a combat helo at one time in the past. The other was a white-and-silver Bell Longranger helicopter. Jake would be happy to fly either of them around the area in air-conditioned comfort, instead of heading out in a car in this suffocating heat.

"Well," Kai said, dropping her hands from her hips. "I guess I have to figure out where we go to find Kalduke and this Ooranye woman." She swung her gaze around, trying to grasp the enormity of the Red Center. She saw red sand dunes in the distance that were anywhere from three to fifteen feet in height. The sand ridges seemed to ripple like the skin of Mother Earth, or maybe a sidewinder moving, Kai imagined. She'd read that these ridges had been formed more than thirty thousand year ago by the strong southerly winds. Well, it was still windy here, if today was typical.

The land was scattered with rugged vegetation, from wildflowers to clumps of grass, shrubs and even mystical looking oak trees, which was surprising to her. These plants had hardy spirits to survive this oven, for sure. From the air, as they flew over the national park, Kai had seen ditches, dried up stream courses, vast lake beds that were the color of bleached bones. She'd seen mines, a few water holes with lurid green water in them, and the red sand that reminded her of Mother Earth's blood. For indeed, Mother Earth's bones were composed of rock, and her skin was considered the soil and vegetation.

"I'll pick up our rental car," Jake said. "You watch the luggage?"

"Sure." Kai watched him saunter back inside the airport. Frowning, she tried to ignore all the emotions that Jake's continued nearness brought up in her, all the yearning. Oh, Great Spirit, she felt a longing in her heart and an ache in her body for Jake. Kai didn't like herself very much. One moment she was grumpy with him, the next, she tried to be nice—her way of apologizing for her prickly emotional state. It wasn't his fault that he'd been ordered on this mission with her. He was as much a pawn in it as she was at the moment. Still upset with Mike Houston and Morgan

Trayhern because of their stupid insistence that every team need a male and female, she looked around at the departing bus engorged with tourists wanting their first look at Uluru, the heart of the world for Aboriginal people in the Northern Territory of Australia.

As they'd flown in, Kai, who had the window seat, had caught her first glimpse of the magical Uluru. The rust-colored monolith looked exactly as she'd seen it in her dreams. It rose out of the flat desert terrain, a geological jewel—regal, solitary, awe-inspiring. No wonder the Aboriginal people called Uluru the "heart" of the world. She was big, red, smooth and magnificent.

Ayers Rock rose forty-one-hundred feet above the basin. Thirty-six miles west was a set of stone formations that looked like giant red marbles that had been dropped carelessly onto the desert floor by some unknown giant. Kai acknowledged she had a vivid imagination, but that's what those round red rocks looked like to her as she saw them in the distance. From Jake's travel guide, Kai learned that they were called Kata Tjuta, or "many heads" by the Aboriginal in the Pitjantjatjara language.

Kai had been struck by the feminine, smooth and softly rounded curves of Uluru, and pointed them out to Jake. He'd said that Kata Tjuta reminded him of male energy. The fact that they were the only geological monoliths for hundreds of miles made them hugely significant, Kai was sure. Male and female. Even the rock structures below her conspired to remind her of the necessary union of male and female—on this mission and in life. She understood that the natural world reflected the two-legged's world. And though she didn't want to acknowledge that male-female duality, she was in awe of the dramatic and powerful Uluru, which called to her, tugging strongly at her heart.

The wind slapped at Kai, bringing her back to the present. She winced in the heated breeze, which felt like a blow dryer on high being aimed at her. There was very little humidity out here, probably less than ten percent, judging from the dryness in her mouth. Rows of silver-leafed eucalyptus trees surrounded the parking lot, providing patches of badly needed shade. Still, the black asphalt wavered in the heat.

The odd-looking desert oaks that stood here and there beyond the airport drew Kai's interest, for she'd been reading about Outback vegetation on the plane. Instead of leaves, they had long, dark green needles that hung in clusters and moved gracefully in the breeze. They looked a lot more like pine trees than the oaks she knew in North Carolina. But pines couldn't live in this scorching desert, where summertime temperatures reached one hundred thirty degrees. Yet there were plenty of these trees dotting the gently rolling dunes surrounding the airport. *Amazing.*

The sky was pale blue and seemed to stretch endlessly, with not a single cloud. Lionel Smythe had warned them that they were going to the Red Center at the hottest time of year. He'd suggested Kai bring along a long-sleeved, white cotton shirt so she wouldn't get badly burned by the scorching rays of the southern sun. Kai had scoffed, but now realized he had been right.

Jake drove up in a white Toyota Corolla sedan and parked at the curb. She picked up their navy-blue and green canvas bags and put them in the trunk when he opened it.

"I hope that sucker is air-conditioned."

He grinned and closed the trunk. "Oh, yeah. I got it on high. Hop in. We're staying at the Yarrageh Hotel, run by Aboriginals."

"Spirit of the Stream Hotel," Kai confirmed, opening the passenger door and sliding in. "Helluva name, but out here, it sounds good, doesn't it? I don't see water anywhere." She had a small handbook of Aboriginal words and phrases that she'd also studied on the flight. Kai liked the idea that the Aborigines, who had been subjected to terrible prejudice by white Australians, were finally bouncing back, and owned their own hotel as well as worked with the government to protect their sacred land.

The coolness of the car felt marvelous. When Jake got in and shut the door, she said, "I never thought I'd appreciate air-conditioning, but if there's a place on earth that needs it, it's here. It doesn't even get this hot in the cockpit of an F-14 on its worst day on a carrier."

"Right on." He got out the local map and looked at it, memorizing the route to the hotel. Yulara wasn't very big, maybe five thousand people. The man who'd briefed them for the mission had told them that the place was a tourist trap and the population consisted mostly of people who worked at the hotels and restaurants. Few people were crazy enough to live out here for the love of it. Jake understood why. Putting the car in gear, he pulled away from the curb.

Kai looked around at the airport landscaping. From her tourist book she identified Desert Grevillea bushes sprouting bright yellow-and-orange flowers that resembled bottle brushes. Purple flowers hugged the ground like a rich carpet beneath the tall, many-limbed Grevillea, suggesting a bright, almost surrealistic painting. Tall, swaying clumps of what could be spinifex grass were planted all around the perimeter. Each one looked like the hair of a woman who'd stuck her finger in a light socket and gotten electrocuted, Kai mused. She had read that the native grass, although beautiful, was dangerous because it was sharp-bladed and could cut a person's flesh as easily as a filet knife. Furthermore, spinifex had topknots like barbed wire that would cling to a person's clothing and then work their way in, abrading the skin.

A two-lane asphalt road pointed toward the village in the distance. After they'd left behind the spinifex barrier around the airport, they found the desert alive with many interesting plants and a surprising rainbow of colors. Kai was amazed anything grew here, and she knew the plant spirits had to be tougher than nails to survive such a harsh environment. They had her respect.

"You any good at driving on the wrong side of the road?" she asked Jake, glancing over at him.

"No, but I learn fast." Like their British forefathers, Australians drove on the left side instead of the right. Jake found the switch uncomfortable and paid much more attention to his driving than he usually did. "It's only a few miles to Yulara. And there's not much traffic, so I don't think I'll plow headlong into anyone." He smiled briefly when he heard Kai's "humph." If she didn't trust him to drive, she'd do it herself, Jake knew. Such was her independence. Kai wasn't one to wait on decorum. That suited him. He'd been raised to respect a woman's opinions as much as a man's.

"Gawd, I'm beat. All I want is an air-conditioned room, a cold shower and about twelve hours' sleep."

"Makes two of us." He braked the Toyota at a stop sign and then turned left. Ahead of them he saw fifteen or twenty buildings huddled together roughly four miles away—Yulara Village.

Kai settled back, her eyes closed. "What do you think about Smythe's comment about watching out for the bad guys?"

"Probably on the mark. We don't know who stole the totems yet and that's what has me on high alert. We could have flown in with one of the robbers." He looked in his rearview mirror. "No one is following us."

Mouth twitching, Kai muttered. "No one knows who stole them. Grams doesn't know. The res police are throwing up their hands. And who would be interested in them, anyway?"

"According to Smythe, there are some rich men who will pay big bucks for Native American objects for their personal collections. They'd be at the top of the list of suspects. Houston is running that list right now, and maybe he'll have some names for us shortly." Jake glanced at Kai. She was lying back against the seat, her eyes closed, her hands resting in her lap. He could see the dark shadows beneath her eyes. And couldn't help noticing how long and thick her eyelashes were against her coppery cheekbones.

Snorting, Kai growled, "His explanation felt right to me, but this is another world I know nothing of. Rich millionaires paying thieves to steal Native American power objects to gloat over?" She glanced toward Jake through slitted eyes. "Smythe was hard to take. I hope not all Aussie males are like him. I could barely tolerate his overinflated ego."

Chuckling, Jake said, "Mike Houston did warn us ahead of time, remember? He said some Aussie men were throwbacks to the 1950s when men were like Neanderthals. They haven't yet learned to evolve like American guys and become humble. I'm sure it will happen over time."

Kai joined his laughter. Her heart twinged as she looked through her lashes at Jake's strong profile. Oh, he was terribly handsome, there was no doubt. Those high cheekbones and his aquiline nose proved his Cherokee heritage, and he had his mother's eyes. Kai remembered Jake's mom. She'd had the largest, most beautiful golden eyes Kai had ever seen—so full of life, sparkling with intelligence and wisdom. Jake had inherited her gentle wisdom, too.

For that, Kai breathed an inner sigh of relief. He could have been like Lionel Smythe, who thought he was God's gift to women.

When Smythe had given her an obviously ogling look, Kai had glared back at him, with such fierceness the man practically went ashen. He got the not-so-subtle message that she wasn't the least bit interested in him. Right now, men weren't on her list of favorite subjects. Well…most weren't. Jake was okay, but he was an old friend from her past—although it was a past she wanted to forget. Having him on this mission stirred up painful memories of her childhood. Kai sighed, desperately wanting to sleep. "Are we there yet?"

"Yep, we are. Take a look, here's the hotel. Nice design. We're home…." He turned the car onto the asphalt driveway. Ahead was a red stucco building with walls shaped in curves, reminding him of a woman's wide hips. Or of the smooth, feminine curves of Uluru, perhaps. There was a huge fountain of water on one side of wide stairs leading up to double glass doors. The water trickled down in a three-foot wide channel over smooth red rocks.

Everywhere he looked, Jake saw dark-skinned Aboriginal people, from teenagers to the elderly. They were dressed casually in everyday Anglo clothing, with no hotel uniform in sight. A youth of about eighteen, with curly black hair tamed into a ponytail at the back of his head, came forward with a wide smile on his face.

"Welcome! Welcome! We are glad you had arrived…." He opened the door for Kai.

She couldn't help but return the young man's infectious, toothy smile. His dark brown eyes were filled with genuine warmth, and as she unwound from the car, she felt her tiredness receding. After all, his people were *her* people, and she never forgot that. Indigenous people around the world were all connected on a much deeper level.

She saw him look at her with admiration and he pointed to her skin. "Your color is familiar. Are you Native American?"

"Yes, I am. Eastern Cherokee."

Thrusting his hand out, he said, "I'm called Sam. We are one."

Gripping his large hand, Kai shook it warmly. "Yes, we are one," she said, suddenly choked up by the young man's sincere demeanor.

"Come, come, I will take your bags. We have cool lime water with honey waiting for you inside."

Jake smiled at Sam as the two of them shook hands. "Sounds good to me."

Kai nodded. "I'm so thirsty I could drink a gallon of it right now…."

The dream began again. The same dark, roiling storm clouds filled the sky, the same growling thunder beat against her ears. Kai was deeply asleep and yet she tossed and turned as fear filled her once more. This time, as the darkness raced to enclose her and then swirl slowly around her like a gyrating tornado, she saw Ooranye's wrinkled old face appear out of the mushrooming clouds.

"Come to me, child…come to me. There isn't much time. You must come right away. The *gwai gubbera* awaits you…."

Moaning, Kai rolled to her side. She saw the woman's form begin to appear as well. The elder wore a loose, dark green gown, with bright yellow embroidery around the scoop neck that fell to her ankles. Her curly hair, a gunmetal gray, framed her face like a hundred coiled snakes. Kai was entranced with that visage. It was stern, yet filled with incredible kindness. Through her fear, Kai felt the old woman reach out and touch her heart. Instantly, her fear dissolved. In its place, Kai felt hot tears building beneath her closed eyelids.

"Come to me, child. Time is precious…. You must get to the *gwai gubbera,* the magic stone, before they do. Come to me…."

The old Aboriginal woman lifted her arm to point, and Kai looked in that direction. In the distance, she saw the dramatic shape of Uluru rising out of the desert. And then

Ooranye pointed to the north where two camels suddenly appeared, heading in a northerly direction. They kept walking, and Kai saw two sunrises and sunsets pass in her mind's eyes. At the end of what would be the second day, she saw a small community appear on the horizon. As the camels approached, she saw Ooranye standing there, waiting for her. The old woman was gesturing for Kai to hurry toward her. As before, Ooranye kept chanting *"Kalduke."*

Slowly, the dream began to dissolve, and Kai woke up with a start, feeling a sense of urgency and of danger.

The next morning over breakfast, Kai related the dream to Jake. They sat at a small square table in one of the many alcoves in the pleasant hotel restaurant. It was 7:00 a.m. and the day was still cool. Probably in the eighties, she surmised, as she wolfed down her eggs, bacon and toast. There were many other hotel guests present, but conversations were muted due to the many thriving plants strategically placed to give everyone a sense of privacy in the large, airy room.

"What do you make of it?" Kai asked, sipping her coffee. She had written down the words phonetically as she'd heard them in the dream. Jake sat opposite her, dressed in a pair of khaki chinos, leather boots and a long-sleeved white cotton shirt with a khaki shooting vest over it. They had special police permits to carry revolvers, but at the moment they had left their guns in their rooms, concealed from view. Members of the public weren't allowed to carry a weapon in Australia, so when Kai and Jake wore theirs they'd have to hide them beneath their clothing.

Jake cut into his French toast, which was smothered with green kiwi sauce. "It sounds like she knows you're here. And that Kalduke is the village where she's waiting, as you predicted. I'll put a call into Smythe and try to track what the other Aboriginal words mean after breakfast."

"Okay. And camels…I know *nothing* about camels, except that they're light brown and they spit."

"Yeah," Jake said, eating his French toast with relish. "There are actually two colors. The common variety are tan. The others are white, a special breed of racing camels, that comes from Saudi Arabia."

"Why would I be seeing camels in my dream, do you think?"

"Because Australia has camels, lots of them. They were brought here in the 1800s and put to use by the British Army. Right now, there are a quarter of a million feral camels running loose right here in the Red Center." He saw the look of surprise on her face. "I think we ought to check at the hotel desk and see if there's a camel station around here that rents them to cross the Outback. If they do, then that means your dream is real."

"A double check."

"Exactly."

Kai sat back in the white wicker chair and sipped her coffee, deep in thought. "Grams always said that some Cherokee people possessed a special skill in dreaming."

"Right. Lucid dreaming abilities."

"Can you do it?"

"No. My mother had that skill, though. But you seem to have the ability up and running. Ooranye has always connected with you in your dream state, so you must have the skill yourself."

"Humph. I wonder if Aboriginal Dreamtime is the same as what we call our dream state?"

"Maybe," Jake said. "I've done enough research to know that Indian nations have different words for the same thing. It wouldn't surprise me at all if Aboriginal Dreamtime was similar to Cherokee lucid dreaming." He wiped his mouth on the white linen napkin and reached for the delicate white coffee cup painted with red-and-black flowers known as Sturt Peas. "My mom told me that our dreaming facility is a gift from our heritage. And lucid dreaming, the ability to change things while in the dream state, is considered a great talent. Did your Gram ever train you how to lucid dream?"

Shaking her head, Kai said with derision, "You've got to be kidding me. I wanted *nothing* to do with these things. Both my parents could lucid dream, so I guess I got the genetics for it."

"I guess you didn't want to learn the medicine way because of how your mother, however gifted she was as a medicine woman, suffered under your father's hand." Jake spoke the words softly and with great understanding, yet he saw Kai's face go stony and her eyes flash with anger. Every time he mentioned her past, she bristled like a threatened porcupine raising its considerable array of quills to defend itself.

"Let's just talk about the present, shall we?" Her words were clipped and brittle sounding.

"Sure, no problem. Looks like we're done with breakfast. How about I go call Smythe from my room and you check with the concierge about camels in this area? I'll meet you back here in, say, fifteen minutes?"

"Fine," Kai grumped, shoving her chair away from the table and standing. She drew out an olive-green baseball cap and settled it on her head. Smythe had given them each a specially made nylon cap that allowed the head to breathe through the fabric while protecting against the brutal sun. In the worst of the heat, flaps could be lowered to shade their neck and shoulders from the glare.

Kai adjusted the cap on her head and, with a wary nod at Jake, left the table.

Jake saw Kai sitting in the lounge of the hotel when he returned from his room. She had a bunch of brochures in her lap and was looking at one of them, in keeping with their cover as tourists. Jake saw she was wearing her Rail Riders, boots, and a long-sleeved white shirt she'd bought at the store with a green nylon vest hanging open over it. Nothing could hide her sensuality or femininity in his eyes.

She looked up as he approached. Jake took the over-stuffed chair next to hers near the glass coffee table. "Well, we've hit pay dirt," he told her quietly. "Kalduke is a small Aborigine village two days north of Uluru, just as your dream told you. Congratulations. Looks like you've got an open pipeline to Ooranye in the dream state."

Raising her brows, Kai sat up and placed all the brochures on the coffee table in front of her. "That's wild, because I don't normally dream at all. When I was flying F-14 Tomcats, I hardly ever dreamed. Probably because I spent most of the time flying and trying to keep my ass in one piece when the Iraqis fired SAMs at us."

Smiling briefly, Jake opened his thighs, folding his hands between them as he leaned forward. "You have the gift, there's no question. Smythe is faxing us a map of how to get to this village. He said that in the Red Center many of the Aboriginal people want nothing to do with white men, and have basically discouraged the building of roads or airports near their enclaves. So…" he smiled more widely "…the only way to get to this village is by…"

"Let me guess. Camel."

"Yep." He was grinning now. "And I gave him the other words that Ooranye said to you. He had a little trouble with them at first because you'd spelled them phonetically." Jake crouched down in front of her, holding out a piece of paper. "Ooranye means rainbow in the local Aboriginal language."

Kai blinked. "Rainbow?"

"Yeah. Their names are probably like ours, and all mean something. It appears that some, if not all, are derived from nature."

"Rainbow. That's a beautiful name…." Kai looked down at his scrawl across the paper. "What else did you find out from our Neanderthal?"

Grinning, Jake tapped his finger over the next set of words. "You heard her say *'gwai gubbera'*?"

"That's right. So you got the translation for that, too?" Her heart lifted. It was beyond Kai to think that what she was dreaming was in fact real. She'd never had this happen before in her life, and it seemed to have opened up during the four days of her vision quest, on the mountain above Grams's cabin.

"We're on a roll, Kai. Yeah, it means magic stone."

Gasping, Kai sat back. "The quartz crystal mask?"

"I think so. I asked Smythe if there was an Aboriginal word for crystal and he said no, that they'd refer to it as a 'stone.' This is only a lead," Jake cautioned her. "Smythe isn't an expert on the Aboriginal people. He's not sure if they work with quartz crystal or not."

"I'll be damned," Kai whispered, picking up the paper and looking at it. "Then I'm not just dreaming. This is really happening…it's real! I'm not just making it all up…."

Slowing unwinding from his crouching position, Jake went back to the overstuffed chair next to hers and sat down. "Why are you surprised, Kai? I'm not."

She shook her head. "Because…well, because I just never thought I had the skills to do this sort of thing. I never had training…."

"But you've got the genes, as you said. You have the memory in your DNA. Why couldn't it happen?"

Giving him a pained look, Kai whispered, "I thought that when my mother died, everything else had died, too, Jake. My heritage, my past."

Pain stabbed his heart. For the first time, Kai's voice, usually strong and confident, had softened. He heard her anguish. The past wasn't buried with Kai's mother at all, he realized in that moment. No, it was alive and twisting and turning in Kai like old grief that had never been given voice.

Without thinking, Jake reached out and settled his hand briefly on Kai's slumped shoulder. Her skin was warm beneath the soft cotton shirt. How he wanted to embrace her! Their past was eating at him like a hungry wolf. Jake saw that in this unguarded moment, Kai needed to be held. He could do that for her, but his heart cautioned him to go slow, so he lifted his hand away. He had seen Kai's eyes go wide and then narrow as he'd touched her. Jake wasn't sure if she was offended or not.

"Genes don't care," he told her, trying to make light about the subject, to lift her spirits. "You have your parents' abilities. Both of them were medicine people. *Something* had to pass on to you, whether you had the training to bring it out or not."

Shaking her head, Kai muttered, "I'm the last person to honestly believe this about myself. When I left the res, I left everything behind, including the beliefs I was raised with." She flexed her hands and frowned. "And here I am, the prodigal daughter, coming back to the clan to supposedly find the crystal mask for our people." Her skin still riffled pleasantly from his unexpected touch. Without thinking, Kai rubbed her shoulder. The truth be known, she wanted more contact with Jake, but it scared the hell out of her. That meant she'd have to trust someone outside herself once again, and she just couldn't do it.

"I'd say we're off to a good start. The Aboriginal village is real. And Smythe said it took two days by camel to get to it. That's where we should go, I think. Maybe Ooranye is there, waiting for you. She's calling you to her home to talk to you about the sacred mask." Jake saw the disbelief in Kai's turquoise eyes even as her mouth softened. "You're getting enough outside double checks on this, Kai, to know that your dreams are giving you the right direction. You can't fight the evidence much longer, can you?"

Giving him a mirthful look, Kai muttered, "I've been fighting and rebelling since I was born. Why should I be any different now?"

"Because the game has changed, that's why," Jake told her in a low, serious tone. "This is no longer about you. It's about our nation, and the implications for our people if we don't bring peace and harmony back by bringing home the totem. Isn't *that* worth letting go of some of your rebellion?"

"Yes…yes, it is. I still can't believe I'm the right one for this mission, though. I'm such a flawed person…."

Chuckling, Jake said, "Not in my eyes. You're a brave woman warrior who can take on the world if she needs to. I'm just glad I got a front row seat to watch it happening."

"You're so full of it, Carter." Her heart swung open as he gave her a boyish grin, his gold eyes sparkling with warmth. It was impossible to stay gruff beneath Jake's sincere charm and sunny smile.

"Maybe." He laughed softly. "Let's talk about camels, shall we?"

"Do we have to?"

"They're a fantastic animal to ride."

"How would you know?" Kai demanded, picking up one of the brochures and handing it to him.

"I was stationed in Saudi Arabia on a special ops assignment two years ago. I made friends with a local sheik who breeds racing camels. I got to ride them a lot, as well as watch them race. You know, over there, camel racing is like

Thoroughbred racing in the States. A lot of money passes hands, and let me tell you, those racing camels are extraordinary animals. Talk about moving fast. Whew!"

"Give me a horse anytime," Kai said dryly. "But you were right—look at this brochure. There's a camel ranch about two miles from here. And check this out…" As she handed the brochure to Jake, their fingers touched momentarily. Kai reluctantly pulled her hand away. She wanted to touch Jake. Her skin prickled pleasantly and her heart beat hard in her breast as she sat back. If Jake had felt their brief touch, he didn't show it as he rapidly scanned the colorful brochure.

Jake took care to keep his expression neutral. He could feel Kai studying him for a reaction to their accidental contact. How was he going to keep a lid on his need for her? Gently putting those heated thoughts to one side, he said, "Hey, this is great! Look, this guy rents out his camels to tourists." He looked up. "Let's go find out if he'll rent us two to ride to Kalduke."

"Just what I wanted to do—ride a damn camel," Kai griped as she stood up, but she was grinning. Truth be told, she liked challenges, because at heart she was a fierce competitor.

Laughing softly, Jake tucked the brochure in a vest pocket. "Hey, they're beautiful animals! Smart. Savvy. You know they have the intelligence of an eight-year-old child? And they're very affectionate if they like you. The ones I knew were very, very curious, as well as patient, self-possessed, hardworking and endlessly fascinating. There is never a boring day with a camel."

"And then there's that charming tendency to spit...."

Jake grinned wickedly. "Well, yes, they can regurgitate their slimy green cud and heave it all over you if they're pissed off at you. Sometimes they'll do it when they're afraid, too."

"Great. Covered in green slime. Just what I've always wanted." Chuckling, she added, "I've heard they often bawl in protest."

"Camels are very astute, Kai. If they've had too much weight put on them to carry, they'll balk and object by bellowing loudly, for sure."

"And they're arrogant."

Jake pulled his hat from his back pocket and settled it on his head. The lobby was filling up with guests heading to the restaurant for breakfast. "It's true, they are very self-possessed and know they're the king of all the four-leggeds."

A grin edged her lips. "I think the word you're searching for is *haughty*."

Chuckling, Jake walked with her. "They clearly believe they are the Great Spirit's favorite animal. But to side with them, I have to say you won't find an animal kinder, more interesting or more beautiful."

She gave him a dirty look. "Did they tell you this or is that your opinion of them?"

"Well, let's go find out, shall we?"

"Camels," Kai muttered, striding down the highly polished, white marble floor toward the door to the parking lot. "Who would ever have *thought* I'd be riding a camel?"

Jake kept pace with her, careful not to get too close. "They weigh, on average, two thousand to twenty-five hundred pounds. The ones they have here are one-humpers, like those I rode over in Saudi Arabia."

Wrinkling her nose, Kai pushed open the glass door and continued down the red-tile sidewalk bordered with flowers. "Why can't I ride a horse to that village?" The heat was already building. It felt like someone had opened a blast furnace door and she was standing right in front of it. Like yesterday, the sky was a pale blue and cloudless.

"Because there's probably no water along the way. No oasis," Jake told her, getting serious. They walked around the redbrick building to the large parking lot. "Camels can take on a load of water and walk for days or weeks without a refill. A horse can't. I asked Smythe about any oases between Uluru and Kalduke and he said there was none. There is a well at the village, though—a natural spring where water bubbles up year-round."

"Why can't we *drive* there?"

"You see the consistency of this red sand?" Jake asked, opening the door of the Toyota. "It's too fine a grit. The car would sink to its axles the minute we drove into it. We'd get nowhere."

"And walking is out of the question," Kai muttered, sliding into the car.

"That's an understatement." Jake started the car and drove slowly out of the parking lot. "Camels are our only way to the village."

"Why couldn't we rent one of those choppers I saw back at the airport?"

"Because this village doesn't allow any aircraft to land there. Smythe said a number of Aboriginal people want nothing to do with any modern conveniences or white culture. We'd get put in the slammer by the Aussie police if we tried that stunt. So we're not flying there."

"Well, I can't blame them for not wanting planes or choppers around," Kai said. "It sounds like they're basically isolating themselves so they can get back to the way of life they had before white men arrived."

"Exactly," Jake told her. He turned down the main highway. "This camel rental place is five miles from Uluru. It's called the Mulga Camel Station. Did you know that mulga is the name for the king brown snake, which is found all around here? It's highly aggressive and always ready to strike."

"Snakes don't bother me. It's the two-leggeds that get my attention, pronto."

"No argument there. Hey, I wonder why the guy who owns that station calls it 'mulga'?"

"Maybe he had a bad meeting with one of those king browns?"

"Dunno, but I'm going to ask him."

Kai stared at the beautiful smooth sandstone rock, which she'd read contained feldspar and quartz. Uluru rose silently and majestically out of the crimson desert floor, an overwhelming red giant dwarfing everything around it. The red rock stood alone. True, there was the cluster of round egg-shaped stones thirty some miles to the west, Kata Tjuta. The Aboriginal people claimed those rounded rocks were actual eggs laid by the Rainbow Snake during the Dreamtime. Kai liked that story better than "many heads" theory. "Okay, looks like this little adventure is going to get humorous. I can just see myself on a camel."

"Let's hope your camel likes you."

Snorting, Kai muttered defiantly, "If it doesn't, we'll have a little talk. No one's vomiting green crud on me."

Jake smiled. He had a feeling camels weren't the only new thing Kai would have to learn to deal with on this journey.

Chapter 5

"**G'**day, mates. I'm Coober Johnson, owner of Mulga Camel Station."

Kai approached the short, lean man, who was wearing an Aussie canvas hat with the brim rolled up on one side. He was in his forties, his skin dark brown and wrinkled from many hours out in the brutal sun. He wore a short-sleeved khaki shirt and shorts, long socks of the same color that came to his knees, and a pair of dusty, well-worn boots.

"Hello. I'm Kai Davis. This is my husband, Jake."

"Nice to meet you, Missus Davis." He released her hand and offered it to Jake as he walked up. "And you're the mister. G'day to you, mate."

Jake nodded and gave a slight smile. "G'day, Mr. Johnson."

"Ah, call me Coober. Everyone else does, mate."

Releasing his strong, lean hand, Jake looked around at the camels, kept in five-foot-high pipe rail corrals. He was almost close enough to the nearest ones to reach out and touch them. There were several aluminum Quonset hut buildings that held fodder for the thirty or so camels, Jake noted. All the animals were the single-hump variety, as he'd read, and the five camels in the nearest corral were crowding toward them, full of curiosity about the new visitors.

"You've come out for a ride on my mates, here?" Coober asked with a quick grin. He threw a thumb over his shoulder, his back to the corral. The camels all extended their long, yellow necks toward Coober, nuzzling him affectionately and nibbling on his hat with their thick, floppy lips.

Kai stood respectfully out of range and gazed up at the huge, leggy animals, while Jake let himself be nuzzled by a tall gelding. *Some kiss,* she thought, eyeing the streak of slobber on his right shoulder. Disgusted by the animals, she eyed them with distrust. They were huge! Like a body on four thin stilts. Their feet were gargantuan, rounded and cleft, and she'd hate to be stepped on by one.

"Well," Jake murmured, reaching up to run his hand along the camel's rounded ears and gently scratch them, "we're looking to rent two camels to take to an Aboriginal village about two day's ride from here. Maybe you've heard of it? Kalduke?"

Coober eyed him, rubbing his stubbled jaw. "Mate, I don't generally hire out my boys to tourists to go gallivantin' off into the Red Center alone. I offer one-, two- or three-hour rides, where each camel's nose peg is hooked to the saddle in front of 'em, and I'm leadin' the line. There's not a Buckley's chance of renting them for that kind of hike."

Jake nodded. That was an Aussie idiom for no chance at all, he knew, but he held aces up his sleeve, and Coober might change his mind. "I understand, but I've had quite a bit of experience with racing camels in Saudi Arabia two years ago. Maybe you know Sheik Abdul Mohammed? He's one of the top breeders, raising and selling the best racing camels in the Middle East."

Coober's green eyes widened. "I'll be gob smacked, mate. Of course I know of 'im!" His voice rose in excitement. "Why, I have four of his offspring right here! Two geldings and two broodmares."

Grinning, Jake said, "I'd like to see them. Are they back there?" He pointed to another group of barns and corrals partially hidden behind a high brush hedge.

"They are, mate."

Jake felt Coober testing him, probably trying to figure out if Jake was being honest. It was one thing to be a name dropper, quite another to be proficient enough around camels that Coober might rent two of his animals for them to take to Kalduke.

"If I show you that I know how to ride a camel and take care of it, would you reconsider renting us two of them?"

Again, Coober rubbed his spiky jaw. "I dunno, mate."

"We're willing to give you a thousand U.S. dollars a day to rent your animals. I promise we'll take good care of them."

Eyes lighting up at the promise of good money, Coober grinned. "Well, mate, now you're talking. But listen, these camels are my friends, and I can't just let you walk out of here on your word alone. I won't rent to roughies."

"I understand," Jake told him solemnly. Aussie slang was a world of its own, and Jake knew "roughie" meant a rough or wild, irresponsible person.

Several camels had gathered around Coober, and one was nibbling playfully at his hat, another tugging at the damp red-and-white kerchief around his neck. Camels were like curious children, and Jake was thrilled to see such intelligence in their dark brown eyes—eyes framed with the longest, thickest black eyelashes in the animal kingdom.

"Tell you what, mate," Coober said, "how about I take you and your missus back there and watch you groom, saddle and then ride them? Once you've got them properly saddled and all, we'll take a short ride so I can see how you handle them."

Kai opened her mouth to protest. No way was she climbing up on a camel! Not without adequate preparation and instruction first!

Jake gave Kai a glance, his voice apologetic. "My wife is just getting over a nasty migraine from our sixteen-hour flight, so she's not up to riding today, mate. We were planning on starting this trip tomorrow, when the doctor gives her the go-ahead. Would it be okay if you watch me go through the motions? Decide whether or not you want to rent us two of your camels, based on my performance?"

Kai snapped her mouth shut. Jake was fast on his feet, she'd give him that. She sent Coober what she hoped was an appeasing smile.

"Oh…sorry, missus. My wife, Darla, always gets them head-bangers, too. Nasty roughies, they are. Lay her up a day or two. So you have my condolences."

"Yes…well, er, I'm not feeling up to riding much of anything today, Mr. Johnson. But my husband is an ace at handling camels, so I think you'll be convinced that we'll take very good care of your friends here."

Nodding, Coober smiled a little. "I understand, missus, I really do. Well, come on, mate, let me show you my four racing camels. They're in the back…and they're beautiful. Did you know I've won nearly every race here in the Outback with my two geldings? They're as fit as a mallee bull. They come straight from that sheik's bloodstock."

Jake gave Kai a meaningful look and reached out to grasp her hand. She complied somewhat reluctantly and fell into step beside him as they headed off between the rectangular corrals, trudging through the loose red sand. Holding Jake's hand after so many years brought back poignant memories to Kai. His grip was strong, firm, and yet he monitored the amount of pressure he exerted so he didn't hurt her. Heart hammering, Kai swallowed. She didn't know what to do. She was drawn to Jake, and a huge part of her wanted to reignite her friendship with him…and more. But that scared the hell out of her. She'd had a terrible, wrenching relationship a year ago, and was still healing from it. Yet her heart was starting to yearn for Jake.

He slowed the pace until Coober was a good twenty steps ahead of them. "I didn't think you wanted to show Coober how awkward you'd be on a camel," Jake told her in a whisper. He liked having Kai's hand in his. For so long, after both of them had left the res, he'd pined away for her. And later, as a man, he could never fully forget her. Feeling as if he were in a dream, he squeezed Kai's fingers gently. For a moment her eyes went soft with longing, making his heart race with joy. Trying to keep his emotions at bay, he gave her a boyish smile.

Kai grinned and shyly squeezed his strong fingers in return. Something was happening. It was almost magical. And scary. "Good thinkin', camel cowboy. I'll just watch what you do and try to pick it up real fast, so by tomorrow morning I can convince Coober I've ridden them half my life."

Jake caught her glinting gaze. Taking advantage of their cover as a married couple, he squeezed her hand tenderly once more. For him, it was a powerful moment, one that made his heart open and sing like the sun rising at dawn.

Kai wanted to hold Jake's hand forever. From time to time, Coober would turn to make sure they were following. Maybe this cover of being married wasn't so bad, after all. Jake smiled merrily at Coober and walked with a plucky stride that made her think he really did enjoy holding her hand. Did he? Or was it an act? Kai couldn't be sure, but she knew it was genuine from her end.

"Here they are, mates. My pride and joy!" Coober halted at a pipe fence and gestured proudly to the animals. Inside were four white camels with single humps. Two of them, the females, were on one side of a barrier, the two geldings on the other.

Jake reluctantly released Kai's hand, moved up to the fence and rested his arms on the top rail. "Both of your girls are pregnant," he observed, seeing the swollen bellies of the camels in the left side of the enclosure.

"Yes, they are," Coober said. "Bred to the best bull in the Outback, Sheik Wind. You heard of 'im?" Coober rested his hands on the fence a few feet from where Jake stood.

"Sure have. That bull came directly from Sheik Mohammed's core stock. Do you own him?"

Coober grinned proudly. "Yes, I do. My missus thought

I was fair dinkum about putting out the money to buy him when he was a yearling. I told her he had the goods. And most of my business is using him as a breeding bull for other racing stock here in the Outback. There's quite a race circuit in the Red Center. Not much else to do out here, and racing camels is big."

Jake eyed the two white geldings. Racing camels were more trim, athletic and slender than normal camel stock. "These must be from your bull, too? They look like him." Jake knew that Coober would want him to be savvy about anatomy and breeding as well as care and handling. He now thanked his stars that he'd spent that stretch of time working with the sheik and his boys. It was going to pay off handsomely.

"Hooley dooley!" Coober said, growing excited again. "It's just incredible that an American bloke would know so much!"

"So who do I get to work with here?" Jake asked, gesturing to the two racing geldings.

"Well, mate, I'm gonna let you work with Freddy here. The gelding closest to you that's eyeing you in a friendly fashion."

"You've trained them yourself?"

"That's right, mate. With love. I don't believe in beating a camel into submission. There's galahs—foolish people—at other camel stations out here who do, but I don't do it."

"The sheik taught me that love and firmness are the only way to train a camel," Jake told him seriously. Camels were too damn intelligent to take a whip to. They could strike not only with their front feet, but with their rear ones as well, and they could kill or badly injure an unsuspecting man with a sideways strike, too. If a camel didn't like you, it would lie in wait to nail you with one of its deadly kicks. Jake had seen one handler, a kid of ten, go flying six feet into the air. The boy had smacked a racing camel in the nose as punishment one day, and came away with a broken leg. No, camels were not animals to push around. Sharing peaceful coexistence based upon trust, respect and appreciation, was the best way to raise and train them.

Kai watched from outside the corral as the two men slipped between the pipe rails. She admired Jake's confidence as he walked right up to the proud, arrogant looking camel. Freddy lifted his furry neck high and then tilted his head to one side to gaze down upon him. Kai had to admit that the camel's huge, sparkling eyes were beautiful. She admired the animal's grace. When Jake stretched up his hand, Freddy opened his huge, cavernous mouth, revealing large yellowed teeth. Then, with his long, thin pink tongue, he licked Jake's palm.

"Beauty! You do know your camels, mate," Coober noted in a pleased voice. "All camels like the salt on the palm of your hand. Camel handlers know that, too. Come on, let me take you into the barn. They'll follow us like children."

Kai decided to head to the barn as well to watch what Jake did. Coober might have them saddle the camels tomorrow, and she had to know how to do it. Stepping into the shade of the building, near the gaping doorway, she felt the hot, dry breeze sweep past her, cooling her slightly.

Coober had brought out brushes, a hoof pick of some sort and an odd-looking saddle. Kai wondered how one could saddle a single-humped camel, but now she saw the ingenuous device.

The saddle had a hole in the middle that fit over the camel's hump. It was thickly padded, of course, so that the animal's back wouldn't be rubbed raw by the metal frame, which was covered in thick, soft red leather. The saddle had two seats, one in front of the hump and one behind. The contraption reminded Kai of a pair of English saddles, with stirrups, and girths wrapped beneath the belly of the camel. This was going to be interesting! She hooked one booted foot up on the fence rail and watched, fascinated.

Jake was a pro at grooming a camel, she realized as she watched him pick up each of the animal's huge feet and rest it against his hard, curved thigh. Then he used the hoof pick to clean between the clefts of the velvety, thick footpads. Freddy had taken an instant liking to Jake and stood very patiently while he cleaned and brushed him. The gelding had a permanent nose peg made out of wood that rested in one flared nostril. There was a light rope attached to it. That was how a camel was steered, Kai realized. A horse had a place in its mouth where a bit could rest, but a camel chewed a cud, which would make a bit uncomfortable. So a simple nose peg was the "bit" that guided this twenty-five hundred pound animal.

"Whoosh!" Jake ordered the camel.

Kai frowned attentively.

Instantly, the camel began to buckle his long, lean front

legs. After Freddy settled on his front knees, he folded his back legs and tucked them beneath him.

That was pretty cool, Kai thought. The word, whatever it meant, had made the camel rest in a sitting position for mounting purposes. She saw Jake carefully place the thick wool padding around Freddy's hump and then, very gently, place the saddle on top. Soon Jake had it adjusted properly, and gave the order for Freddy to stand. A few minutes later the girths were in place and tightened.

"You want me to mount in here or take him outside?" Jake asked Coober, who was looking very impressed.

"No, that's all right, mate, mount Freddy here. I'll go saddle up Sprite while you take him out of the paddock. Just ride him around the area until I can join you."

Jake grinned and nodded. "Sure thing." He caught Kai's wide-eyed look. There was a mixture of admiration and new respect in her eyes and it made him feel ten feet tall. Maybe Kai would realize that he wasn't just excess baggage on this mission, that he could contribute in some ways, even surprising ones at times. He saw her mouth pull into a smile as he ordered Freddy to lie down again. Nose peg rein in one hand, Jake placed his foot in the left stirrup and lifted his right leg up and over. Settling in the saddle, he called, "Up!" to the camel. Instantly, Freddy's rear legs shot upward like power elevators, throwing Jake far forward. He compensated instantly so that he remained balanced and seated. Then Freddy threw out his front legs and, with Jake on board, rose to his full ten feet in height. Luckily, the barn interior was over forty feet high and the doorways massive, so it was no problem.

Jake grinned down at Kai. She shook her head and rolled her eyes. When Coober went inside the tack room to get a saddle for the other camel, she drawled, "You look right at home. All you need is a sheik's turban and you're set for a bit part in *Lawrence of Arabia*."

Chuckling, Jake turned his baseball cap around on his head. He leaned down and patted Freddy's soft tan fur. "Call me Larry for short."

"You're so full of it, dude."

Laughing softly, Jake lifted his hand. "Why don't you wait for us at the tourist hut? We'll probably be gone about thirty minutes, is my guess."

"Good idea, because I'm not tramping around on foot trying to follow you two."

Jake's laughter was rich and strong as it rolled through the enclosure. Kai laughed with him. She made her way out of the corral area and back to the small house with a wooden porch beneath the shade of a huge silver-leafed eucalyptus, or gum tree. Its white trunk reminded Kai of the white-barked, smooth-skinned sycamores that grew along the rivers and streams of Arizona.

The heat was rising. Kai saw the men on their camels leave the fenced area and head for a high sand ridge nearby. She watched with some pride as Jake, who was in the lead, rode his mount at a loping trot on the red sand dune covered with clumps of spinifex. He looked like he'd been born to ride camels.

Shaking her head, Kai chuckled again and went into the small house where Coober signed up riders. She found bottles of water in the refrigerator and plunked down a couple of Aussie dollars on the wooden counter to pay for one.

The place was cool compared to the outdoors, and she remained inside, studying the hundreds of colored pictures gracing the walls. Many were of rows of tourists sitting on camels, the nose peg of one animal tied to the back of the next one's saddle. Nose to tail, the humped animals stood like proud ships of the desert, bearing their greenhorn cargo.

In a way, Kai was looking forward to this journey. She'd never ridden a camel, but now that she'd seen how well Jake handled the animal, she was eager for this new adventure.

About thirty minutes later, Kai heard Jake and Coober approaching on camelback. Looking up, she saw them trotting between the corrals, heading directly for where she stood on the porch. Jake and Coober ordered the camels to sit, and instantly, both animals obeyed.

"How's your head feelin', missus?" Coober asked as he dismounted.

"It's much better," Kai told him dryly.

"That's great," Coober said, patting Sprite gently on the forehead.

Giving him a brief smile, Kai continued, "I'm almost good as new." She glanced at Jake, who was giving her a narrow-eyed look, his mouth twitching. "Well," he said lightly to Coober, "I hope this means we can rent two of your camels tomorrow morning and take them to Kalduke?"

Lifting the hat off his head, Coober wiped the sweat from his brow. "No problem, mate. Of course. I'll give you Rocket and Booster. They're the best geldings of my herd, aside from these two racing camels, which I won't loan out to anyone. Rocket and Booster were born twins." He grinned.

Relieved, Jake nodded and smiled. "That will be fine."

"Rocket and Booster?" Kai murmured. Those names brought images to her mind—not good ones.

Coober grinned. "Yeah, that's right."

"How'd they get their names?" Kai eyed the herd of camels at the nearest corral.

"They were twins born from one of my best brood-mares, Gracie. From the time they hit the ground after birth, they loved to run. They would rocket around here at a gallop. Though their momma isn't a racing camel, their daddy is and I think they got a lot of their dad's blood in 'em. You want a pair of fast-walking camels to make your trip to Kalduke as short as possible, don't you?"

"We do," Jake said, noting the laughter in Kai's eyes. She was having a tough time keeping a straight face around Coober. "We'll take them, Coober, thanks. Once we put these camels up, let's come back to the office and I'll give you the money."

Brightening considerably, Coober replaced the hat on his head. "Oh, that's all right, mate. I'll put these two away. Let's get the finances out of the way now. I think you should be here at four-thirty tomorrow morning. The best time to make your way across the Red Center is in the early morning hours. You should rest during the heat of the day, and push on in the late afternoon until nightfall, when it's cooler."

Jake nodded and tied Freddy's rope to the back of Sprite's

saddle. That way if Freddy got up, he wouldn't wander off. All he could do was stand and wait. "Sounds good to me."

Kai was glad to get back inside the cool office. As Jake joined her, he slid his hand gently under her left elbow. "Were you bored out of your skull waiting on us?"

Giving him a slight smile, Kai secretly relished his fleeting touch. Coober was still outside. "No. It's pretty here. I had a drink and sat out on the porch, just watching the world go by. I like being out in nature. It's not a hardship, you know."

"It's gorgeous country," Jake agreed with a sigh, releasing her elbow. Again, he'd seen her eyes go soft when he'd touched her. He found himself wanting to do a lot more, but pulled back on the reins on that idea. At least for now. "When you were riding, did you find out why Coober named this Mulga Station?"

"Oh, yeah...I did. He's got a female brown king snake that lives here." Jake pointed toward the porch. "He calls her Wanda, after his deceased sister."

Eyes widening, Kai stared at the porch. "The snake lives *under* the porch? That one I was sitting on most of the time?"

"That's what Coober says. She comes out every evening and he leaves her a dish of warm milk with honey. Wanda loves it."

"Egads," Kai muttered. "What would I have done if she had come out while I was sitting there?"

Laughing shortly, Jake raised his brows. "Scream?"

"Funny, Carter. I'd have run like hell...." Kai laughed then, her warm gaze falling on Jake. She *was* looking forward to their journey together. More than she wanted to admit.

Chapter 6

Kai mounted her camel, Booster, as if it came naturally to her. The lights in the corral area were on, casting deep shadows beneath the inky sky. It was 4:30 a.m. and the stars seemed so close she swore she could reach out and touch them. The sky in the Outback was even more impressive than that of the North American Southwest. Here there was more sky than land, and she felt as if she was part of it. As she swung her leg over the saddle in front of Booster's hump, he turned his imperious head and looked at her. Jake had told her that if a camel felt a person weighed too much, it would start bellowing and bawling. Booster just blinked at her, his black, liquid eyes watching her with childlike curiosity.

Coober finished tying the pack of food, water and sleeping gear on the back of Booster's saddle. Jake checked the snugness of the load.

"Mate, you're going to need an elephant gun out there," Coober announced. Pointing to the leather rifle sheath that hung just behind Kai's saddle, he said, "You know that a feral bull camel with his own herd will charge if he sees you. He regards gelding camels as a threat and doesn't know the difference between them and a solitary wild bull looking for a herd of his own."

"I'll take the gun," Kai said. Last night at the hotel, Jake had steeped her in camel lore until she nearly fell asleep from oversaturation. Kai had been surprised to find out that the wild camels that ranged across the Outback were herd animals, much like a wild stallion with his band of mares. And like a stallion, a bull camel would fiercely protect his herd of females. Only, Jake had told her seriously, a twenty-five-hundred-pound bawling bull charging at full speed would deliberately run into them, killing both her and the animal she rode on impact. That was why having an elephant gun was mandatory—it was the only weapon with a large enough bullet to drop a crazed bull camel in his tracks. Of course, the shooting would go easier if the camel she rode stood still during the charge, but that would never happen. Kai would have to shoot a moving target from atop a galloping camel. There'd be no room for error if the situation arose, Jake had warned. Shoot or be killed. It was that simple.

"Yep, I got it. Hold on a moment," Coober said, and hurried into the tack room.

Jake mounted Rocket and smiled over at her. Kai was wearing her nylon baseball cap with the fabric down, falling to her shoulders like a sheik's headdress. The sun was fierce and the material would protect her vulnerable neck and shoulders. He wore the same type of hat.

In the deep shadows, he saw her smile back. "Ready for this adventure?" he asked.

"I'd still prefer a horse, Carter."

Chuckling softly, he chided, "Now don't go and hurt Booster's feelings…."

Reaching down, Kai patted the camel's soft furry hair just ahead of the saddle. She held a braided cotton rein in her hand attached to the nose peg. Booster's fuzzy ears twitched back and forth with pleasure as she petted him with long, smooth strokes.

"I think he likes you," Jake said, grinning widely.

Grimacing, Kai sat up. She had to make it seem as if she could handle a camel getting up without being pitched off. Jake had drilled her on the procedure last night. She had to make Coober believe that she was just as practiced as Jake was, to convince the man to allow them to take the camels to Kalduke.

"Here we go…." Coober called as he trotted out of the tack room and brought the elephant gun around to Kai's side. "Now, missus, you're sure you can handle this rifle? It's a Remington .416 Safari and when you fire it's got a buck that can knock you off this camel."

Kai nodded. "I'm sure I can handle it, Coober." She took the rifle and opened the breech to make certain it wasn't loaded. When she closed it again, Coober handed her a large box of ammunition.

"My advice is put a round in the chamber and keep it locked and loaded, because a feral bull could be anywhere out there. He'll see and hear you coming long before you spot him, and chances are you'll have seconds to pull this rifle out of the sheath and get a bead on the crazy thing. You won't have time to load the gun before he gets to you."

"You've convinced me." Kai took a bullet and shoved it in place. Locked and loaded the rifle and placed the safety on it, then passed it to Coober to slide into the sheath. When she saw him begin to place the strap across it, she stopped him.

"Leave it off," she commanded. "If I need that rifle in a hurry, I don't want to have to play around with a leather snap."

"Hmm, okay, missus, no problem. Just make sure it doesn't fall out."

"Not a chance," Kai assured him dryly.

Backing off, Coober set his hands on his hips. He looked at the radium dials on his wristwatch. "It's nearly 5:00 a.m. The sky is going to turn purple in about twenty minutes. Dreamtime is what the Aboriginals call it—a stretch of time preceding the actual light of dawn. Very beautiful. Mysterious-looking, like a purple curtain. Let's get your camels up, shall we? I'll open the gate. Jake, you have a compass and a map? You know which track to take out of here?"

"Yes, I do, Coober." Jake uttered, "Up!" to Rocket. Instantly, the camel lurched, unfolding his rear legs. Jake leaned far back in reaction. While Rocket straightened his front legs, Jake looked over at Kai. She had uttered the command, and he saw her gracefully lean back, her shoulders almost touching Booster's hips as he lurched forward. Feeling relief, he saw her take the camel's roller coaster movements in stride, as if she'd done it all her life. Grinning to himself, he waved to Coober, who stood at the gate.

"We're ready, Coober. We've got a satellite phone on us, and we've got your phone number. If we run into any problems, we'll be calling you."

"That's great, mate!" He opened the gate and swung it wide.

Jake kicked Rocket, who took the lead out of the gate. Right at his thigh came Booster, whose slobbering mouth was drooling across his leg, but Jake didn't mind. He'd told Kai to let the camel stay close to him. After all, they were herd-oriented animals, and she didn't really have to guide him with the rein at all; he'd just naturally stick to Rocket's hip like glue. That way, Coober wouldn't suspect Kai had never ridden or handled a camel. She could learn the fine points once out of eyesight and earshot, on the great red desert that sprawled in front of them.

Kai loved the silence. The soft footfalls of the camel's feet didn't disturb the darkness as they moved in a northerly direction. Off to her right, she knew, Uluru sat in the darkness, even though she couldn't see it yet. The gentle swaying of the camel was a huge surprise to her; it was like being gently rocked by her mother in a rocking chair. As they climbed up and over a sand ridge and were heading down the other side, the camels avoiding the clumps of sharp spinifex grass, Kai said, "Dude, this is a cool ride!"

Jake heard the joy in her tone, and his heart lifted. Kai sounded happy. "I told you it would be."

"This is really something! Better than riding a horse, that's for sure." Kai used her heels and nudged Booster closer to Rocket so that they could travel side by side. "I really like this! It's like riding a gaited horse, you know that? On a regular horse you get jostled around when it trots, but not on a camel."

Nodding, Jake kept perusing the area around them. "Because of their size and the length of their legs, camels are the Rolls Royces of riding. Their smooth gait makes horseback riding seem awkward in comparison."

It was still too dark to see much of anything. They had to rely on the camels' eyesight not to fall into a hole or trip over clumps of grass.

"Amazing," Kai murmured. Her foot brushed against Jake's from time to time as the camels swayed in unison down the ridge and back onto the flat desert. "I could really get used to this."

"I told you it would be a lot of fun. No sore butt from riding a camel, that's for sure."

Smiling, Kai looked up. Her smile dissolved. The black sky was changing, in an almost eerie way. "Jake…am I seeing things? Look at the horizon…." Her voice dissolved into an awed whisper, then silence once again surrounded them.

Jake squinted. He saw the night sky about one-third of the way up from the horizon turning a deep purple color. "That is *something*…. Coober called it Dreamtime dawn."

Kai stared in appreciation as the blackness melted almost magically from ebony into a deep indigo color. As the minutes passed, she watched the indigo turn to a soft purple. Within minutes one third of the sky looked like a purple curtain hanging down from space. The hair on the back of her neck stood up, and Kai recognized in some dim recess of her primal self that what she was privileged to see was something so incredible and magical that there were no words to describe how she felt.

As she swayed back and forth on Booster, Kai felt the color surround her. The sensation was unexpected. Startling. When she looked around, she found that the entire horizon was purple. In the distance she could see ghostly silhouettes of haunting, ghostlike desert oaks and cork-wood trees, plus the stiff arms of the spinifex grass, re-minding her of giant crochet needles sticking up everywhere. The world, it seemed, had come to a halt to honor Dreamtime.

"Stop," she urged Jake, and pulled on the rein to halt Booster. The camel slowed to a standstill. They were on top of another sand ridge, with the mystical, silent curtain of purple surrounding them. Everything, including them, became washed in that ethereal, otherworldly color.

Jake pulled Rocket to a stop. He drew abreast of Kai and saw the rapt attention on her face as she stared, wide-eyed, into the purple curtain of Dreamtime. Looking around, he realized all sound had ceased. It was silent in a way he'd never heard before.

"It's like we're in a vacuum," Kai whispered. "No sound, nothing, between here…and somewhere else…. I feel like I'm not here, not there…." She gestured to her body and the camel she rode.

Nodding, Jake felt the same almost dizzying sense of being nowhere and yet everywhere at once. "I can't put words to it, either," he murmured.

Kai sat there, gazing in awe. "Have you *ever* seen any-thing like this in your travels, Jake? I haven't."

He shook his head. "No, not even in the Middle East. I've never seen a purple dawn like this. This is…incredible…."

"I feel like we're in between worlds, between dimensions right now…neither here nor there. It's such an *odd* feeling."

"Yeah, it is." Jake stared wonderingly at the purple curtain. It was getting brighter and brighter by the minute, the purple turning to a lavender hue as the sun continued its march toward the horizon. "I've seen a lot of dawns, but nothing like this…."

Kai felt herself being drawn powerfully into the curtain. "I feel like…well, I could go anywhere I wanted—anywhere at all. That time no longer exists…and that all the dimensions I've heard Grams talk about when I was a kid are here. She told me that the universe is multidimensional, that a shaman who was trained could journey between these worlds…. That's the closest I can come to expressing how I feel about this color and how it's affecting me…."

Jake heard the wonderment in her husky tone; at this moment she seemed more like a child than an adult. He felt like a child, too, looking at this silent miracle before them. "It reminds me of a rift in time opening up to reveal other dimensions that I've read about in science fiction books," he murmured, his gaze never leaving the drama before them. "An opening in time, a door to the other worlds…"

"I don't know anything about Aboriginal Dreamtime, but Coober said this was Dreamtime dawn for them. Do they wait for this opening once every twenty-four hours? And then what do they do? Meditate? Do they use it as an opening and journey into it? I want to reach out and touch it, Jake. And I feel like if I did, I'd somehow connect with it. This is so weird, so incredible…."

"I remember my mother telling me that there are places all over the world where you can find doors that open to the other dimensions. She said that Mother Earth is crisscrossed with lines of energy—ley lines is how she referred to them—and where they cross one another, there's an opening available."

"This is more than a ley line, Jake." Kai swept her hand in an arc. "This is the whole horizon from one end to the other! That's more than just a crossing point, don't you think?"

"Logically, you're right. My mother never mentioned a dawn like this one, or the feelings we are having right now…."

Kai sat back in the saddle and allowed the color to penetrate her. She knew enough from her grandmother to shut off her yappy left brain, which was rooted in the third-dimensional world. Instead, she shifted to her right hemisphere, where Grams had told her all her sixth sense equipment was located. Unfocusing her eyes, she let the lavender color infuse her. Instantly she felt a spinning, whirling sensation at the base of her spine. Heat suffused her spinal column like a pleasant flow of warm water and shot upward. In seconds, Kai felt as if she were going to fall off the camel, the vertigo that followed was so powerful and sudden. Gripping the leather-covered pommel with her hand, she shook her head.

"Kai? You okay?" Jake watched her touch her furrowed brow, her eyes unfocused.

"Uh…yeah, I am. I tried to get in touch with that energy and it knocked me for a loop. I almost fell out of the saddle. I'll be okay. Just give me a minute…."

Jake moved Rocket closer, until his leg touched hers. "My two cents' worth is that this phenomenon only happens here in the Red Center, and the Aborigines know how to access it and use it. We don't. We're not trained for it."

"I sure would love to have Grams see this," Kai muttered. She pulled a digital camera out of a pocket of her vest. "I'm going to catch it on film. When we get back, we'll tell her about this…" And she rapidly took five photos.

"I wonder if it will come out on film."

She laughed briefly. "I don't know." She tucked the camera back into her vest pocket. Looking over at Jake, she said, "Are you ready to walk between the worlds with me?"

Grinning, he answered, "Yeah, in a heartbeat. I can't think of anyone else I'd want to do it with."

"What a glutton for punishment you are, Carter."

"Maybe…" He nudged Rocket forward with his heels and the camel began its downward stroll to the desert floor below.

To Kai's amazement, not more than twenty minutes had passed before the purple hue faded into what she would call a normal dawn—where golden light arced up from beneath the horizon. *Twenty minutes.* Her mind whirled with questions as they rode along in companionable silence. Was it a twenty-minute opening that occurred daily? Coober hadn't said the purple dawn happened every day. Kai was looking forward to seeing if it would happen tomorrow morning, as well.

"There's Uluru," Jake said, pointing off to their right. The huge dome of the mountain was silhouetted against the growing light.

"She's magnificent," Kai murmured. "Grams would say she was the chief mountain spirit of this region. She's the only rock around of that size."

"There's something so peaceful about watching Uluru come out of the darkness and slowly materialize before us," Jake agreed quietly. "She's magical."

"So, you believe the mountain is a she, too?" Kai was beginning to realize Jake was far more confident in his feeling assessment of energy than her. She felt comfortable being instructed by him in such things and was more than willing to learn from him.

"Feels like it to me. How about you?"

Kai shrugged helplessly.

"My mother taught me to open my heart and send a stream of green color into whatever I wanted to 'feel,'" Jake stated. "She told me that all things in nature are either male, female or androgynous. Try it. See what you sense."

Mouth quirking, Kai muttered, "You got a lot more training in this than I did." And right now, she was glad of it. Jake could be her eyes and ears on the more spiritual vistas of this trip. He was more than that, she acknowledged. He, too, flew a combat aircraft, and was a crack shot just as she was. In so many ways, Jake complemented her. And without his knowledge of the camels, she'd be at a loss over how to reach Kalduke. No, Morgan Trayhern's order that all teams consist of a man and a woman was seeming more and more intelligent. She'd make sure on her return that she apologized to Morgan and Mike Houston. They were right.

"I'm sure your Grams wanted to share this stuff with you, but you really didn't want to hear it," Jake said.

Kai gave a muffled laugh. "That's the truth! Okay," she sighed, "I'll try it…." And she closed her eyes and shifted her consciousness down to her heart. Imagining a beautiful apple-green stream flowing out of it, she sent the ribbon of color toward Uluru in her mind. As she saw it connect and flow around the red sandstone mountain, she felt suddenly suffused with incredibly nurturing warmth and love.

Shocked by the sensations, Kai opened her eyes. Her heart was pounding in her chest, and she felt a wave of soothing, cool energy wrap around her, lingering like a mother holding her child in her arms. Blinking, Kai looked toward the dark shape of Uluru in the distance.

"What happened?"

Giving Jake a disgruntled look, Kai said, "I don't know…."

"Describe it to me." He noted the confused look on Kai's face, the way she frowned and rubbed her chest above her heart.

"When I connected with Uluru, I felt an immediate response from her. Warmth, like a wonderful blanket, encircled me. I mean…I *felt* it, Jake. And then a cooling, soft sensation came next, making me feel so peaceful. It was *real*. It wasn't my imagination…."

"What else?" He saw Kai shake her head, a mystified expression on her face.

"Well…love, I guess. I felt like I was a little child again and my mom was rocking me in her arms. It was such a strong, powerful feeling…."

"Uluru likes you."

She stared at Jake's stoic profile as he rode next to her. "What?"

"Mountains are like people, you know? Each mountain has a spirit. They like some two-leggeds, and others they don't. When you connected energetically to Uluru, her response was to send you her love." He smiled. "See? You called her a 'her,' too. She is female. Now you know how you can tell."

"I thought it was my imagination," Kai grumped. She was relieved that Jake knew what gender the mountain was.

"Where does imagination end or begin? You know, in physics right now, quantum theory scientists are calling what you just experienced the realm of the imaginal world. They've shown that molecules do respond to us when we imagine something…so imagination may not be a figment, after all. It is connected to our real world in some magical way. So what you imagine can be just as real as you touching your skin with your fingers, Kai."

Giving him a flat look, she stated, "You're sounding more and more like a medicine person every moment."

Jake reached down, pulled his water bottle from the pack and took a swig. After wiping his mouth with the back of his hand, he screwed the cap back on. "I was interested in what my mother did, and I hung out a lot with her. In the end, my desire to fly was stronger than following the medicine path, but I did listen…." He smiled wolfishly. "That's probably why Major Houston chose me for this mission, Kai."

"It was a good choice. Maybe between us we can find the crystal mask."

Jake watched as the horizon grew brighter and brighter. "So, I'm not just baggage on this trip?" he teased.

Kai managed a humble smile. "Far from it, Carter. And you know it."

"Guilty as charged," he chuckled. With the growing light, Jake could see the plants around them in more detail. The camels were walking at a good, swift pace and he was amazed at how they avoided the nasty hooks on the tops of the spinifex grass that proliferated in clumps as far as the eye could see. Glancing at Kai, he said, "After the sun rises, we're going to wish it were dark again. Coober said it will be a hundred thirty degrees out here today, no problem. As a matter of fact, they've had temperatures reach a hundred and forty or fifty, too."

"We'll have to endure it."

"And we're going to have to stay alert for feral camels," Jake warned. "Coober said there are plenty of roving herds between Uluru and Kalduke. Every bull has his own territory, and we'll never know where one ends and another begins...."

"Until it's too late," Kai added. Grimly, she looked around. The silence was now broken by the trilling songs of birds. Flocks of black-and-white zebra finches rose from the desert floor, flitting up to land in the trees and shrubs. A pair of orange-and-green mulga parrots flashed by overhead. "For a desert, this place is really alive with animals and birds."

"Coober said it was." As they passed a yellow flowering waxy wattle bush, a group of button quail exploded from it, startling the camels. The birds hurried skyward in a flurry of beating wings.

"Was the Middle East desert like this one?"

"No, vastly different. There was a lot less vegetation. The sand was a gold color, too, not red like this."

"I've never seen sand this hue."

Jake nodded. "It has a high iron content, that's why it's so red." As the dawn brightened and the sun's rays were minutes away from flooding the desert plain, he said, "This place feels sacred to women. Red sand. Red dirt. Uluru is red. There's no doubt in me that this is feminine energy at its finest."

Kai gave him a slight smile. "I feel right at home." And she did.

"When we reach Kalduke, it will be interesting to see if we can find this elder woman, Ooranye."

"I really don't know if she'll be there or if she's a figment of my imagination."

Jake reached down and patted Rocket's flank. The camel flicked his ears appreciatively. "Remember, imagination is now considered the realm of what's possible."

"We'll find out soon enough, Carter. So far everything I've been dreaming about has come true—much to my amazement."

"If she's there, I really want to find out about this purple dawn thing. I'm fascinated by it."

"Makes two of us, but we can't forget our real objective—the crystal mask."

Jake looked around at the awakening desert. The sand ridges reminded him of waves on an ocean. "My gut tells me that some Aboriginal people live in a magical out-of-time place, and my bet is she'll know where the crystal mask is hidden."

"Let's just get through this first day, shall we? Between worry over hormone-driven bulls coming out of nowhere, and this murderous heat, I've got my hands full just surviving in the present."

Laughing, Jake agreed. "By the time we stop after dark,

we'll be so tired we won't be able to put two coherent sentences together...."

Kai gratefully sipped the strong billy tea. She sat as far away from the small fire as she could. Fire was necessary to boil the water and cook their food, but it was throwing off heat she didn't want after a day spent in the blast furnace of the desert. Tiredness made her thinking groggy. Jake had just come back from hobbling the two camels so that they could forage on the grass around them before they hunkered down for the night.

"Gawd, it's hot," Kai griped, watching as he sat down cross-legged on the sand nearby.

"Coober warned us," he said, pouring the tea from the old copper teakettle sitting on the wire grate across the fire. Jake looked around. The sky was dark now, the stars like huge, glittering globules, so close that he swore he could reach out and wrap his fingers around one of them. Sipping the fortifying tea, he looked over his tin cup at Kai. Her face showed her exhaustion. The temperature gauge on the saddle had registered one hundred and thirty-five degrees at midday.

They'd finally found a grove of wattle trees to provide enough shade to wait out the hottest hours. Then they'd remounted the camels and continued their trek north until dark. They sky had been bright and clear all day, with nary a cloud to provide shade overhead.

Rubbing her arm, Kai hated the feel of grit on her skin. No matter what she did to protect it, it was coated with the fine sand. "What I'd give for a cold shower right now...."

"Makes two of us." Jake set his cup down and opened the saddlebags. "I'm glad Coober suggested we bring along kangaroo jerky as a protein source. I wouldn't want to cook anything over that fire."

"Roger that." Kai reached out and took a huge piece of the dried kangaroo meat, which resembled a piece of fried bacon in shape and color. Chewing on the salty meat, she muttered, "Tastes a little like a cross between beef and chicken."

Jake took a bite and chewed it a long time before swallowing. "Know what the Aussies call kangaroos?"

"I can hardly wait for you to tell me."

"Desert rats. Can you believe that? I guess they do a lot of damage all over the country eating crops, and people hate having them around."

"Humph." Kai eyed the jerky. "I think they're beautiful."

"I liked seeing them off and on today. I didn't know they were out here."

"We saw a lot of wildlife today. More than I expected." Kai watched the play of firelight across Jake's strong face. She was struck by the tenderness in his gaze when he glanced at her. Her heart responded and she tried to ignore it. Jake had been considerate and sensitive toward her throughout the day. Kai found herself wanting to trust him once more, as she had when they were childhood playmates. Could she, with her heart so badly scarred?

Though she hadn't told Jake yet, she had suffered heartbreak more than once after leaving the res. Ted was an F-14 Tomcat pilot in another Navy squadron, and she'd loved him. Yet he'd walked away from her, deciding he couldn't handle her brazen independence. Surprised now that her heart was responding to another man at all, Kai wondered if she was truly healing from the past. She must be.

Jake leaned back on his saddle, his head resting in the center. He gazed up at the canopy of stars. "This is an incredible place," he murmured softly. "It sort of reminds me of when we were kids sitting in our safe place." Slanting a glance to where she sat with her legs crossed, Jake said, "Remember that place we used to meet? That old gray-skinned beech tree that sat halfway up Raccoon Mountain? We had a nice slope to sit on beneath the trunk and branches."

"Yeah, I remember…." She would never forget.

Hearing the tenderness in Kai's tone, Jake lifted his gaze toward the stars once more. "There were nights when I'd go up that hill to the beech and wait for you. While I was waiting, I'd lie on my back in that small opening between the trees, my hands under my head as I gazed up at the night sky."

Brows knitting, Kai chewed on her jerky. "You never knew when I'd be up there or not."

"That's right." Jake chuckled fondly. He finished off his jerky and slid his hands beneath his head. "We didn't have phones on the res at that time, so there was no way to communicate. At least, not that way."

"I was always surprised to find you up there more times than not," Kai admitted haltingly. "I sometimes wondered if you were a mind reader."

"No, it wasn't that, Kai."

She studied Jake's face in the semidarkness, the light from the flames playing against the clean, sharp planes of his features. His eyes were half-closed and he was looking at the stars. There was such a sense of safety with Jake; there always had been. Now Kai fought that feeling like a wild horse with a rope thrown about its neck. She told herself sternly that not all men were trouble. Over the past year, men had caused her nothing but pain, one way or another, but it hadn't always been that way. Pursing her lips, she finished her jerky and wiped her fingers on her trousers.

"What was it, then? How did you know when I was coming up there?" A part of her was more than a little curious. Another part didn't want to know. Because Jake never presented a threat or challenge to her, Kai felt safe enough to allow her curiosity to show.

She watched as he closed his eyes, and she heard him laugh softly. When he opened them again he looked directly at her.

"I'm not a mind reader, believe me. No, I went up there every night my mom would let me. I didn't know if or when you were coming, but I always hoped you would…."

Stunned, Kai stared at him. "You mean…you were up there almost every night of the week?" That seemed impossible. Yet she lived on the other side of Raccoon Holler, a huge meadow surrounded by old-growth trees. Jake and his family lived three miles on the opposite side. When she was six years old, after being beaten with a leather strap by her drunken father one afternoon, Jake had found her sobbing in the woods about a half mile from the log cabin where she lived. He'd taken her hand, leaned down and tried to dry her eyes with the red-and-white-striped T-shirt he wore. She remembered vividly that he'd pulled it out of the waist of his jeans, hunkered over her and tugged on the end of the material to awkwardly dab the tears from her face. No words had been spoken, but his actions had expressed volumes. He'd then pulled Kai to her feet and taken her to the huge old beech tree where he'd built a playhouse in the branches. They'd climbed the rickety wooden ladder to the platform among the spreading limbs, where they'd sat together.

Jake saw the shock in Kai's widening eyes. "Yeah, I went up there almost every evening after doing my homework."

"Even in winter?" she asked, amazed. It snowed often in the Great Smoky Mountains, and it was a cold walk from his cabin up that slope to his playhouse.

Gently, Jake whispered, "No, not during the storms. But when the weather was nice, yeah, I'd tramp up to that old beech. I knew your father had drunken rages, and he'd blow up and beat the hell out of you at any time, in any season. For me, it was important to be there if you needed someone…."

Kai closed her eyes to avoid his searching look. She turned her face away from him, her hands clenching into fists. Forcing herself to relax her fingers, she opened her eyes and stared sightlessly into the dark. Somewhere in the distance, she heard the bark of dingos, wild dogs of the Outback that were similar to the coyotes of North America.

"I can't believe you did that."

"I did."

"All those years?"

"Yeah."

Heart pounding with uncertainty, Kai couldn't stop the tendrils of warmth blossoming within her. "You were almost always around when I'd run up there after a beating. I used to wonder how you knew…."

"I didn't. But I cared for you, Kai, and I didn't ever want you to cry alone again, as you did that first afternoon I found you…."

"Why?" Kai wanted to cry, but fought the desire with everything in her. Her feelings for Jake swelled and that scared her more than anything she'd ever experienced in her life. She wasn't ready for another relationship. And she knew so little about Jake. He could be married, for all she knew, although he wore no ring on his left hand.

Lying down, her head on her saddle, her back toward him, she muttered, "Listen, I'm going to sleep. I'm beat. Wake me up at 4:00 a.m.?"

"Sure. Good night, Kai…."

"Night…" She closed her eyes, hoping sleep would bring her escape from her escalating emotions. Being around Jake was stripping her down, making her vulnerable, and Kai just couldn't handle that. She had a mission to accomplish. The crystal mask had to take priority over everything, despite the longing she had to feel Jake's embrace once again.

Chapter 7

"Look," Jake said, pointing toward the northern horizon. "Kalduke." He grinned triumphantly at Kai, who was riding at his side. "We made it."

"I never thought I'd be so glad to see civilization again. Do you think they'll have a shower?"

"Don't count on it."

Grimacing, Kai wiped the sweat from her upper lip one more time. It was near four in the afternoon, and the brutal heat of the day was pounding down on them. She felt sapped of strength from the relentless ovenlike temperatures. The camels, though, seemed completely adjusted to it and had kept up a fast, steady walk toward their destination.

Pulling out a pair of binoculars from the saddle pocket, Kai tried to peer through them despite the constant swaying of the camel. "All I see is a lot of small, dome-shaped brush huts. Not too many people, either. This is a really small village…." She placed the binoculars back in the tan leather case at her side and snapped it closed.

"Don't expect much. There's a rock hole spring here and

they'll have water for the camels to drink. Coober said that many of these remote aboriginal villages are built around water sources."

"I'd give anything to fall into a water trough at this point." Kai touched her cheek, which was rough with fine grit. Rock holes, she'd discovered, were just that: holes in the ground where water poured upward like an artesian well from an underground lake below—a continual source for those lucky enough to find them in this hot, dry desert.

Chuckling, Jake nodded. "Makes two of us. Let's hope that your Aboriginal elder, Ooranye, is here."

"If she isn't…" Kai clenched her teeth momentarily. "That means we've wasted two days out in this oven." She didn't have much faith that Ooranye would be here, but the rest of her dream had come true, so maybe, just maybe, the woman really did exist. Kai hoped so, because she didn't want to ever have to make this kind of trip again.

"Well, we'll soon find out." Jake saw a small group of people of different ages gathering at the outskirts of the village, which was built more or less in a circle. He counted seven individuals watching them as they drew closer and closer.

Kai halted Booster and instructed him to kneel. Leaning back as the camel dropped to his front knees, Kai kept her gaze on the Aborigines who stood looking at them. Once Booster was on the ground, she dismounted from the saddle. Riding a camel was somewhat like riding a horse, yet different. Her muscles weren't in terrific shape for this, so her legs were stiff and sore.

Jake dismounted in turn, and together they walked toward the group. Kai had been studying a bit of the local Aboriginal language on her way here. They didn't have a word for "Hello." Instead, they always asked, "What's up?" That seemed odd to her, but it was their custom, and she had to try and fit in so that they would trust her.

Kai saw several white- and gray-haired elders, both men and women. They were dressed in sun-bleached and well-worn but clean cotton garments, all colorful. The men wore trousers that were ragged on the bottoms. The women, all rotund, wore skirts that hung to their knees, and white blouses. None wore shoes, and Kai could see the thick calluses on their feet that enabled them to handle the burning heat of the desert.

"What's up?" she said, greeting them in their language. "I'm Kai and this is my friend Jake. We're looking for Ooranye. Is she here in this village?" Heart beating a little harder, Kai waited. She knew her ability to speak their language was very poor.

One man, stooped with age, his gray hair hanging around his shoulders, hobbled forward. "Yes, Ooranye said you were coming," he told her in pidgin English. With great effort, his words slow and halting, he said, "Follow us. We will take your camels to the rock hole. Come…."

Relief exploded through Kai. She looked at Jake as the small entourage of adults surrounded them.

"Pay dirt. She's here." Kai was amazed and stunned by the discovery. Her dreams weren't just her imagination, after all. That made her uneasy, for she'd never had dreams come true before.

Grinning, Jake said, "I never thought she wasn't."

Eyes round as they walked slowly with the group, Kai said, "Well, I didn't have that kind of blind faith, Carter."

Wiping his face, Jake replaced his baseball cap, still grinning. "I probably have more faith in you right now that you do yourself."

"No argument there." From her vest, Kai brought out two sticks of sacred sage from her home in North Carolina. It was good manners when visiting a medicine person to honor them with sage. It was like a calling card. Kai wasn't sure Ooranye would know her people's customs, but that didn't matter. She would honor her anyway.

Entering the village proper, Kai saw that the homes were mostly makeshift and created out of wattle brush. Others were lean-tos with woven grass roofs to give shade from the merciless heat. She knew from her research that, before white men came to Australia, the Aboriginal people had moved with the seasons, without any fixed dwellings they called home. Instead, as they traveled about, seeking food and water, they created brush huts when necessary, and used them as transitory housing to escape the heat. Half the village was comprised of such huts, some of them quite large and well made. The other buildings were of corrugated tin panels cobbled together, the metal dulled from time and age. Nothing looked very solid or stable. But then, the Aborigines didn't want permanent dwellings, so this building style suited them just fine.

Kai's heart bled for these magnificent people, who walked with their heads up and shoulders back. They shared a common history with Native Americans. In both cases, Europeans had come and heartlessly destroyed their cultures without a backward glance. So many Aboriginal children had been stolen from their parents, cruelly taken and placed in schools to "civilize" them, just as Indian children had been similarly wrenched away. There was indeed an unspoken bond between Indians and Aborigines.

The Aboriginal people were trying to reclaim their culture now. They had fought for their rights in courts of law, as well. Kai felt very close to these people, even though she lived half a world away.

"Here," the male elder said, pointing to a large brush hut. "Ooranye expects you to come in…."

"Thank you," Kai said in English, knowing that in their language there was no such term. Bending down, she entered the opening. Surprised at the coolness that greeted her, she realized that the loose branches provided shade, yet let in every breeze.

In the light filtering in through the branches, Kai saw a very old woman sitting on a green blanket opposite the doorway. Kai's heart sped up. It was Ooranye! She looked exactly as Kai had seen her in her dreams. Ooranye lifted her round, black face, and Kai could see that her eyes were completely covered with a whitish membrane. Startled, Kai realized the old woman was blind.

"Welcome, child. We are grateful you have arrived. Come. Come and sit down…."

Kai went forward, crouching down on her hands and knees because of the low ceiling. The hut was less than six feet in height. Ooranye herself didn't appear to be more than four and a half feet tall. She was dressed in a dark blue shift, her legs crossed under the fabric, her toughened feet sticking out from beneath. To Kai's surprise, Ooranye's English was halting but understandable.

"Grandmother Ooranye, I bring you a gift from my people." Kai gently placed the dried sticks of sage in the woman's short wide hands.

"Ahh! Yes…" She smiled a toothless smile and lifted the sage to her wide, flat nose, her nostrils flaring as she inhaled deeply. "Mmm, this smells good."

Jake moved into the hut and saw Kai crouched before the old woman. He knelt quietly and said nothing. The rapt look on Kai's face told him that this old, gray-haired woman smiling over the sage in her hands was indeed Ooranye.

Kai heard Jake quietly enter the hut and kneel nearby. She spoke slowly in English, knowing it was a foreign language to Ooranye. The old woman set the sage in her lap, her gnarled hands resting over it. She tilted her head to one side birdlike, as Kai introduced Jake.

"You have come a long way, my grandson," she greeted him, turning her head toward him. "Be at peace. Sit here with us."

Jake wondered how Ooranye could know where he was sitting. She was obviously blind. When she patted the blanket at her left side, he moved over to her and sat down.

"Granddaughter, come and sit here, beside me."

Kai did as she was bid when Ooranye pointed to her right side. As she made herself comfortable in the large, airy shelter, Kai saw another woman, perhaps half Ooranye's age, come to the entrance. She was carrying a wooden pitcher and three wooden cups in her hands. Entering and kneeling before Ooranye, she murmured something in their language that Kai couldn't decipher.

"Are you thirsty, my children? My daughter Yirrkala has made us a sweet, cool drink from the flowers."

"We'd love some," Kai murmured. "Thank you." She watched as Yirrkala, who was probably in her sixties, poured them each a glass. The first one went to Ooranye, who took it, nodded and smiled. Kai was served next. She held the rough-hewn wooden cup and looked into it. Bits of crushed yellow flower petals were floating on top of the beverage.

Jake took the last cup and thanked her.

"Drink, children. There is more if you want it." Ooranye lifted her cup to her lips and drank deeply.

Kai didn't know the protocol of these people, but she waited until Ooranye was drinking before she did so herself. To her surprise, the drink tasted like honey. It was delicious. Kai drained her cup and held it out to Yirrkala to fill it again.

"Is there enough of this for everyone?" Kai asked. She didn't want to be a pig or seem rude.

Smacking her lips with pleasure, Ooranye set her cup aside. "Yes, we have plenty, child. This is made from the Grevillea bush. The nectar of their long yellow flowers is what you are tasting. The women gather the blossoms just after the sun rises, mash them and pour water over them in a bowl, then let them sit half a day. We enjoy the sweetness. Drink until you are filled."

Kai drank three full cups before her thirst was stated. She hadn't realized just how parched she'd become, although she'd been drinking regularly from the water bottles tied to Booster's saddle.

When Yirrkala left, another woman—Akana—came in, bearing a round wooden platter filled with cooked kangaroo meat, bush honey and bread.

"I know you are tired," Ooranye said to Kai and Jake. "You are not used to our heat. Come, eat your fill. Our hunters have prayed that a kangaroo would give his life so that we may live. This meat is freshly cooked for you. My little granddaughter, Ulpundu, found the honey nearby by talking to the bees who made it. They led her to the hive, so that you may put honey on your bread. My other daughter, Mararu, has made flour damper here, or what you call bush bread. Come, eat...."

For the next half hour, they feasted. Kai reverently made sure that the elder was served first. It was a custom of the Cherokee that the old ones and growing children ate before anyone else, to be assured a full stomach. Adults were the last to eat, consuming whatever was left.

There was no talking during the meal, only the sounds of them eating with great enjoyment. Kai found the tender kangaroo meat tasted like the jerky she'd eaten the last two days—a cross between beef and chicken. The flour damper bread was surprisingly delicious and warm. She smeared the bush honey across the firm crust with her finger. Outside the hut, Kai heard quiet sounds of people talking to one another as they passed. Every now and again there was laughter. The homey setting and warm welcome made Kai relax. She had been worried about what kind of reception they would get. Little by little, she was feeling relief—a profound relief. She hadn't realized how tense and anxious she'd been about the whole journey.

As Kai sucked the last of the honey from her fingers, Yirrkala reentered the hut. She removed the platter, cups and pitcher, and left the three of them alone once more.

"Bush food is best," Ooranye told them in halting pidgin English. "When I was very little, white men came and stole me from my mother and family. I was taken to Adelaide, where I was taught English and told that my own language was never to be spoken again."

Kai's heart ached for the old woman.

"I spent the next twenty years as a servant to a rich white man and his family. Always, my heart yearned to come home to here." She pointed to the red sand with her index finger. "One day, I got the courage to escape and I ran. I would rather die in the bush than be made into a person I was not. I finally found my way here, to my home. My mother was alive and so happy to see me. All my brothers and sisters were still missing, so she was very glad to have me return."

"And you've lived here in Kalduke since then?" Kai asked. Outside, the sun was changing position, slanting ever westward, she noted. Even though the day was still hot, the interior of the hut was cool. Surprisingly so.

Chuckling deeply, Ooranye said, "Oh, no! This place is where the government asks us to have an 'official' village. Our people follow the Rainbow Serpent's instructions, which she gives to us yearly. She tells us where to go and when. We have only come back to this place because I knew you were coming. No, we are usually out there." She gestured toward the desert that surrounded them. "The government needs us to have a place we call home. They do not understand that home for us is all over the bush, not just here." She chuckled again and shook her head.

"I'm sure your mother was overjoyed to have you back," Kai said, suddenly emotional. She couldn't imagine being torn away like that. But in a way, she could, having lost her own mother at age nine and living in a foster home until age thirteen. After her parents' death, the state had felt Grams was too old to take care of her, so Kai had been sent to a foster home. Grams had eventually proved to the officials that she was more than capable of caring for her, so Kai was able to go home to the res once more. But Kai refused to be taught anything about medicine even though Grams had offered.

Reaching out, Ooranye patted Kai's hand. "All things have purpose, child. We do not know the answers to why they happen, only that the Rainbow Serpent has a greater plan and path for us to follow." Her fingers curled around Kai's. "And just like I was, you are lost, child, and yearn to go home."

Uneasy, Kai wondered if the elder could read not only her mind, but what lay in her wounded heart. She knew enough not to try and lie her way out of this, for there was an incredible energy swirling around Ooranye. Kai recognized it as the kind of nurturing, loving energy that Grams also possessed. It told her that Ooranye was a very adept medicine person who knew a great deal of magic. Kai was sure that the elder understood the world of metaphysics as few could, and had likely completed decades of work on herself to lighten her spirit and make a powerful connection to the Rainbow Serpent so revered by her people.

"Grandmother, in all honesty, I do not know why I was chosen for this mission. I am not whole. I don't walk in balance as I should. My people seek harmony and wholeness, but I possess neither of those things…."

Patting her hand again, Ooranye whispered. "That is *why* you were chosen, child. You have the heart of Kuniya, the woman python or Dream Snake, and the humility to admit that you do not know everything. Do not feel bad about this. When I was stolen, I used to sit in a school that had bars over the windows to stop us from leaving. I cried nightly to the Dream Snake and asked why this had happened to me. Now I understand why I had to be taken. There is a greater plan for all of us, so do not feel bad about where you are presently. In time, all things heal within us, if we allow it. Everything is more than it seems…."

Hot tears stung Kai's closed eyes. She felt such gentle love flowing from Ooranye as she held her hand. The heat was alive and she realized that there was a healing going on between them. Sitting quietly, Kai closed her fingers around the old woman's gnarled and callused ones. Once the heat reached her heart she felt pain so sharp that it made her gasp out loud.

"Just accept it," Ooranye counseled gently. "The hurt will go as you give it back to the Rainbow Serpent to digest…."

Breathing shallowly, Kai felt the pain in her heart arc upward. Was she going to die of a cardiac arrest? With each indrawn breath, she felt the ache go deeper. It hurt to inhale, it hurt to think. Gripping Ooranye's hand, Kai bowed her head, her other hand pressed to the center of her chest. Was she going to die?

The moment she thought it, the pain began to ease. Over the next few minutes, the hurt dissolved, and soon Kai could once more take in a full, deep breath of air without resistance. Gradually, she loosened her grip on the elder's strong hand.

"There…" Ooranye murmured. "It is done. Now you will feel better, a little more each day."

Kai looked at the woman, whose ebony face shone with an ethereal glow. Blinking, Kai realized that the glow went beyond her head, surrounding her whole body in a golden, oval-shaped aura. Kai sent Jake a quick glance, wondering if he saw it, too. He did, she realized. His eyes were wide with awe and surprise.

Sitting back, Kai gulped. Only once, in her late teens, had she seen Grams's aura. It had startled her, almost frightened her, until she'd remembered as a child seeing an icon of the Mother Mary with just such a halo of gold light around her head. When it happened with her grandmother, Grams had just finished conducting a sacred ceremony for their clan.

Understanding that Ooranye was a sacred person, someone holy in the tradition of her people, Kai gulped again. She felt so far below her, spiritually speaking, that she had no right to even be near her. Kai knew her life so far had been one of bruising pain and nonstop suffering. She was not a light to the world, as this Aboriginal elder certainly was. And as was Grams.

"I came into your dreams, child, because the Rainbow

Serpent told me it was time." Ooranye looked directly at Kai. "Last year we had a dark-hearted man near here. He had stolen a sacred object, and it was made of stone. That much I know."

"You mean the quartz crystal mask we're looking for?" Kai asked, unable to keep the excitement out of her voice. She gave Jake another quick look. He, too, was leaning forward raptly.

Nodding, Ooranye said, "I have seen this stone face. It has come to me often in the Dreamtime. It cries out to go home."

"We're here to bring it back to our people," Jake told her. "It's the Paint Clan crystal mask. A sacred totem for our people."

Unable to contain her excitement, Kai whispered, "You know it's here?"

Ooranye nodded. "Yes. But to get it back will be very, very dangerous. You may lose your life trying to rescue it…."

Chapter 8

"Did you sleep well, child?" Ooranye asked the next morning as they sat in her brush hut.

Kai nodded. "A dreamless sleep." She smiled at the old woman, who now wore a crinkled but clean pink shift.

"No, I wasn't in your dreams last night." The Aborigine chuckled indulgently.

Jake sat a few feet away from Kai. They'd been given a brush hut with a grass mat to sleep upon last night. Kai hadn't protested about sleeping in the same space with him. Given the fact that they were exhausted from the journey and the murderous heat, neither of them had anything on their mind but deep, healing sleep. Shortly after they had awakened, Kai had been given a hand-hewn wooden bowl of fresh water, and she'd eagerly washed the grit from her face, arms, neck and hands.

Jake had gone to the rock hole about a quarter of a mile from the village. Kai had wanted nothing to do with the murky looking pool of water. At the spring, Jake had found a large wooden dish that was curved enough to hold water, and he'd bathed as well as he could. It felt good to be clean, the salty perspiration cleansed from his body.

"You feel refreshed now?" Ooranye asked Kai kindly.

"Yes, Grandmother, thank you." She sat cross-legged, her elbows resting on her knees, hands folded in her lap. The morning sun was shining through the east-facing door. Outside, Kai could hear the soft chatter of villagers as they went about their day.

Jake pushed his fingers through his recently washed hair. This morning, Kai's hair was neatly combed into a thick black braid that hung between her shoulder blades. She had on clean clothes—a pink silk, sleeveless top with a scoop neck and another pair of Rail Ryder nylon pants. He tried not to allow his gaze to drift to the swell of her breasts, the nipples clearly visible against the soft fabric. Last night had been a special kind of hell for him, with only a foot or so of space between them. Kai had fallen asleep immediately, but he'd lain awake for a long time, aching to roll over and pull her into his arms. Would she have come? No. He had to talk with her first. He thought what he saw in her eyes was yearning for him, but he couldn't be sure. He could be misreading her.

Kai quashed her impatience to know about the crystal mask and its whereabouts. It wasn't polite to push elders to speak on any topic until they were ready to. Kai was finding that Aboriginal culture was very similar to her own in that way. Younger people were taught to wait until an elder asked before they gave their thoughts. Young people were expected to sit at the feet of wise elders to listen and learn.

"Your eyes are beautiful gems," Ooranye said. "They remind me of when I stood on the shore of Mother Ocean and saw that amazing color in the water."

"How can you see me?" Kai asked, stymied.

Chuckling, Ooranye tapped her brow. "Child, we have three eyes, you know? There are two here—" she pointed to her milky, sightless orbs "—and a third one that is unseen, yet works just as well as the others. I had fleshy tumors grow across my eyes when I was middle-aged. The doctor call them pterygiums. From then on, I was blind. Over the years, with my mother's instruction and help, I was able to develop my ability to see with my middle eye. When I finally went blind, I simply switch to seeing with this other one, and it serves me just as well. I can see you as clearly as you see me."

Shaking her head, Kai smiled at Jake, who had a surprised look on his face, too.

Ooranye said, "In order for you to find the stone mask, you must be prepared to die."

Gulping, Kai whispered, "Die?"

Nodding, Ooranye looked at Jake. "Yes, and I must warn you that there is darkness that wants to surround you."

Jake frowned. "What do you mean by darkness, Grandmother?" He felt terror deep in his heart as he looked over at Kai. She seemed surprised, too, by the elder's statement.

"We are given glimpses of things, of possibilities…but that is all." She sighed and folded her hands, her voice lowering. "Here is what I have been shown. I see dark clouds gathering on the horizon, racing toward you. I sense that a person or group of people wants the crystal mask you speak of. They know about you. How, I do not know, so do not ask me. This darkness wants the crystal mask because it represents power. The dark ones are always enchanted with power. If this man finds the mask before you do, he will exploit it for his own selfish greed and desire. They know who you are and they track you now as a dingo tracks her quarry. Are you aware of them?"

Shaking her head, Kai murmured, "No, Grandmother, we aren't."

Jake scowled. "Have you seen them?" he asked the old woman.

Shaking her head, she said, "I see them only as a symbol. That is all I am being shown."

"How dangerous are they?" Kai asked, glancing toward Jake, who returned her worried look.

"They will kill for this stone mask. They have been searching the Red Center for over a year and have not found it."

"It means that we have to stop being lackadaisical about our welfare," Kai told him. "We both thought there was little danger to this mission."

"We didn't think anyone would care," Jake muttered. "Obviously, we were dead wrong." His heart pounded. The thought of Kai being killed alarmed him as nothing else could. Jake knew she could take care of herself. Kai was a warrior through and through, yet Jake wanted to be there at her side. Together, they would stand a better chance of survival.

Ooranye smiled, brushing a fly away from her face. "Children, you underestimate the darkness of man. Earth is a school, where we come into a physical body to learn certain lessons. There is light here, which we represent, but also a darkness that cares nothing for those within the circle of life. We are learning lessons about the use and abuse of power, about greed, lust, desire, prejudice and all the other harmful human emotions we encounter."

Kai sighed and gave Jake a searching look. "We'll have to stay on guard twenty-four-seven until we figure out *who* is behind this."

"Yes," he agreed grimly. "I've been racking my brain just now, trying to think if we were followed and didn't realize it."

"No other camels or riders followed us here, that's for sure."

"True," Jake murmured with a slight smile, "but there are satellites up in the sky that could track us."

"Those are defense satellites," Kai objected.

"So what? What if our enemy is military?"

Scowling, Kai growled, "This sucks."

Raising her hands, Ooranye said, "Children, you do not know who it is—yet. My sense is you will know shortly. Therefore, you must remain alert, like the woma python, which is always stalked by the dingo."

"Don't worry, Grandmother, we will."

Nodding, Ooranye said, "Now, I must tell you about this crystal mask of your people and where it is located. There is a Red Canyon perhaps a day's camel ride from here. At the back of it is a cave—a very deep, old cave. No one goes to it because it is dangerous. We know that others have tried to walk into it in the past, and when they did, they disappeared."

"Because?" Kai asked.

Shrugging, Ooranye said, "It is dark in there. You walk into it and suddenly there is no floor beneath your feet. Many have fallen to their deaths."

Jake glanced at Kai. "And this is where the man who stole the crystal mask went?"

"Yes, my grandson, he did." Ooranye pointed toward the ceiling of the hut. "He came from the sky like a bird."

Frowning, Kai muttered, "In a plane? A helicopter?"

"No, neither of those. It was odd looking. It had wings and a noisy motor...."

"An ultralight!" Jake said excitedly. "It had to be one of those little homemade airplanes."

Shrugging, Ooranye said, "He landed near the canyon. We saw him and his noisy, sputtering bird put down. One of our hunters went to see why he was here. He said the man pushed the bird beneath a large tree to hide it and then ran into the canyon. He was carrying a brown leather sack in his hand. The hunter tracked him. When he came to where the prints of his boots disappeared, the hunter knew he'd fallen into the cave."

"Was he alive?" Kai asked.

"No. The bird man had fallen to his death, as all others have."

"Then the man with the mask is down on the bottom of this cave floor?" Jake inquired.

Wrinkling her nose, Ooranye said, "Yes."

"Are you sure?" Kai demanded.

"The smell of dead, rotting flesh has filled this canyon for nearly a year. Only of late has the odor left. The desert is hot and dries things out. We are sure this bird man is dead at the bottom of that cave. There was a great sandstorm about three months after he died, and it swept away the wings and motor he flew here with. They are no more, torn apart by the winds and buried by the shifting sand. But we found this in his bird." She handed Kai some folded, dusty papers.

Eagerly unfolding the badly crinkled papers, Kai opened and quickly perused them. A feeling of triumph soared through her. She handed them to Jake.

"Look at this!" she said, excited as she tapped her finger on the papers he held. "The man's name was Giles Rowland. And see that? Marston's address is on it!"

Frowning, Jake read the scribbled notes, eyes squinting. "Marston's Hong Kong address. It says here in 'instructions' that Rowland was to fly from the U.S. to Sydney and then to Marston's villa on the island."

Snorting, Kai muttered, "It looks like Rowland had other ideas. He might have landed in Sydney, but he was taking the totem for himself. Why else would he be out here? Probably looking for a good place to hide it where no one would find it until he could pawn it off to some millionaire who wanted to buy it instead of giving it to Marston as he'd agreed to."

"I think you're right," Jake murmured, handing her back the papers. "That's proof against Marston. It also gives you a double check on that one totem where you were told it was on an island where yellow-skinned people lived. That would be the Chinese and Hong Kong is an island." He smiled proudly over at her. "You're batting a thousand on your dreaming ability," he congratulated her.

Feeling a warm flush creep up her neck and into her face, Kai absorbed Jake's warm praise. "I'm still so new at this...." She folded the papers and put them into a zippered pocket of her Rail Riders for safe keeping. This was more evidence implicating Marston.

Ooranye smiled at Kai. "You are a far seerer. And I'm glad these papers mean something to you."

"Did the hunter find the sack the man was carrying?" Kai asked.

"No, he did not." Ooranye tapped her brow between her eyes. "I know the stone mask is down there. I hear it crying. The man is dead and the sack he brought holds the mask you seek. We cannot get down there. We tried and failed."

Jake gave Kai a meaningful glance. "It makes me glad I stowed some climbing gear in our baggage. We're going to need it."

Nodding, Kai pursed her lips. "How are you at spelunking, Carter? You got a degree in that, too?"

Grinning, Jake murmured, "Camels and caves. What do they have in common?"

He saw her eyes dance with mischief. "They both start with a *C*, for Carter."

"Bang on. Yes, I've done my fair share of caving over the years. In the Great Smokies where we were raised there were plenty of limestone caves. I used to explore many of them."

"I didn't."

Chuckling, Jake reached out and gripped her hand for a moment. "I'll teach you." He felt her squeeze his fingers in return. How badly he wanted quality time to talk to Kai of their past and their present.

"Good."

"Rest for today, children. Tomorrow, I will show you how to get to the canyon. That will be soon enough," Ooranye counseled. "You need another good night's sleep to be alert, so you will not die in your attempt to get the stone mask."

"What do you think about someone wanting to steal the crystal mask?" Kai asked. Lying on her back, hands behind her head, she looked up through the brush ceiling, to where stars were winking in the ebony sky. Jake lay on the other side of the hut, with a few feet of space separating them.

Rolling onto his side, Jake used his arm as a pillow. "Rowland could have had help. He could have hired others to help him hide the mask in Red Canyon or Marston realized he took it."

"Yeah," Kai said, "and he's got his men here in the Red Center trying to find it just like we're doing."

"I think you're right, Kai. Your dream is proving to be true and it's gotten us this far." He saw the vague outline of Kai's body near the open doorway. There was a slight breeze and he was grateful for it.

"Having clairvoyant skills is a blessing and a curse," she muttered, closing her eyes. Kai felt comfortable being so near to Jake. She didn't feel threatened by him; on the contrary, she was glad he was here. Somehow, Kai felt he understood her need to be left to make her own decisions and come to her own conclusions. Maybe that's why she felt comfortable asking his thoughts now.

"Ooranye certainly is clairvoyant. It blows me away that she can get around just like us, though she's completely blind. When she took us out to find witchetty grubs earlier today, I watched her listen like a dog with its ears up. And she seemed to know just where to dig under that bush to find those big white grubs."

Wrinkling her nose, Kai said, "It made my stomach turn when she popped one in her mouth. Ugh!"

Laughing softly, Jake said, "Hey, they consider those grubs a big find. I was wondering if you were going to eat one when she offered it to you."

"Carter, I would have to be starving to death, on my last legs, to even think of eating an insect."

"You had survival training in the military, though," he pointed out mildly. "You had to go through a couple of weeks in the woods or desert, didn't you?"

"Yeah, I did," she muttered, frowning. "I didn't like it."

"You ate insects then, didn't you?"

"No...I managed to kill a rattlesnake. It was good food. I avoid eating the Little People, the insects."

"I'm impressed."

Kai snorted. "I'm sure you had to go through survival training as a combat helicopter pilot."

"Yes, I did. I ate night crawlers."

"Dude, let's talk about something else, anything but *this,* okay?"

Chuckling, Jake controlled his urge to reach out and touch Kai's shoulder. She had stripped down to the sleeveless, low-cut pink tank top and a pair of silk shorts that barely covered the tops of her curved thighs. He'd like to explore those legs slowly and in great, lingering detail. Kai was in superior shape, her limbs firm and tight. Jake was glad she couldn't read his mind or he was sure she'd deck him with those kick-boxing skills of hers.

"I want to call Mike Houston tomorrow morning on the satellite phone, Kai. I think he should be alerted that we've got some bad guys hanging around. We need to tell him we've discovered where the crystal mask is located, the information on Rowland and Marston, plus that we're going to have to spelunk to get to it."

"That's a good idea."

In the shadows, Jake saw Kai's narrowed eyes, her lowered brows. His gaze trailed to her mouth, which was pursed and puckered. A mouth he'd like to brush with his own. Poignantly recalling when he'd shyly kissed Kai one day at the old beech tree, Jake remembered how he'd felt as he'd touched her soft, tearstained mouth. Her lips had clung to his briefly, and the wild, euphoric feelings that bolted through him had made him jerk away in complete surprise. He'd seen that his kiss had made Kai feel better, because she'd reached up with her long, thin fingers and touched her lower lip, a look of awe in her flawless blue eyes as she'd stared at him in wonderment.

Jake gently tucked that memory away. That was then. This was now. Kai's mouth used to be full, the lower lip slightly pouty. These days her lips were often thinned, and she was tense and on guard. Right now, though, the starlight revealed how relaxed she was. An ache centered in his heart as he yearned, once more, to give her respite from a world that kept her constantly on guard.

Raising his brows, Jake lay down on his back, hands behind his head. "Kai, I need to talk to you." His mouth was dry, his heart pounding like a scared rabbit in his chest. He saw her turn and look at him. "About the past. The present. Us." There, he'd gotten it out. How would Kai react? Jake was terribly unsure, but something powerful was pushing him to broach this supersensitive topic with her, because he wanted her in his life in the future. Would she have anything to do with it? With him?

Chapter 9

"I don't want to talk about it, Jake." Kai felt bad because she'd heard the hope in his husky tone. "I—I just can't. Not now…"

Jake tried to squelch his disappointment. "Okay, Kai."

"I need to sleep," she muttered, apology in her tone.

"No problem…" Jake stared sightlessly through the darkness. Pain flowed through his heart and he felt it keenly.

Nostrils flaring. Kai stared at his long, powerful form silhouetted against the hut wall. She saw his rugged profile and how his mouth was compressed with unhappiness over her decision.

She closed her eyes. Old memories came floating back to her, of Jake's skinny but strong arms around her, holding her, rocking her while she wept her heart out, her face pressed against his youthful chest. One memory, painful and strong, came back to her as she stared at him. Her father had just beaten her with his old, cracked leather belt. He kept the belt hanging on a hook behind his bedroom door, and he used it to beat her with when he decided she needed a lickin'. And that was often enough, because Kai couldn't keep her rage suppressed and she'd confronted him daily, mouthing off to him, much to her regret.

Closing her eyes, Kai dragged her arm across her eyes as the memory overwhelmed her. Her father had gotten drunk on moonshine. He'd had a still where he made "white lightnin'," and would go to it every night and down a couple of slugs of the stuff. Then he'd stumble back to the cabin and start a fight with her mother. Kai remembered those nights all too well. She would stay in her room, do her homework and try to ignore the screaming and yelling that went on. Some nights were worse than others. Her mother would stand up to her father and then he'd hit her and knock her down. Even after she'd stop fighting back, Henry would continue to strike her as she crawled around on the floor, shrieking and trying to evade his pummeling fists.

It was those nights, as Kai hunkered at her small desk near her narrow pine bed, that her stomach became tied in knots. She'd grip the pencil so hard that her knuckles would whiten, and she'd wait with dread, hearing her mother's pitiful shrieks and her father's angry roars rising in a crescendo. Kai always knew when her father was going to beat her mother. She had a sixth sense about it. Henry would stalk her for days, goading her, being verbally abusive before she'd fight back, and then he'd beat the hell out of her.

One night, when Kai had heard the crack of her father's hand slapping her mother's face, she'd rocketed out of her room, shrieking in uncontrolled rage at him. She'd found her father hunkered over her mother, who had been knocked to the white linoleum floor, her head against the cabinets. When Kai saw blood flowing out of her mother's nose, her mouth open and contorted with pain, tears trailing down her copper cheeks, she had mindlessly launched herself at her father, arms flailing, fingers arched like claws as she landed on his back. Kai had beaten him with every ounce of strength she'd had that night. She loved her mother and could no longer stand to have her crying or bleeding.

Something had changed in Kai that night. Had it ever, she thought, looking back on that terrible moment.

Turning her head, Kai gazed up through the hut's ceiling at the blinking stars. She didn't want to relive the minutes after her sudden and unexpected attack on her drunken father. She'd never hit her dad before, and it had caught him off guard. But not for long.

After he'd used the belt on her, Kai remembered staggering out of the house near dusk and running blindly toward the beech tree on the mountain. It was a good mile and a half away from their cabin, which sat on the floor of the valley, but Kai didn't care. As she ran like a deer, her skin smarting and swelling with thick purple welts, she sobbed. And when she ran up to the tree's sheltering arms, there was Jake, waiting for her. Kai was always amazed that he seemed to know when she'd be coming. Grateful that he was there, she had flung herself against him, crying wildly, like a wounded animal.

Oh, she remembered how gently and awkwardly Jake would pat her heaving shoulders, whisper broken, tearful words meant to heal her. Often he would sit down, his back against the girth of the old beech, gently gather her into his arms and simply hold her.

Jake jerked awake. Sitting up, he heard Kai's soft sobbing. What time was it? he wondered. Getting to his hands and knees, he realized it was dawn, the horizon outside the door a pale gold color. Kai was curled in a fetal position, her body turned away from him. He reached toward her.

"Kai…?"

The moment Jake's hand connected with her shoulder, she awakened, sitting up quickly to face him. "Don't touch me!"

Recoiling, Jake sat up in turn. He saw terror in Kai's eyes and heard it in her voice. Holding up his hands, he rasped, "Okay…it's okay. You were just having a bad dream, Kai. You're safe now…you're here with me…." Jake recognized the panicked look in her eyes. He'd seen it so often when she was a child.

Gulping hard, Kai choked down the panic that was clawing up her throat from her knotted stomach. Her breathing was chaotic, and she so desperately wanted to fall into Jake's arms. His face was sleep-ridden, his eyes puffy as he sat tensely no more than a foot away from her. His voice was low and gentle. She clung to his words, words that he'd crooned to her so many times so long ago. She hated her past! She hated the pain she carried in the name of her drunken father. The son of a bitch! Even now, after his death, he was hurting her. Why should anyone have to suffer that kind of pain over and over again? She was the victim, not the perpetrator. Life was so damn unfair and vicious, in her experience.

Kai took a deep, shuddering breath. "I'm okay, Jake…."

"Can I get you something? Some water?"

Shaking her head, Kai pulled her knees up to her chest and crossed her arms over them. She forced herself to stop reacting like a scared little girl. She was a mature woman, a fighter pilot. It was funny how, in the cockpit, she was like steel behind the stick, not this mushy, emotional woman she was currently. Kai decided it had to be the circumstances.

"I don't want to be *here!*" she whispered harshly.

Jake sat patiently. Kai's hair was in disarray. She'd loosened her braid sometime after he'd fallen asleep, and her hair was like a shining cloak around her shaking shoulders. How badly he wanted to touch her, to soothe her. Jake knew he could; he'd done it as a child. Yet she'd spurned his attempt just now. Bitterly, he sat there, knowing he could do nothing except be a silent witness to her suffering.

Lifting her face, Kai wiped the perspiration from her brow and cheeks with several swipes of her trembling fingers. When she looked at Jake, she saw he had moved closer, his face deeply shadowed with concern.

"Was it a dream?" he asked quietly. To hell with it. He reached out and placed his hand on her shoulder.

"Something…" she croaked. His touch was warm. Supportive. More tears leaked from her eyes. She didn't try to hide them from him. Seeing the agony in his own narrowed eyes, she sniffed and gulped.

"Was it a new dream? Not the same as the ones before?"

Just hearing his quiet, low tone helped soothe Kai's fractious state. She pushed her fingers through her hair and squared her shoulders to rid herself of the fear that inhabited her. His hand left her shoulder. Jake reached for a wooden pitcher and poured some water into a wooden cup. He held it toward her and Kai humbly accepted it.

As she gulped the tepid water, several drops spilled from the corners of her mouth and splattered on her pink silk T-shirt. Finishing it off, she wiped her mouth with the back of her hand. Giving the cup back to Jake, she whispered, "Thanks…."

"Sure." Their fingers touched briefly as he took it. There was such anguish in Kai's shadowed blue eyes that Jake ached for her.

"You know what I'd like to do for you right now?" he whispered unsteadily.

"No…" Kai sniffed and looked into his eyes. She saw such care in them, just as there had been in the past.

"I'd like to hold you. Like before. When we were kids…"

The words strung hauntingly between them and Jake wasn't sure if the offer would soothe Kai or hurt her. He watched her face, holding his breath.

Without a word, she crawled over to him. She saw the relief on Jake's face as he opened his arms wide to receive her.

Oh! The past was never far away! Kai realized. But she didn't care. Her dreams had been too virulent, leaving her feeling stripped and alone. She nestled in his arms, feeling the warmth of his strong body as she placed her head against his shoulder, nose pressed against his neck. She sighed. It was a sigh that felt old, as if it had been held for a long time within her. As Jake's arms moved around her and he brought her fully against him, Kai closed her eyes, feeling the solid beat of his heart against her hand as she slid it across his chest.

"When will the past stop haunting me?" she whispered brokenly, new tears leaking out from beneath her lashes.

Jake shook his head, lifted his hand and gently stroked the silken length of her hair down her back. "I don't know, Kai, but I do know one thing…." He looked down at her. In the grayness of the dawn light, she seemed more like a vulnerable child to him than the woman she was. Here eyes were closed. There were wet tear tracks down her face, her soft lips parted, the lower one quivering.

"Wh-what?" she asked quietly.

"That I want to be here with you. That I like holding you as I did when we were kids. For me, holding you again is a dream come true. I might not be able to chase the demons from inside you, but at least by holding you I can give you a moment's rest from them…."

Nodding, she savored Jake's quiet tone as it washed away her terror. "You've always been my safe haven, Jake."

He chuckled quietly. "Some things don't change, Kai. And I'm glad they don't."

She opened her eyes, pulling her head away just enough to look into his narrowed, smoldering gaze. Oh, how close his lips were! How she ached to kiss him. "When you left, I lost track of you. I tried to find you, but I never did…."

Nodding, Jake touched her cheek and brushed the tears away with his fingers. "I tried to find you, too, but it didn't work."

"We went our separate ways, Jake."

"And look what happened." He felt the soft strength of her beneath his trembling fingers. Touching Kai was like touching life itself. Never had Jake felt so good, so happy, as right now. "We thought what we had was gone, but the Great Spirit has brought us back together again. I'm grateful for that, Kai."

Nodding, Kai closed her eyes and felt the hurt rising in her chest. "I don't even know if you're married. Or what's happened to you since…since we last…"

Jake shifted position and eased Kai against him as he supported himself against the wall of the hut. "That's easy to share with you." Closing his eyes, he rested his head against Kai's. "When my dad got orders from the Air Force, we picked up and left the res. That was about a few weeks after your parents died. He was sent to Germany. I kicked around Air Force bases until I was eighteen, when I went into the U.S. Army to learn to fly helicopters. I like what I do, Kai. I like flying the Apache combat helicopter. I'd like to think I make a difference in the world."

"You've always been a warrior, Jake. Like me." Kai melted into him, her heart beating time to his. "I guess it shouldn't have been a surprise to me that you went into the military."

"I was surprised you did," he murmured. Giving her a gentle squeeze, he rasped, "I had all kinds of crazy dreams about you when I was growing up. I wondered if you were okay. I figured your Gram would take care of you. She's a good person, so I knew you would be okay. At least—" he grimaced "—she wasn't an abuser like your father. She's always loved you."

"Yes, she does. She helped me to see that not all men are bad like my father was. I owe her a lot, Jake."

"She's the best," he agreed.

"Are you married? Have a bunch of kids?" Kai's throat ached with tension. She didn't want to think of Jake as married, but he was such a wonderful person that she couldn't imagine some woman hadn't snagged him yet.

"No. Oh, came close a few times, but…" he smiled distantly "…I had this blue-eyed Indian girl who stole my heart long ago, and I just never got over her or forgot her through all these years."

The words were spoken haltingly and with great emotion. Kai moved her hand up around Jake's neck and pressed herself more closely to him. She couldn't believe that he had been thinking of her all these years. That he'd felt so much for her. "You never married?" she asked in disbelief.

Shaking his head, Jake said, "No. I had some good relationships, Kai, but none so serious that I wanted to walk down the aisle. Once, when I was twenty-one, I lived with a woman, but that broke up after a year because she found someone else who had more money and prestige."

"Good riddance."

He chuckled. "Yeah. At the time, it hurt like hell, but afterward, I realized it was a good thing." He opened his eyes and lifted his head to look down at Kai. "How about you? I didn't see any wedding ring on your left hand, but nowadays you never can tell what that means. You have a steady other in your life?"

Shrugging, Kai whispered, "Two years ago, I did. Lieutenant Ted Barnes. He was an F-18 Hernet pilot. We met on the carrier I was on. I fell in love with him…or thought I did."

"And now?" Jake didn't want Kai to be engaged to another man. Not with her in his arms for the first time in so many years. This was like a dream come true. Jake had lost count of how many times he'd dreamed of this. He knew it was selfish of him to hope she hadn't found someone else. After all, Kai deserved happiness after the hell of her growing-up years.

"I broke up with Ted a year ago, Jake. We went our separate ways." Her mouth thinned. "He couldn't handle a fully independent res girl." She felt Jake laugh, the sound vibrating through her like warm honey across her scarred heart. "And to tell you the truth, I'm still recovering from it." Kai looked up at Jake and absorbed the burning tenderness in his golden eyes. "That's why I didn't want you on this mission with me. I—I was afraid of myself, of my reactions to you. The past I thought I'd buried and left behind came roaring back at me. I was so cold to you when we met in Montana. I—I just couldn't handle the past, even though you were the only positive thing in my life at that time."

Lifting his hand, Jake removed a strand of hair from the side of her face and slipped it behind her ear. "I saw your eyes, Kai. I saw the look in them. I knew you were glad to see me. Well…at least a part of you was. I sensed it."

Though his touch soothed her ailing heart, her mind screamed at her not to get involved with anyone right now. Closing her eyes, Kai focused on his fingers sliding across her hair in such a gentle fashion. "You knew…."

"I knew I'd never forgotten you, Kai. Or what we shared."

Opening her eyes, she held his gaze. "And now? Is that what you want? What we had in the past?"

Shaking his head, Jake whispered, "I want only those things from the past that were healthy and positive for us, Kai. We can't forget it. All we can do is learn from it and use our experiences wisely for the present—and maybe the future...." How badly he wanted to tell Kai what lay in his heart, but Jake knew she wasn't ready to hear it. Not now. Maybe never. Everything was so tenuous with her. Realizing she was still reeling from Ted walking out of her life, Jake felt some of his hope for them crumble.

"The only part of my past I don't hate is the part that had you in it, Jake." Kai gulped unsteadily. "But I'm scared. Really scared. Me! I can fly an F-14 around in the skies, get shot at by SAM missiles and still not be half as scared as I am right now."

Jake understood. "Listen," he whispered, giving her a tender look, "let's take our time. We're together again. We have a job to do here. Let's take this relationship of ours one step at a time, okay?" He didn't want to. No, Jake was ready to go full throttle to the firewall in a relationship with Kai, but he could tell she wasn't there yet. Holding his breath, he watched many emotions cross her face. Once again, Kai was allowing him to see the real her. Before this, she had kept her expression carefully arranged so he couldn't see how she really felt. Now she was allowing him that privilege. He considered that a huge victory.

"One day at a time, Jake. That's all I can handle right now." She searched his face, her eyes meeting and holding his. "Can you deal with that? With what I need?"

"In a heartbeat, Kai." Jake looked around. The hut was growing brighter and brighter by the minute as the sun continued to inch toward the horizon. The purple dawn had begun. "To tell you the truth, I never thought you'd come into my arms again, so what I have right now is a precious gift, and more than I ever thought I'd receive from you."

Kai nodded mutely. She briefly touched his jaw, finding the skin sandpapery and in need of a shave. "I want to go for a walk, Jake. I have to feel my way through all of this…." She slowly extricated herself from his arms and shifted away from him. It wasn't what Kai wanted to do, but she knew under the circumstances she had to or she was going to kiss Jake, and that would signal a depth of commitment her heart simply wouldn't allow her to make right now. Slowly getting to her feet, she picked up her Rail Riders and drew the pant legs on one at a time.

"Want company?"

"No. I need some time alone, Jake…."

Jake watched helplessly as Kai quickly got dressed and slipped out of the opening. He heard her booted feet head off toward the north, away from the small village. Scratching his head, he decided to get his own boots on and just hang around outside the hut. His job was to be Kai's wing man, her eyes and ears. Then he remembered Ooranye's assertion that there was someone out there who wanted that crystal mask as badly as they did, and he quickly pulled his boots on, deciding he should follow Kai. Not too closely. No, he'd shadow her, so that she could have the time alone she needed. Was she deciding about them? About whether to ever allow him to hold her again? It was a burning question for Jake as he crawled out of the hut and stood up.

The eastern horizon was a deep purple now, the ebony of the night slowly releasing its grip. Around him, Jake noted some villagers were already awake and going about their morning activities. In the distance, he saw the silhouettes of the hobbled camels, grazing about half a mile from the encampment. Kai was out there with them, patting Rocket on the nose. Warmth encircled Jake's heart as he stood there, hands stuffed in the pockets of his trousers. At least she didn't distrust animals as she did the men who had scarred her heart. Hanging his head, he scuffed the toe of his boot into the red sand. Somehow, he wished he could ease Kai's tortured past, but he knew he couldn't. Her drunken father had hurt her so grievously.

Lifting his chin, his eyes narrowing, Jake saw Kai walking away from the camels. Both began to follow her. Smiling wryly, Jake took his hands out of his pockets and followed at a leisurely pace. Would Kai continue to open up to him? Trust him as she had before? Allow her heart to reach out to his? He hoped so.

Chapter 10

"There is a place nearby that I want to take you to. The ground is good and flat and I can draw you a map with my fingers. I'll show you how to get to this cave in the canyon where the sacred stone mask is located." Ooranye stood up and dusted off the dark green shift she wore.

The morning sun was strong and they'd just finished a delicious breakfast with the wise woman in her hut. Ooranye carried a huge loaf of damper bread in one hand and a bowl of bush honey in the other as she slowly walked toward the spring. Jake walked beside Kai, his heart still warm with the memory of holding her that morning. He had noticed during their breakfast with Ooranye that Kai seemed softer, more open than before.

The old woman led them to a spot near the Anangu rock hole where Jake took his sponge baths twice a day. The area was just right for scratching pictures into the soil. Around the water hole in the gray stone grew a circle of white-barked River Red Gum trees. Their long, graceful limbs spread above the spring that Jake had come to appreciate so much. The eucalyptus trees with their broad, reaching limbs made it one of the few places where shade was available on the Gibson Desert, a miniature oasis. Their two camels were nearby after drinking their fill, hidden in the deep shade of the thick grove of trees.

Ooranye settled herself on a smooth red rock that was flat on top. She placed the flour damper on a similar one nearby, and gestured for Kai and Jake to join her. Sitting back, Jake enjoyed the morning, the birds singing…and then his sharp hearing caught an unnatural sound. Turning, he scanned the pale blue sky to the south.

"You hear it, too?" Ooranye murmured, cocking her head to listen. Her frown deepened.

Kai was the last to hear the sound. She got up and placed her hand against the trunk of a gum tree, looking at the southern horizon. "What is it?"

Jake moved closer to Ooranye. "Sounds like an engine…maybe a helicopter?"

Frowning, Kai said, "Yeah, for sure, an aircraft. And it's coming our way. Are the binoculars nearby?"

"No, they're in our hut," Jake said unhappily. The sound was growing stronger. "That's a helicopter," he told them, sure of it now. Moving to Kai's side beneath the spreading arms of the red gum, he saw a black spec on the horizon. "There it is."

"I see it…." Kai turned and looked down at Ooranye. "Do you get aircraft out here often?"

Shaking her head, she said, "No. We live very far away from where such craft fly. We do not like the sound, so we make sure we stay away from them. The government has promised that none would come near our village, so this is strange...."

The hair on the back of Kai's neck stood up. She got that same sensation when a SAM had been aimed at her as she flew over the skies of Iraq. Worriedly, she glanced at Jake. Hands on his hips, he stared at the approaching aircraft. "Could it be a tourist chopper?"

"I don't know...."

"The darkness has found you...." Ooranye muttered.

Kai's heart thudded with fear. She saw Jake's eyes narrow and his lips thin.

"It's that Huey from the Yulara airport," Jake said in a low tone.

"Yes," Kai agreed tensely. "I wish I had my pistol on me now...."

"Children, you must go!" Ooranye warned. "They must not see you. They are darkness. I feel it strongly. Hurry! Run to your hut and stay there. If they land, they will be looking for you, and we will take them off your scent. The camels will remain here with me."

Kai glanced again at Jake. He held out his hand toward her. "Let's go."

Kai nodded, and they turned and quickly jogged toward the huts that stood a quarter mile away. "I wonder if they have infrared on board."

"I doubt it," he said, breaking into a run. Feeling sure they could make it before the helicopter pilot saw them, he kept up the steady pace. Kai ran fluidly at his side. "That's a 1970s model, Kai."

Nodding, Kai narrowed her eyes. It felt good to run, although fear was shooting through her. They were without weapons, which made the situation more dangerous. Her heart actually slowed in beat, adrenaline flooding her bloodstream, readying her to fight. "There were two choppers there," she huffed. "I didn't pay much attention." The copter was drawing closer by the moment, but they were nearly to their hut. A number of the Aborigines were looking toward the sky as Kai and Jake approached.

"I did. There was this Huey with a blue-and-yellow paint scheme, and a Bell helicopter, a silver Bell Longranger."

"Good memory," Kai said huskily. The whapping of the blades began to make the early morning air tremble as the helicopter sped nearer. Kai glanced back at Ooranye, who sat dipping her fingers into the bowl of bush honey and methodically spreading it across the damper bread held in the palm of her hand. She was pretending nothing was wrong. Wise woman, Kai thought. Acting as if nothing is out of the ordinary. Maybe if the pilot thinks nothing's out of place, he'll just go away.

"Jake? Can you read the numbers on the fuselage? And do you have a pen or paper handy once we get to the hut?" She didn't, and again Kai berated herself for her lack of preparedness. If someone was really hunting for her and the crystal mask, she had to get off her duff and stay more alert. No pistol. No binoculars. Nothing. She felt frustrated at her own incompetence under the circumstances.

The helicopter was behind the grove of gums now. "Yeah, when it passes by, I'll try and get a look at it without giving away our hiding place."

Kai spied a group of Aboriginal women walking toward them, water jugs in hand. Whoever was in the helo would certainly see them and know they were heading to the rock hole oasis. Maybe that would throw them off Kai and Jake's scent. The helicopter was less than a mile away and flying at three thousand feet. Kai wasn't completely convinced they were hostile. Ooranye hadn't been wrong yet, but something in Kai didn't want to believe that anyone would challenge her quest for the crystal mask.

Ducking quickly into their hut, she got down on her hands and knees and reached for her pack. Unzipping it, she grabbed her holster and pistol. Jake did the same. Their breathing was heavy as they silently but quickly worked to arm themselves. Would the copter land? Kai wasn't sure. She turned, inching back toward the opening, where Jake now crouched, looking skyward.

He lifted his head as the Huey flew low overhead. The whole area trembled in the wake of the turning blades. "Got it!" he said to Kai. Memorizing the numbers on the fuselage, he watched as the pilot, who sat in the right-hand seat, banked the helo and flew in a circle around the oasis. Jake quickly scribbled the numbers down on a small notebook and shoved it into the pocket of his white, short-sleeved shirt.

"They're looking for *something*," Kai muttered, her voice grim. Indeed they were. She could see the copilot craning his neck as he looked around. Kai couldn't make out his features because he was so far away.

After circling the oasis three times, the helicopter landed near the rock hole where Ooranye was calmly eating her bread. Kai peered through the cracks in the hut wall and saw two men emerging from the helo as the blades swung sluggishly, the engine shut down.

"They're armed," Jake hissed. He rose on one knee, his pistol held high, a bullet in the chamber.

"They're walking over to the rock hole where Ooranye's sitting," Kai said, worried for the old woman. She still couldn't see the men's faces clearly.

Jake turned, rummaged through his pack and pulled out a pair of binoculars. "I want to see who they are," he muttered, raising the field glasses to his eyes. They wore civilian clothes. The pilot appeared to be in his thirties, with black hair and brown eyes. He was deeply tanned, and Jake saw that he wore a pistol at his side. The other man was taller, leaner, red-haired and carrying an AK-47 military rifle. Looking closer, Jake saw there was a small label on the left-hand side of their red polo shirts. A name. What was it? Sharpening the focus, he honed in on the label: Marston Enterprises.

"It says Marston Enterprises," he told Kai, watching as the men approached Ooranye.

Shaking her head, she said, "Same Marston who Giles Rowland worked for?"

"That's the label on their shirts. They're both wearing that name on it." Pursing his lips, he whispered. "They're talking to Ooranye. She seems to be playing dumb."

Kai squinted and looked through the cracks of the hut wall. The men were too far away for her to see facial expressions, but she saw the rifle. The camels stood in the shade calmly chewing their curds, disinterested.

"Why would this dude be carrying a rifle around with him?"

"Hunters?"

"Of us? Or animals? Besides, who hunts in the bush with an AK-47? No, he's no hunter of animals." In her gut, she knew the men were looking for them. Mouth dry, Kai wiped her lips with the back of one hand, her pistol ready in the other one.

"Hang on—the red-haired guy is looking around... toward the village. I think he wants to check it out...."

"Yeah, and he's raised the rifle, ready to be fired," Kai growled. Her hand began to sweat around the handle of her pistol. She was glad there was a nine-bullet clip in it. "If they come into the village..."

"Then there's gonna be a shoot-out."

"Yeah..."

Jake watched Ooranye. By now, several of the other women, all relative of hers, had reached the spring and begun filling their jars with water, acting as if nothing was out of place. The two men appeared irritated. The red-haired one kept looking their way, impatience stamped all over his narrow face and close-set eyes.

"That guy wants to come into the village. The one with the AK-47," Jake warned her quietly. His heart was pounding with dread. The last thing he wanted was a firefight in this village. With bullets flying, the possibility of innocent people being wounded was very real. Yet there was no place for them to run and hide, either. This village was their only cover. If they took off, they'd be seen, and those two would hop in their chopper and hunt them down from the air. No, there wasn't much choice left to them.

Gritting her teeth, Kai watched the red-haired man with

the rifle take a couple of steps toward the village. Her breath hitched and she tensed.

The pilot who was talking to Ooranye called him back. A breath exploded from Jake. "They're leaving!"

Relief shot through Kai. Eyes slitted, she watched the two men reluctantly turn away and walk back to the Huey. "Thank the Great Spirit…."

"When they've left, we'll find out from Ooranye what they wanted," Jake murmured. He continued to watch the men, still not assured they would leave. Only after the copter was airborne and heading back in the direction of Yulara did he relax.

Kai sighed and gave him a tense look. Then she strapped her holster around her waist and put the pistol in it. Jake did the same. He kept the binoculars around his neck as they emerged from the hut and quickly walked back to the water hole to speak with Ooranye. By the time they arrived, the three women with the water jugs were sitting with the wise woman. They nodded respectfully as Kai and Jake approached, and chatted animatedly with Ooranye, who had continued eating as if nothing had happened.

Kai walked at Jake's side. "We weren't at all prepared for this incident."

"No, we weren't." He frowned. "We're not exactly cloak-and-dagger types, are we?"

A sour smile tugged at Kai's lips. "No…we're on a steep learning curve here, for sure. But I don't want to be caught like this again."

"It wouldn't make sense for a helicopter to come out nearly a hundred miles from the airport to this place," Jake told her in a low voice. "Not unless they wanted something real bad—like us."

"We can check all this out when we get back to Yulara. As soon as we get done talking with Ooranye, I'm going to call Mike Houston. You can give him the fuselage numbers on that Huey. Plus the name Marston Enterprises. Maybe he or someone else can run down the numbers and name and we'll get some info."

Nodding, Jake said, "That's a good idea." And then he gave her a silly grin. "The satellite phone is back at our hut, too."

"Lesson number three—don't leave home without it."

"Yep, that's right."

Ooranye welcomed them back. She gestured for them to sit before her, and they did. Licking her fingers free of the bush honey, she said, "These white men wanted to know about you. They asked for you by name, so they know who you are."

"Did they ask about the crystal mask?" Kai inquired.

"No," the wise woman murmured. "But they saw the camels. They asked if you were here and I said no, that we'd bought the camels in a trade with some white men many months ago." She grinned. "They believed me."

Jake smiled briefly. "I know you can't see them, Ooranye, but they wore red shirts with a label that said Marston Enterprises on it. Do you know about that company?"

Wrinkling her brow, Ooranye said, "No. But Robert Marston is a very rich white man. We know of him because he sends his men to steal our sacred objects. He collects them because he wants their power. He is a two-heart, a man of darkness."

Jake gave Kai a meaningful look. "This could be the same guy that sent men to steal the totems from our nation."

"That's what I was thinking," Kai said. "I'll give Mike the info and have him do some serious snooping on this Marston guy."

"These men are dark," Ooranye murmured. "They are looking for you. That means you must get to the canyon and into the cave to find that stone mask quickly. I have a feeling they will return or keep looking for you no matter what I told them. There is much danger around you."

Kai reached out and squeezed the elder's wrinkled, callused hand. "Thanks for all your help. We're going to make a phone call and then we'll return to you."

"Of course. I need to draw you a map of how to reach the canyon. You must go by camel. It is too far away for you to walk there."

"Okay…" Kai turned and fell into step at Jake's side. "I hope Mike is up."

As they emerged from beneath the silver-green leaves of the shady gum and into the sunlight spilling across the land from the eastern horizon, Jake smiled. "We're half a world away and too many time zones to count. We have his personal number and I think you should use that one to call him." As they hurried back to their hut, the sun was already heating up the red desert. It was beginning to feel like another blast-furnace day.

Kai crawled back into their hut. All their gear was packed in a large green canvas bag. She unzipped it and pulled out the satellite phone. Getting up, she slipped out of the hut, walked to a nearby gum tree for shade and dialed the number that would connect them with Mike Houston.

Jake stood nearby as Kai talked to Houston on the phone. He took from his shirt pocket the notebook where he'd scribbled down the fuselage numbers earlier, and he handed it to her. Kai gave him a slight smile, her eyes warm as she held his gaze.

"Hold on, Mike, Jake has the tail numbers on that Huey for you...." She passed the phone to him. "You talk with him."

Jake was pleased to see that Kai would entrust him to do some things on this mission. Until now, she'd been a control freak about handling everything herself, but he understood why. This was her mission and she was in charge of it. He gave her a nod of thanks and took the phone. The fact that he'd held Kai earlier was changing their relationship remarkably. Miraculously. He only hoped they would survive the dangers that lay ahead to see what the future held.

Chapter 11

Kai looked around as Jake continued to speak with Mike on the satellite phone. Rocket and Booster were foraging nearby on the thick clumps of ever-present spinifex. How the camels could eat that grass was beyond her. Their muzzles were so soft and velvety, and she wondered how they could handle the sharp blades of grass, which reminded her of tiny razor blades. Still, their camel friends seemed very happy here at Kalduke and enjoyed going over to the rock hole whenever they wanted a drink of water. It must be heaven for them, Kai thought, resting her hands on her hips.

She heard Jake's low voice in the background. A gray bird with a black face flew overhead. Kai had seen one yesterday, and Ooranye had called it *dulloora,* or "small gray bird." She had looked it up in the bird guide she had brought along and knew it was a black-faced cuckoo-shrike. The bird headed directly for the towering, graceful River Red Gums. Kai was sure it had a nest somewhere in the arms of one of those magnificent trees ringing the rock hole.

"Kai?"

Turning, she saw Jake handing her the phone.

"Oh...thanks." She took the device back. Again their fingers touched, and again that pleasant tingle raced up Kai's arm. She pulled away and focused on speaking with Mike.

"Can you call us after you run those helo numbers?"

"I'll have my assistant, Jenny, research it tomorrow morning, Kai. She'll call you just as soon as we stumble on to something. It would be one thing if this aircraft was registered in the USA. The FAA mainframe computer could spit this info out in a heartbeat. As it is, we're going to have to go through the CIA and then to Australia's spy system to get it. And that will take some time."

"Okay, no problem," Kai murmured. "And what about this Marston guy? Marston Enterprises?"

"I'll put one of my other assistants on that immediately. I'll wake him up and get him over to the office to start running an Interpol check on this dude. As soon as we have something on him and his activities, I'll be back in touch with you."

"Thanks for everything. We'll wait for that call. Out."

Jake pointed to an orange-and-yellow lizard that was taking its time crossing the red sand.

Kai hitched the phone into the belt of her Rail Riders and walked over to him. The giant lizard was about four and a half feet long. "They grow lizards Texas-size here in Australia, don't they?" she said, amazed.

"Yeah. Did you read about them in our manual? They grow five feet long. They look like miniature dragons, if you ask me. I sure wouldn't want to bump into one in the night."

"Yeah, I think it's called a giant perentie, and you're right, I wouldn't want to run into one, either."

Jake smiled wryly. "Ooranye said they're all over the area."

"I hope that cave where the crystal mask is doesn't have any. Who knew a lizard could be as tall as a person?" She grimaced. "Let's get back to work. Ooranye is going to show us where that canyon is."

Kai lay awake on her bedding that night. It was too hot to have any kind of blanket, so she had unrolled her thin sleeping pad and was using the saddle as her pillow. They'd spent most of the day repacking and getting ready to go to the canyon, after Ooranye showed them where it was located. In Jake's estimation, it was a full day's ride away and they'd hurriedly left in the late afternoon, when the brutal heat of the day was beginning to ease off. They'd traveled one-third of the distance to the cave before night had fallen around them. After they'd set up camp, Kai had cooked succulent kangaroo meat over a small campfire. Now, as she looked at the luminous dials on her watch, she saw it was nearly midnight. They'd gone to bed at 9:00 p.m. The stars in the black sky above were so close and bright. Kai couldn't sleep. Her mind was going in a hundred different directions. Mike Houston had not called them back. He'd said it would take time, but she was impatient by nature. Her gaze shifted to Jake, who lay a couple of feet away on his sleeping pad.

"Are you asleep?" she asked.

"No."

"I didn't hear you snoring, so I figured you were still awake."

Kai heard him chuckle. "I don't snore."

"Dude, you do."

"Well, okay…you do, too."

Her brows lifted and she laughed. "I do *not!*"

"Trust me, I can tape record it some day if you want."

Laughter gurgled up through her chest and Kai grinned lopsidedly. "I know—snoring is a gender-neutral thing all two-leggeds do."

"Oh, so you'll admit it?"

She heard the smile in Jake's low voice. When he spoke like that, her flesh riffled with pleasure. As a little girl she had loved his voice; even then he'd had a soothing quality to his tone that automatically alleviated the coiled tension she felt all the time. He was doing that now, whether he knew it or not. Kai was grateful, but she didn't voice it.

Sighing, she turned on her side to face Jake, who was barely visible in the starlight. "I can't sleep. My mind won't shut off…."

Jake studied Kai. The moon was in the sky, shedding just enough light for him to see her serious features. "Let's talk then. We have a lot to catch up on between us."

Nodding, Kai said, "I know so little about you since… well, since I got sent to that foster home in Asheville, after my folks died. You said your dad was stationed in Germany when you were a kid?"

Pleased that she was asking, Jake said, "Yes. After you left the res, like I told you before, my father, who was in the Air Force, got orders to go overseas to Germany. We followed."

"That must have been really exciting, a chance to live in Europe. But leaving the res would have been tough in some ways...." Kai tried to put herself in Jake's shoes.

"It was. I had no way to contact you. I sent a letter to your Gram, but it never reached her, I guess. Did you try to contact me after you got situated with your foster family?" Jake knew he was on fragile ground with her now. He remembered only too well the day when Kai had been taken by the state. It had torn his heart in half. He'd cried right along with Grams on that rickety old wooden porch of her cabin. She'd held him and he'd clung to her, both of them feeling bereft over losing Kai.

"I—well, I was in shock for a long time, looking back on it, Jake. I was thrown into a new family, given a 'new' mother and father, along with three stepbrothers, and I didn't even think about contacting you...."

"Understandable," Jake murmured. He heard the pain in her voice.

"I wanted to...."

His heart thumped hard in his chest. "You did?"

"I was lonely. I missed you...." There, the truth was out. Kai felt her heart throb with pain from the past, but admitting it seemed to soothe some of it away.

"I missed you, too. I was lonely without you in my life, Kai." Jake grappled inwardly with memories from that time. Looking back on it, he realized he'd had a childhood crush on Kai, a case of puppy love. Only, he realized, he'd never outgrown his love for her.

Had she ever loved him? Jake wasn't sure. There was a huge difference between her needing him as a safe haven and loving him. Kai had never told him she loved him. Not then and not now.

"The state took me away because they felt Grams was too old to care for me, as I told you before. I was thirteen when she finally convinced the court she could, raising a hell of a fuss in the process. She was smart—she went to the newspapers and television stations and told her story of how they'd taken her granddaughter away from her because she was considered too old." Chuckling, Kai said, "I stayed in contact with Grams by letter. You know, she's never had a phone. Still doesn't. About once every three months, my foster family would take me out to visit her on the res for the day, and that was great. Sometimes Grams's friends, who had a car, would bring her for a visit in Asheville. I always loved those days when she came…."

Jake closed his eyes and felt Kai's pain at the separation from her grandmother. Grams's address read "Rabbit Holler, North Carolina" and that was all. People knew where the cabins were by names of the meadows, hills, mountains and hollows where they were situated. "I'm glad you kept contact with her, Kai. That was important for both of you."

"It was my lifeline, Jake. By the time I was sent back to the res to live with Grams, you were long gone. I asked her about you and she said you'd left shortly after I did."

"Yes. I didn't want to go, though…."

Kai stared at his darkened form. She heard sadness in his husky voice. Afraid to ask why, she muttered, "As exciting as it would be to live in Europe, I don't know how you adjusted to a foreign country as a kid, Jake. I found it hard enough going from my warring family into the foster home, which was so different from what I knew before. Culture shock, I suppose."

Feeling a warmth in his chest over Kai's decision to share on a personal level with him, Jake said, "It wasn't easy for either of us. My mother took moving to a foreign country as an adventure and an opportunity. Her enthusiasm was infectious, and it made me feel a little better about leaving the res. She had me learn German and French. There were a lot of Moroccan people outside the base where we lived who spoke only French. So I picked up two extra languages. She made the transition a lot easier for me with her attitude." Jake was starving for information on Kai—her life since he'd left the res, how she'd coped, what experiences she'd had along the way, what she had learned from life thus far because of them. Everything about her interested him. Still, Jake knew he had to quell his curiosity. If he was too forward, too aggressive in asking questions, she'd retreat from him.

In some ways, Kai was like a wounded animal who trusted no one outside herself. Why should she? She'd grown up in a war zone, a dysfunctional family, and was the only survivor. Jake knew Kai didn't have a lot of social skills when it came to interacting with people. All she could do was fight to survive daily in that toxic household. Still, the fact that she was reaching out, considering his welfare, showed that she was trying to be sensitive toward other people rather than just focused on herself.

"Do you know what my foster family taught me?"

"No. What?"

"My foster father, Al Goodings, was a pilot for a major airline. He used to often go to the Asheville airport to fly his Cessna, a small plane he owned, and would ask if I wanted to go along. The three boys that they'd adopted had no interest in flying, but I did. I jumped at the chance." Kai's voice softened. "He was a straightlaced, retired military dude, but he let me sit in the copilot's seat when he flew that plane. When we got up to altitude, he told me to put my hands on the wheel and hold it. I remember taking command of the plane with his direction and thinking that I'd died and gone to heaven." Kai chuckled. "So talk about making changes. You went to a foreign country and learned new languages, and I went to a foster home where I was taught how to fly a plane. By the time I was eleven years old, I had my private pilot's license. I was one of the few kids of my age in the U.S. that held one. My foster dad was my first positive male role model. I love him for what he did. And he never fought to keep me when Grams got the right to bring me back to the res. I continued to learn how to fly. He paid for my lessons. Every week he'd drive out to the res and take me to the airport for another hour or two of flying. By the time I graduated from high school, I had six hundred hours in single-engine planes. I still keep in touch with my foster parents to this day. They are good people."

"Even adversity hands us gifts," Jake murmured, closing his eyes. He was happy that Kai had had something good happen to her after losing her parents in that terrible crash.

"Yeah," she sighed. "Al instilled a hunger for flying in me that I carried back to the res. When I lived with Grams

I worked to get a 4.0 average in school, and then went on to college to get a degree in aerodynamics. I joined the ROTC at Ohio State University, and after I graduated, I was taken into the U.S. Navy for flight training at Pensacola. The rest is history." She smiled and rolled over on her back. "Isn't it funny how life twists and turns like a snake?"

Jake smiled sleepily at her. "Yes. And I'm glad this latest twist brought us together again."

Chapter 12

Just past noon, Kai sat on Booster beneath the spreading arms of a River Red Gum at the entrance of the colorful canyon. Jake came up alongside her, halted and looked around. The remarkable canyon walls rose five hundred feet on either side and towered above them. To Kai, it was as if a giant had slashed open the red desert and created the colorful marvel. The entrance was nothing more than a well-trodden rocky path that could barely be discerned to anyone but trackers. One thing her father did was teach her how to track. Now that skill had come in handy.

The canyon was U-shaped, the walls of red, yellow and white sedimentary deposits stacked up like a layer cake. It reminded Kai of a colorful torte cake, with scraggly, tough gum trees around the top like frosting.

As she studied the landscape, her stomach knotted with dread. Dread of failure, of disappointing Grams and the Cherokee nation. Would Jake and she find the crystal mask here? Anxiety riffled through her.

Then she spotted the dark mouth of the cave at the far end of the box canyon. "There it is," she murmured to Jake. "The cave."

"Yeah, I see it." He patted his camel. "Let's get to it. Maybe we can have that mask in an hour or two." He looked upward. "The sky is turning a funny color, did you notice?"

Kai nudged Booster forward. "Yes, I've been watching it. Looks weird. You were out in various deserts. Does it remind you of some kind of special weather condition?" Kai swayed from side to side as the camel picked his way along the stony path that led to the cave.

Jake frowned and studied the sky. It wasn't clear blue any longer. As they'd rode throughout the morning, it had seemed to be tinged with a reddish stain, making the blue look dirty. "Well, every desert is different, but if I'm right, I think we've got one helluva sandstorm coming our way."

"Never been in one," Kai said, looking back and flashing him a slight smile. Jake was still studying the turgid sky, obviously concerned.

"There are all kinds, Kai. A big one can kill you if you aren't in the right place at the right time. The frontal winds blast at over a hundred miles an hour, and the sand flies like sharp shards of glass into your face. If it doesn't suffocate you, it cuts you like a thousand razors."

"Oh…." Kai frowned. "How soon will we know?"

"Not long from now, I'm afraid. Sandstorms move at different velocities, too. Judging from how quickly the sky is changing, I'm guessing this one is pretty big and fast."

"Are we in a good place to be when it hits?" The canyon looked like a safe place if sand was flying like glass at a hundred miles an hour.

"Yeah, we are. This canyon could mean the difference between life and death."

Kai patted Booster's neck affectionately. "What about these guys?"

"They can handle any and all storms. See their nostrils? How they're shaped like vertical slits? They can close them down so the sand won't get in and choke them to death."

"I see! Too bad we don't have nostrils like that."

"Right. But that cave coming up could be an ideal place to wait out a sandstorm. Also, it looks big enough to bring the camels inside, to protect them, as well."

"If the storm hits soon, will it cause us problems finding the mask?"

"It could. We'll have to wait and see…."

As the camels moved with ease over the rocky ground, Jake studied the cave's oval entrance. Bushes crowded around the front, but it was still going to be easy to access. The cave appeared to be about forty feet in height, with two very different colors of rock on the walls inside. He could barely make them out because the darkness became total at the rear. The cave seemed to be about fifty feet deep, wide and dry.

They halted the camels at the cave mouth and ordered them to sit so they could dismount. The canyon was a lot cooler than the open desert thanks to the shade cast by the south wall and by the trees that grew profusely there. Obviously, water was close to the surface in the area, judging from all the greenery surrounding them.

Kai moved forward. Halting at the cave entrance, she saw what looked like a ledge at the back end abruptly. Jake came up alongside, a set of heavy nylon ropes slung over his right shoulder. Noticing the frown gathering on his face, she asked, "What do you think? You're the caving expert."

"I think that's a trick shelf at the rear of the cave," he told her, pointing toward it. Leaning down, he examined the prints of a man's boots in the red sandy soil. They were barely visible, the wind having blown most of them away over time. "I wonder if this is the dude that ran in here with the mask. I see animal tracks around, but only his prints go straight back and disappear."

Kai knelt down, her eyes narrowing. She might not be a spelunker, but she knew tracking. Jake was right: a lot of small animal tracks dotted the sand, but only one set, a two-legged's, went anywhere near the end of what appeared to be a ledge. "I wonder if it's a straight drop-off."

"I don't know." Jake put the nylon rope down and smiled at her. "Who's going down and who's staying up here?"

Kai rose to her full height. "You know more about belaying ropes than I do. How about if you teach me the rudimental rock climbing and I go down? You can stay here and anchor me."

Jake swallowed his fear for her safety. Kai was grown-up now, not a little girl needing his protection any longer. "Sounds like a plan to me. I'm going to set up a makeshift winch and ropes by using these nearby trees to haul you up and out of there."

Kai looked around. "Good." The day was growing darker by the moment. The sky, which was mostly hidden by the amazing number of gum trees growing in the small canyon, seemed to be turning a brownish color. Sand was in the air. She also noticed that the birds were no longer singing. More than likely they were finding somewhere to hide from the threatening storm.

Looking around the cave, she saw there was nothing other than that one ledge to indicate the danger Ooranye had warned them about. Jake quickly fashioned an aluminum "come along" device between two huge gum trees that grew in front of the entrance. He expertly wove the nylon ropes around their stout trunks and threaded them through the metal device that would help him lower and raise her without a lot of physical effort on his part.

Jake knelt down and, using a series of carabiners, metal locks, created a harness for Kai to step into. He motioned her into the contraption and trussed her up from the waist downward. When Kai put weight on the harness, it would place her in an automatic sitting position when she was suspended in midair. Jake had one headlamp and she slipped it on, adjusting the elastic to her head size, grateful she had arranged her hair in one long braid earlier. Making sure all tendrils of hair were out of her face, she slid on leather gloves to protect her hands from potentially sharp rocks.

"How long will this headlamp battery last?" she asked, adjusting the harness around her waist.

"Probably two hours at the most. And we have no idea how this cave twists or winds." He grimaced. "Or if that ledge falls off into never-never land. The first thing I want you to do once we've got you safely harnessed up is move forward on your hands and knees to the rear of the cave.

Look over that lip. See what you can see. But be careful. That ledge could be real brittle and not support your weight."

Kai nodded. Jake's hands flew with knowing ease across the rope harness, double-checking all the knots and carabiners. The thick, soft nylon felt snug but comfortable around her thighs and butt. Luckily, he'd brought along walkie-talkie radios. He handed one to her and made sure it was on the same channel as his own.

"As you descend, stay in touch like I taught you, okay?" He wiped the sweat from his brow as he straightened and looked at her. She appeared proud and confident. Still, it didn't stop him from being scared for her.

"I will." Kai leaned over and adjusted her leather holster, making sure the pistol was strapped in snugly. She wasn't going down into that cave unarmed. She didn't know what—or who—she might find once inside. She cast one more glance at the sky. "You're right about a sandstorm coming, Jake. Look at it now."

Jake nodded. "Yeah, no doubt about it. The sky's already turning a dirty brown. Wait until it hits. You won't be able to see your hand in front of your face."

"What about the camels? Do you want to put them inside just in case?"

"Yeah, right now. Hold on…." He trotted over to them, got them up and led them into the cave. Rocket and Booster settled side by side near the entrance, chewing their cuds.

Jake walked quickly to a huge, white-barked gum tree just outside the entrance and double-checked to see that the series of ropes were tight around the thick trunk, and the pulley and winch were secure. Picking up an extra saddle blanket he'd retrieved, he handed it to Kai.

"I need you to put this on that cave ledge. If you have to go straight down, the ropes need to stay on this pad so they won't be sawn through or cut by the rock and sand on that lip. This blanket will protect the ropes."

"Got it," Kai said, taking the pad.

Jake gave her a critical look. "You have water on you?"

Kai patted the two quarts of water hanging from the rear of her belt. "Yeah. Some protein bars in my pockets. Hopefully, I'm not going to be gone that long to use any of them." She gave him a quick grin.

Kai saw the worry in Jake's gold eyes. Reaching out, she gave his hand a quick squeeze. "I'll be okay...."

He squeezed her gloved hand in return. This was the first time Kai had reached out to reassure him. It felt wonderful. "Yeah, I know. Just be careful, okay?" Jake didn't tell her how concerned he was about the coming sandstorm. He didn't want her to worry about that, too.

Kai nodded. "I will," she promised softly, and turned and walked into the shadows of the cave. Getting down on her hands and knees, she dragged the pad alongside until she got to the ledge. Testing the ground by pounding her fist ahead of her, she discovered the area was solid. She felt fairly confident in going to the edge. Turning on her headlamp, Kai saw that the lip did indeed fall off into darkness.

"This is a cliff," she told Jake, raising her voice. The sound echoed strangely around the cave. "My headlamp won't penetrate the darkness below the lip. I see nothing.

No bottom. No…nothing. It's probably a helluva fall from here. Maybe a hundred feet or more, would be my guess."

"That's what I thought," Jake called, standing by the gum tree, the ropes in his gloved hands. He was about ten feet outside the mouth of the cave. "Put the pad down and place the ropes on top of it. Once you do that, just belly up to the edge, swing your feet over and point your head in my direction. I'll keep tension on the ropes so you can't fall. Once you get in that position, I'll slowly ease the ropes and begin to lower you when you give the signal."

Kai did exactly as Jake said. With her legs dangling over the maw, she shouted, "Go ahead, on belay. I'm ready!"

"On belay," Jake said, speaking into the walkie-talkie. The special winch as well as the two gum trees he'd used as anchoring points would easily hold her weight. The "come along device" held the tension and also released it. Jake tucked the radio in his pocket and slowly eased the handle forward. Kai disappeared over the edge. The nylon rope swiftly began to play out.

Kai coughed violently as she slid over the edge, raising clouds of sand by her movements. Bits of grit showered around her. Closing her eyes, she dangled a few feet below the lip, slowly swinging back and forth above the dark abyss. Finding the switch, she turned on her headlamp. The darkness seemed to swallow the weak beam of light like a hungry monster as she turned her head, one hand on the ropes above her, to explore her surroundings.

"Kai?" Jake's voice sounded worried.

Fumbling for the walkie-talkie, she turned it on. She'd tucked it in the pocket nearest her mouth so she could

speak directly into it, and decided to leave it on for the du-
ration of the descent.

"I'm here. I'm okay." She coughed again. "Damn
dust… Everywhere I look, I see only darkness. This headlamp is like shining a penlight into a cavern. The beam
doesn't go very far."

"Don't worry about it. That light has a seven-foot radius.
It's strong enough for you to see a wall or floor coming up,"
Jake said. "I'm going to slowly start lowering you. If you
see *anything* below you, or if the sides of the cave come
in around you, holler."

"Roger that," she said, feeling the ropes begin to slide,
taking her slowly downward.

Darkness consumed Kai. The daylight at the ledge was
growing dimmer and dimmer. It was much cooler in the
cave, and felt delicious compared to the heat out in the canyon. Continuing to swing her head from side to side as she
descended, Kai still saw nothing. The silence was overwhelming. Had the man who'd stolen the mask run into the
cave, thinking he'd hide, and then failed to see the ledge?
Tumbled to his death? Kai estimated she must have
dropped a hundred feet. Still no bottom. Was there a floor
to this cave?

"Anything yet?" Jake called, his voice scratchy because
the radio signals were weak.

"No, not yet. There's a hell of an updraft of wind down
here. I'm almost cold." She gave a strained laugh. "The
cave walls are narrowing, from what I can see, Jake. They
have all kinds of spikes and nobs sticking out from them."

"Those points are called stalagmites and stalactites

formed when this cave was wet a long time ago," he said. "You got enough room to maneuver or are you brushing the sides?"

"No, plenty of room. At least six feet on either side. How about you? How's that weather stacking up around you?" She heard him grunt and then laugh.

"Let's just say I'd rather be *in* the cave at this point. Sand's starting to fly thick and fast around here."

"Bad?" She twisted to look down.

"Not yet. It's a nasty storm, though."

"Then the sooner I can get to the floor and get out of here, the better for you. You're standing outside the cave."

"Don't worry, I got my goggles on and my kerchief wrapped around the lower half of my face. I'm breathing just fine, thank you very much."

Some of her worry for Jake dissolved. "I like your drop-dead sense of humor, Carter. You're such an optimist."

"What's the other choice, Ms. Alseoun?"

Chuckling, Kai turned and leaned out, her hand wrapped tightly around the rope. She aimed her headlamp downward.

"Jake! I see the floor!"

"How far?"

"Maybe seven feet…" She swung her head in a slow arc, the weak light barely penetrating the sand drifting down around her from the turbulent storm above. "I see—oh God…Jake, I see a body…." She squinted hard to see the darkened form.

"Human? Animal?"

Hearing the dread in his voice, Kai rasped, "Human. And dead. The poor bastard fell and landed on a stalagmite.

He was impaled on it through the center of his body."
Gulping, she saw the man's shrunken form, the leather
bomber jacket he was wearing, the denim jeans looking as
if the cotton fiber had been partially eaten away by bugs.
"He looks like an Egyptian mummy—all dried out." He'd
landed on his back, arms and legs splayed outward in
death. Kai could barely see his face in the grayness. It was
shrunken, the skin pulled tautly against the bones, mouth
open in a grotesque scream that she realized no one but the
denizens of this cave had heard.

"In this hot, dry climate that's about all you could expect. Do you see anything around him?"

The ropes brought her closer and closer to the bottom.
"The floor has all kinds of spikes rising up from it, large
and small. Like lots of needles. Not something you'd want
to fall on...."

"Yeah, stalagmites. And the dude? Where is he in relationship to you?"

"To my left. He's suspended about six feet above the
floor." Her heart was pumping hard. Anxiously, Kai looked
around. The light from her headlamp was minimal in the
pitch blackness that surrounded her. Pink and red spikes of
calcified minerals thrust up like dozens of fine, thin needles
of varying heights. Every time the light from her lamp swept
an area, it illuminated that spot briefly and created shadows.

"Stop belay!" Kai called. Her booted feet landed on the
cave floor, spikes crunching noisily beneath the soles. She
remained in the harness and carefully surveyed her surroundings. A cooling breeze continued to move past her. It
was impossible to see more than six feet in any direction.

"Jake, I'm down and standing on the floor. I'm going to remain in the harness. I can't see very far, but I'm going to walk slowly and carefully toward the body. If he had the crystal mask in a pouch, it's probably going to be somewhere around him."

"Okay, test *every* step you take, Kai. Don't assume that floor is solid. Please…"

Kai could hear the frantic concern in Jake's voice. A warmth stole into her heart. "I'm following your orders to the letter," she promised.

There were plenty of bugs on the floor that scurried in every direction as her boots crunched the stalagmites. She saw scattered remains of a number of animals and human skeletons, the bones bleached or crumbling into powder from old age. Kai headed straight toward the body. She would have to create a search pattern around it in order to locate the pouch—if there was a pouch. Every time she thrust out the toe of her boot she automatically set all her weight on her heel in case the ground before her cracked and fell away. That way, she had a chance of falling backward, not forward.

"Anything?"

Jake's voice was muffled. Kai halted and looked upward. Far above she could see a faint light. "No…not yet. You sound awful. What's going on up there?"

"The full brunt of the sandstorm just hit—winds clocking around sixty or seventy miles an hour…."

Frowning, Kai shook her head. "Is anything left standing?"

She heard him chuckle. "I'm clinging to this gum tree for dear life right now. There's an initial wind gust from the rolling cloud carrying the sand. It'll last anywhere between five to fifteen minutes. After that, the wind slows down a little. I'm crouched between the gums, trying to protect my head from the flying sand. It gets into every nook and cranny of your body."

"Makes me glad I'm down here," she remarked dryly.

"Trust me, I'd join you if I could."

"I believe you," Kai said softly. "I couldn't ask for a better partner."

"Aww, you're only saying that because I'm the one who's going to winch you up and out of that place."

Laughing, Kai felt her heart burst with an incredible joy. "Carter, what did I *ever* do when you weren't in my life? You always make me feel better, even if I'm in deep shit."

His laughter lifted her. Happiness threaded through Kai as she continued toward the large spire.

"Misery loves company."

"Ain't that the truth. Wait…Jake! I see something…." Kai's breath hitched. Her eyes rounded. There on the floor, about five feet away from the spire the dead man was impaled on, Kai glimpsed two objects: a wallet and a dark brown leather pouch.

"What? What is it?"

Hearing Jake's concern, Kai said, "Jake, I think it's the pouch! And a wallet! Hold on…it's just a few feet away…."

"Take your *time,* Kai. Don't rush!"

"I hear you…." She carefully detoured to the right. As she focused her headlamp on the pouch, she could see that the thick yellow rawhide drawstrings were still knotted around the top of it. Heart hammering, she crouched down and reached for it. Was the crystal mask in there? Was it?

Her fingers slid across the rough leather. As she curved them around the dusty exterior, she could feel a solid object within it. Not recalling if she'd ever seen the mask, she wasn't exactly sure what it looked like. She undid the knots at the top of the pouch and, with a tug, opened it. Breath suspended, Kai stared at the pouch. There was no way in hell she was sticking her fingers into the bag. For all she knew, there could be a deadly scorpion or centipede making its home in there. Instead, she aimed her headlamp into the opening.

"Oh!" she whispered. There, gleaming in the light, was the smooth edge of a crystal object. Carefully investigating the inside of the pouch, she found no insects. Reassured, Kai stuck her fingers into it. With great care, she gripped the crystal with her thumb and fingers and drew it out. The light glanced off it, as if sunlight were striking it.

"Jake…I found it! It's the mask. It's so beautiful…." she said in a hushed, reverent tone. As she held it, her fingers began to tingle. The mask had been fashioned to fit over the upper half of the face; it was perhaps four inches wide and curved so that the holes would fit over a human's eyes. Turning it, Kai saw the lightning bolt that had been carved diagonally across it.

Slowly getting to her feet, she couldn't take her eyes off the precious, sacred totem.

"You got it? Is it in one piece?"

"Yes, it is. I don't know how, but it is…." Her voice was filled with wonder. An incredible warmth spread through her fingers and up her arm to her fast-beating heart. A sense of incredible peace filled Kai as she stood there looking down at the heritage of the Paint Clan. *Her* clan. A sense of victory, of satisfaction at doing something good for once, filled her. Kai used her fingers to wipe away the dust that had settled upon the sparkling mask. It was hauntingly beautiful. Someone had fashioned this mask by hand thousands of years ago. And whoever it was, man or woman, had done an incredible job. The mask probably weighed close to three pounds; it was no lightweight. Holes at each side were obviously for leather thongs, so that a medicine person could wear it over his or her face during ceremony.

"It's in perfect condition, Jake!" A thrill ran through Kai. She turned and gently slipped the mask back inside its leather case. "I'm putting it back in the pouch and then sliding it into my vest. Now for the wallet." She leaned over and picked up the dusty black leather wallet. Tucking it into her vest, she took one more look around. All she saw were the grayish bones lying like a disturbed graveyard on the floor. "I'll be ready in just a minute. I want to take a drink of water before I get hauled out of this place."

"Sounds good to me. I can hardly wait to see it—and you."

Chuckling, Kai carefully tucked the mask inside her canvas vest. It rested perfectly over her left breast beneath the thick, protective material. And it was out of the way of the ropes.

"Who do you want to see first?" she teased, pulling a water bottle from her belt and uncapping it.

"Who do you think?" Jake chuckled, his voice muffled but joyful.

Wiping her mouth with the back of her hand, Kai grinned up at the light far above her. "I don't know. This crystal mask is really a knockout, dude. Priceless. Sacred. And that wallet, who knows if there's money in it?"

"You're what I want, Kai."

More warmth poured through her heart. Hooking the bottle back onto her belt, she called, "Belay on…."

Chapter 13

Jake was never so glad to see Kai as now. Once she crawled away from the ledge, he ran into the cave to help her to her feet. The air inside the cave was dusty, but a helluva lot more breathable than that outside. Kai's hair was in disarray, and a light coating of dust covered her from head to toe. She coughed violently a few times and sat up as he trotted toward her.

She had the biggest grin on her face as she took the pouch from her vest. "We got it!"

Jake pulled off his bandanna and knelt down in front of her. Wiping the sweat off his brow with the back of his arm, he grinned and took her proffered gift. Their fingers touched, and a powerful sensation of love ripped through him as he met and held her intense blue gaze, which mirrored his joy.

"Yeah, we did it," he murmured. "Let me see this mask…." He carefully removed it from the pouch.

Kai pulled the water bottle from her belt again and chugged down the rest of the contents in a few gulps. Wiping her mouth, she looked outside the cave. There was nothing but darkness, the wind wailing and screaming so loudly it shocked her. Rocket and Booster were well inside the cave, quietly chewing their cuds and acting as if nothing was wrong. Swinging her gaze back to Jake, she saw he was covered with red sand. His face was grimy with sweat and dirt.

"You need a bath," she chortled, watching his face light up as he removed the crystal mask from the pouch.

Grinning, Jake nodded. His eyes, however, never left the mask in his hands. "This, is beautiful…. And it's just like I remember. It's real, Kai… You did it…." Looking up at her, he saw the crazy smile on her lips.

"No, *we* did it, Jake. We're a good team." She drank deeply from the second bottle of water, then stopped and offered the rest to him.

"Thanks," he murmured, taking the bottle. "I didn't have much time out there to drink in that sandstorm." He put the bottle to his lips and finished off the contents in a hurry.

Kai sat resting on her heels, her hands on her thighs. Watching Jake's Adam's apple bob up and down with each gulp, she was once again reminded of his maleness. Something warm and good stirred deep within her body, a yearning for him—in all ways. Taken by surprise, she avoided his hooded eyes after he'd put the bottle aside. Did Jake feel it, too, when their fingers met? That feeling, crazy as it was, of goodness? Hope for the future? She hadn't been very optimistic lately.

"Well," she said, pointing to the mask, "what do you

think? The real McCoy, right? You're the one who's seen it before—or at least remembers it."

Cradling the mask gently in his hands, Jake nodded. "Yeah, it's real, Kai. I know this is going to make the elders back at the res *very* happy. Not to mention every member of the Paint Clan."

Frowning, she ran her fingers over her hair and felt the grit on her scalp. "We have to get home first. What about this storm? How long do you think it will last?"

Shrugging, Jake replaced the mask in the pouch and gave it back to her. "Could be hours. I don't really know. Cold fronts create these storms, and if it's a major one, the storm could go on for the rest of the day before it loses power." Wiping his face with his fingers and feeling the grit on his flesh, he turned and looked out the cave mouth. "Seems to be lightening up a little, however. Maybe, if we're lucky, it will run out of steam in another hour and we can head home to Yulara today."

"Let's see who this wallet belongs to," Kai murmured, withdrawing it from her vest and opening it up. "Hmm… Giles Rowland…"

"The guy skewered on the point down there?" Jake asked, looking at the wallet in her hand. She pulled out several pieces of identification. There was a huge amount of bills in it as well.

"Yeah, the wallet was right next to the pouch. It probably was in his back pocket when he hit that point…" Kai narrowed her gaze on the credit card. "Look at this—Marston Enterprises." She looked over at Jake. "Robert Marston?"

"I'd bet on it. Looks like Rowland had his boss's credit card and the stolen totem."

Nodding, Kai looked at a white business card. "Here it is—Robert Marston. His Hong Kong address. And phone number. The works." She handed it to Jake.

"That pretty much implicates Marston to this theft. Chances are he was the one who hired Giles here, and two other dudes who have the other two totems."

"Well, we know where Giles ended up," Kai murmured, looking back at the darkened lip.

"Got what he deserved," Jake said in a growl. "Here's another pieces of evidence—A business card for antiques down in Lima, Peru." He saw Kai's eyes go wide with surprise. His mouth twitched. "Your dream showed another totem going to Peru." He waved the card toward her. "And here's your double check. You're on a roll, Kai."

Hearing the pride in his voice, she managed a slight smile and studied the card in disbelief. "This is just amazing, dude."

"Yeah, I know. When you're in the flow, as my mom would say, synchronicities and double checks abound right, left and center." Jake pulled out the wad of U.S. dollars. "Must be at least ten grand here by my estimate," he said, fingering through the one-thousand-dollar notes.

"Marston probably gave him the credit card and cash to make sure he'd get to Hong Kong to deliver this to him."

"Yeah," Jake said dryly, "but Giles had other plans for that mask and himself. He was on the lam until he screwed up thinking this cave was a great place to hide his asset. The only mistake he made was not realizing the floor didn't go all the way to the wall back there…pity."

Kai couldn't disagree. "Once we get mounted up and out of here we need to call Mike and tell him what we've found."

"Right on. Pieces of a puzzle is what we're finding."

Looking at her watch, Kai realized that barely an hour had passed since they'd arrived. "Seemed like I was down in that cave a lot longer than this indicates," she muttered, pointing to the watch on her wrist.

"When you're in a cave, time stops existing," he told her, getting to his feet. Holding out his hand to her, he said, "Come on, let's dig into our supplies on the camels and try and clean up a little."

Without hesitating, Kai took Jake's hand. How good it felt to wrap her fingers around his, dirty and gritty as they were. She felt his strength and saw the tenderness burn in his eyes as she rose to her feet. Releasing her, Jake helped her climb out of the harness. Her hand tingled as she helped him roll up the nylon ropes. Hefting one of the rolls over her shoulder, she walked through the cave with him to the camels, who lifted their heads and watched them with interest.

"You grab some water and a washcloth? I'll put these ropes into Rocket's supply pack."

"Right." Kai went over to Booster and patted his fuzzy head. The camel's ears moved back and forth, his huge brown eyes adoring as he gazed up at her. As Kai opened one of the saddlebags she heard the howl of the wind begin to abate. Looking out the cave entrance, she gasped. "Wow! Look, Jake!"

He turned. "Good news. Looks like the worst of the sandstorm is over. Why…I even see some patches of blue sky up there…."

Laughing, Kai quickly pulled a gallon of fresh water from the bag and placed it on the ground. "That means we can leave real soon."

"Yeah." Jake grunted, strapping the buckle shut on the canvas container. "I'd like to get out of this canyon before nightfall. If any of Marston's guys come flying around looking for us, we'll be long gone."

"I seriously doubt those boys would be flying in this, wouldn't you?"

Jake turned and walked over to where Kai was squatting. "They can't fly in it. That sand would pit the blades of their helo so fast they'd fall out of the sky. Besides, those kinds of copters don't have the instruments to fly in a sandstorm." He knelt down next to the wide metal bowl Kai had filled with water. She was already scrubbing her face and arms to get rid of the sand.

"Then, assuming they are still hunting us, we'd be wise to leave here and ride until dark. They won't be in the sky until tomorrow morning at dawn at the earliest."

Jake took the washcloth. The wetness felt good against his face, which smarted and burned from being pelted with sand. No fool stayed out in a sandstorm, but Kai had needed his help with those ropes.

"Right," he murmured. The coolness made his skin feel better. Kai was drying her face and arms. She looked beautiful to him. "We need to take a different route back. Throw them off our track. We'll figure out another way to Uluru. Go a direction they aren't expecting."

Kai handed him the towel. "You think they'll try to find us?"

"I think we'd better assume they will, don't you?"

Grimly, Kai stood up. Resting her hands on her hips, she saw that the sky was becoming more blue by the minute. The trees were barely moving now, the shrieking wind a mere inconstant breeze. "Yeah, we'd better."

"Just keep that elephant gun handy," Jake warned her. Standing, he tossed her the towel and took the bowl of dirty water outside, emptying it on the roots of one of the gum trees that had held the ropes.

Forewarned was forearmed. Kai saw the grim look on Jake's reddened features. She took the headlamp and stuffed it in her pack. "Do you think I should carry the mask on me? Or should I put it in the pack here?"

His mouth twitched. "I don't know. Do what you feel?"

Following her intuition, Kai gently eased the mask back into her vest. It fit beautifully, and she felt better that it was on her person.

"Okay, let's mount up and get out of here," Jake told her, throwing his leg over Rocket's back.

Turning Booster around, Kai followed Jake and Rocket out of the cave. The path was now covered with an inch or two of red sand that the storm had carried in. It didn't matter; there was only one way in and out of the box canyon.

Shutting her eyes, Kai tried to deal with an unexpected and overwhelming emotion that surged within her now that her quest was half done and she had time to think. Ooranye reminded her strongly of Grams in so many ways. Their skin color might be different, but their hearts and minds were similar. Did all medicine women grow into this kind of loving being? What had gone wrong with her mother, then? How could she have made such a bad choice in husbands? Why would she cut her life and possibilities short by staying with a man like Kai's father? The questions pummeled her, soothed only by the gentle swaying, the soft whoosh of Booster's padded feet as they met the desert floor.

Once out of the canyon and into the open desert again, Jake rode up alongside Kai, the camels moving in sync with one another, almost as if they were in a military drill. Jake momentarily absorbed Kai's profile. She wore her nylon baseball cap with the neck flaps to protect her from the blazing sun, her long-sleeved cotton shirt, a pale peach cotton camisole beneath it, along with her Rail Riders and dusty boots.

Jake had wanted to tell her how much he liked sharing the hut with her yesterday afternoon, when she'd combed out her long, silky hair, which reminded him of ebony shimmering between her fingers. Watching her twist the gleaming strands into one long braid between her shoulder blades was a secret pleasure he always looked forward to. Swallowing hard, Jake kept all his revelations to himself. Would there come a day when he could share such observations with her?

"Hell of an adventure we're on," he murmured sympathetically to her. Their legs touched from time to time as the camels swayed in unison.

Shrugging, Kai twisted her shoulders to try to get rid of the grief she felt over leaving Ooranye. "Yeah... unexpected. I'm feeling really emotional about leaving Ooranye and the people of Kalduke."

"I didn't know what to expect from this mission, either. I wish we had time to go back and tell her we found the mask. Goodbyes are always hard."

Kai gave Jake a sideward glance and saw the sadness in his shadowed face. "Did Ooranye remind you of your mother?"

One corner of his mouth lifted. Jake pulled the bill of his baseball cap over his eyes. "Yes, in some ways."

"I was wondering to myself if all medicine people are like Ooranye."

"My mother was like her, but not all are," Jake cautioned. "I've seen some selfish, greedy ones whose main interest is in stalking power. All of them men," he said almost apologetically. "When people connect with the power of Mother Earth—" he gestured toward the sky, now a pale blue above them "—the universal energy is a heady trip for them. As Ooranye said, the energy is neutral. What it becomes is dictated by what lies in a person's heart."

"Well," Kai whispered, blinking rapidly, surprised at the tears that came, "your mother, Grams and Ooranye all have hearts as wide and flowing as this endless desert we're on." Kai gestured gracefully toward the horizon. A flock of green-and-yellow parakeets flew over them, heading, Kai was sure, to the rock hole oasis at Kalduke for their fill of water.

"Don't forget," Jake told her gently, "you have the same heart as they do. It's in your blood, your genes. It's there…." His eyes connected briefly with her blue gaze. He'd never seen Kai so moved as she was now, their conversation touching her in an unexpected way. Jake saw the stubborn set of her mouth, her refusal to cry, and he ached silently for her. He wanted to reach out, drag her over to his camel, set her on the saddle in front of him, so that she could lean back and discover how much love could assuage the pain she always carried.

Of course, all that was fantasy. Still, he held out hope because she'd come to him in the hut and allowed him to hold her. Hope sprang strongly in his chest as he drowned in the aqua color of her eyes, which spoke so eloquently to his heart and soul.

"I look at them and think that's not me. I don't have what they've got. I never did."

"Yes, you do, Kai." Jake gave her an intense look. "You were chosen to find the crystal mask precisely because you *do* have that same wide, deep-hearted compassion that they have. You've never been given a chance to get in touch with that part of yourself. Real life intruded. You made different choices, Kai, but they weren't wrong ones." Jake glanced fondly toward Kalduke, which lay somewhere over the red horizon. "By going on this mission, by finding the mask, you're getting training you never received before."

Kai smiled grimly. "Yeah, dude, it's called 'on the job training' and the learning curve is steep. We could've died if we didn't do things right. We're not out of danger yet."

They had tried to call Mike Houston after leaving the canyon, but the sandstorm had caused local interference. They still hadn't received a call from Medusa to tell them about the helicopter registration or Marston Enterprises, and she and Jake remained very much on guard.

Shrugging, Jake said, "Every medicine person runs that

risk, Kai. And I don't feel you're going to die. You're already successful." He grinned. "You've got the mask." He gazed around the desert, which was coming alive once more. "The energy around us, even though it's invisible, is still here with us. Medicine people have learned how to open themselves up and allow this universal energy to run through them and help them."

"I guess I'm learning how to get out of my own way?" She smiled ruefully.

Chuckling, Jake looked up at the soft azure sky. "It's called life, Kai." He returned the sheepish smile he saw tugging at her luscious mouth. "You're a fast learner in my book."

Kai heard the pride in Jake's tone, and her skin prickled beneath his hooded, burning gaze. "I guess I'm the last to believe in my people's spirituality—or myself in relation to it."

"Life has conditioned you differently," Jake said soothingly, "but that doesn't mean you can't open yourself up to what is a natural heritage for you to tap into and use."

Looking ahead, feeling the heat as the sun's rays burned silently over the undulating landscape once more, Kai said, "I wish Mike would call. I'm sitting on pins and needles about those jokers in the copter."

The call from Medusa came that evening as they sat around a small campfire. Kai was pouring billy tea from the blackened kettle sitting on the grate over the flickering fire when the phone buzzed. She looked up, kettle in hand.

"Answer it, will you?"

Jake nodded and pulled the device off his belt. "Carter here."

Kai heard Jake talk in low tones. She moved away from the fire and poured more of the strong tea into his cup, which he held out to her. Moving to her saddle, she poured some into her own tin cup, then returned the kettle to the edge of the grate to keep warm. As she sat down cross-legged near her saddle and picked up the cup, Jake finished the transmission. He shut off the phone with the punch of a button, folded it and slid it back onto his belt.

"There are two helos at Yulara," he told Kai. "That Huey and the Bell Longranger we saw when we got off the commercial flight at the airport."

"Right."

"The Bell Longranger is registered to a Dudley Dawson, from Alice Springs, the largest town in the Northern Territory."

"It's roughly two hundred miles northeast of Yulara."

Jake nodded. "Yes."

"Anything on this Dawson dude?"

Shaking his head, Jake muttered, "Nothing. He's a local entrepreneur. He also runs a big restaurant in Alice Springs, and hosts one-, two- and three-day treks out into the Gibson Desert for tourists by Jeep, helo and on foot."

"No prison background?"

"He's clean," Jake said. "However, that Huey belongs to Marston Enterprises. Robert Marston is the owner. So those two dudes work for him. He said the Huey is a tourist helo and that it's a legit company at Yulara."

"Bingo," she murmured, sipping her hot tea.

"Mike said Marston is a multimillionaire media mogul from Canada. His passion is collecting museum quality

items from around the world." Raising an eyebrow, Jake
added, "And Mike dug up a lot of stuff on this guy. He's a
shady character. Some of the people who work for him
were caught stealing Native American pipes from the
Blood tribe in Canada at one time. In another theft from a
local museum in the Black Hills, South Dakota, a number
of sacred items to the Sioux people were stolen. The men
were caught with the goods two days later, trying to get
them through Seattle, Washington customs. They didn't
admit working for Marston, but a customs investigator
found a tie with him. The man has never been directly
charged."

"Robert Marston's the one, then. I feel it in my gut,
Jake." Kai stared at the small flames licking up into the
darkness. In the background, somewhere in the night, she
heard the howl of a pack of foraging dingos.

"Houston said Marston's too smart to be caught. He
pays off his henchmen through third- and fourth-hand
sources, so they never know he's involved in it." Jake eased
back on his saddle, which was covered with the thick wool
blanket that acted as a pad for it. "Except this time. Those
were Marston's men. They were wearing the logo on their
polo shirts. They're flying one of his copters but they run
a helo operation out of Yulara."

Exhaustion pulled at Kai. "And what is Mike going to
do? Alert Australian authorities that we're being tailed?"

"He can't go to the police with hearsay," Jake muttered.
"All we can do is stay alert."

Nodding, Kai said, "We know that old helo of theirs
doesn't have night-stalking equipment on board, so we

should try and get a good night's sleep under our belt. Tomorrow, we'll reach Uluru, and five miles beyond that, we'll be at the Mulga Station and can drop our camels off with Coober." She was still sweating profusely. The heat was unbearable. Heatstroke or sunstroke were a genuine possibility in this oven they called the Red Center.

Finishing his tea, Jake got up and brushed the sand off his trousers. "I'm in agreement. I'm going out to check on Rocket and Booster. Hit the sack. We're both ready to keel over."

Nodding, Kai pulled out the saddle pad and stretched it out on the sand to lie on. It was a good seven feet long and three feet wide. The thick wool prevented the saddle from hurting the camel's hump. Lying down, Kai turned her back toward the fire, nestled into the thick, padded saddle that acted as her pillow, and closed her eyes. Within moments, she spiraled down into a very deep sleep. The unbearable heat of the day took a toll on her as nothing else ever had, and the only way she could deal with it was to sleep a good eight hours. Nestled nearby was the pouch containing the crystal mask.

The dream began later. Kai found herself riding Booster near Uluru. Terror sizzled through her. Unable at first to pinpoint why she was so scared, Kai heard the whapping sounds of a helicopter coming toward her. A helicopter? Frowning, Kai twisted around on Booster. The helo was coming in swift and low. There was gunfire! Throwing herself forward on the camel, Kai saw the helicopter zoom past, and someone fire a rifle out the door toward her. Tracer bullets flashed through the darkness.

Then the helo turned and began to fire at another unseen

target. *Jake! Oh, no!* Screaming his name, Kai saw him galloping ahead of her on Rocket. He had a pistol in his hand
and he was firing back at the helicopter. Breathing hard,
Kai screamed a warning. She watched in horror as the
stream of red tracer rounds stalked him. *No!*

Jerking upright, Kai gulped and choked for air. Her
heart thudded heavily in her chest. It was dark. The familiar sounds of crickets singing, a far-off cry of a dingo,
were all that she heard. Perspiration trickled down her temples. Hands shaking, Kai wiped her face and leaned forward as she brought her knees up against her body. The fear
was real. Her stomach churned violently. Forcing herself
to steady her breathing, she finally looked around.

The fire was out, with nothing but a few orange coals
glowing. In the starlight, she saw Jake sleeping on the opposite side of the fire. He was snoring softly. All was right
in his world. Rubbing her face, Kai turned and reached for
her bottle of water near the saddle. She drank in huge
gulps, trying to put out the fire in her knotted belly, to douse
the fear that was eating her alive.

Sitting there, under a beautiful river of stars moving silently above her, Kai wondered what it all meant. All her
dreams had come true, thus far. *Jake…* She groaned softly
and buried her face in her hands. They were in danger. Was
this dream a forewarning? Or just some crazy thing cobbled together by her subconscious that meant nothing?

After capping her water bottle, Kai lay back down. Sighing, she shut her eyes. She had to get some sleep! But for
the first time in a long time, she felt completely vulnerable.

Chapter 14

"Jake, I had a crazy dream last night." They were nearing Uluru in the late afternoon, the sun brutal and hot overhead.

Jake looked over as he gently scratched his camel's neck. "Another dream?" He saw Kai's mouth quirk. Jake knew she wasn't comfortable with the dreams she had. Would he be if his all came true? Probably not.

Kai shared the dream with him. "Jake, there was danger. I debated telling you at all, but we're here at Uluru and I've got a knot in my stomach, and that tells me danger is nearby. I don't know what kind, but I think we should be ready."

Nodding, Jake pulled out his holster and strapped it around his waist. He tapped the Remington Safari rifle that lay beneath his leg in the leather sheath. It had been his turn to carry the gun today. "I think we're armed and ready to roll."

Booster strode a few feet away from Rocket, his ears constantly moving. Kai breathed in deeply and muttered, "I wonder if the dream is true, or if I'm overreacting because the others with Ooranye did come true." She removed the baseball cap from her head, wiped the sweat off her brow and settled it back into place, scowling. Reaching down, she took the water bottle from a nearby saddlebag and uncapped it.

Jake urged Rocket alongside Kai's mount. "Why don't we treat it as real? We'll be better off than if we ignored it." Jake did not want to lose Kai. He'd lost her once, when he was ten years old, and now the Great Spirit had given him a second chance to be with her. This time he intended to stay the course, come hell or high water.

Kai took another swig of water, leaving rivulets dribbling down both sides of her mouth. The slow swaying motion soothed some of her fear and helped her ground herself in the present. She capped the bottle and put it in a side pocket of the saddle. Looking over, she saw Jake studying her from beneath the bill of his cap. There was such concern in his golden gaze that it caught her off guard. It was only then that Kai realized he was genuinely worried. Maybe she *should* take this last dream seriously. Jake wasn't the type to make mountains out of molehills.

The warm presence of the crystal mask inside her vest made her feel more emotional than normal. Kai unconsciously touched the area where the crystal lay against her body. What was going on? Was she somehow being affected by the crystal's energy? Glancing at Jake again, she noted his tender gaze. She tapped her vest where the mask lay.

"I think this crystal is influencing me, Jake. It's weird…."

"Oh?" He looked around, his gaze sweeping the sky for

any aircraft. Glancing back at Kai, he saw confusion clearly registered on her face. "In a good way? Or bad?"

Shrugging, Kai said, "It's making me feel my emotions very sharply, Jake. A lot more, maybe, than I want to."

Chuckling, Jake said, "Welcome to the club, Kai." He saw her give him a questioning look. "You're a combat pilot. You're trained to keep your emotions in check. But you learned how to stuff your feelings down inside you long before that—as a kid. After you went into the Navy, you learned to stuff them even more deeply inside, so you could keep a level head during stressful wartime maneuvers."

"That's true," she conceded.

"What kind of feelings are you having?"

Rolling her eyes, Kai muttered, "I don't know that I want to share them with you, Jake."

He gave her a boyish grin. "Are they about me?"

"I'm *that* transparent?"

"Oh, not usually, but you are right now," he said soothingly. His grin broadened. "Hey, you wear it well, Kai. Even your face is softer, less tense. I started noticing it this morning after we broke camp and you put on that vest with the mask in it."

"Oh."

"It's not a death sentence, you know."

Snorting, Kai shook her head and looked off to the left, across the rolling red desert. "Maybe not…"

"Good feelings about me, huh?"

It was her turn to grin. "There's no shame in you, is there, Carter?"

Jake lifted his hands, laughter rolling out of his chest. "Guilty as charged."

"Yes, they were nice feelings about you."

"See? That wasn't so hard to admit, was it?"

"You're gloating, Carter."

"Yeah, but I won't ever use it against you, Kai." He reached over and captured her hand, which was resting on the round pommel of the saddle. Her eyes widened in surprise—and then pleasure. Jake released her fingers and said, "I'm glad we're together on this mission, Kai. Are you sorry?"

Her voice was hoarse as she held Jake's hooded look. "No…I'm not, Jake. Scared as hell, but not sorry." She saw him give her that little-boy smile. Heat flowed through her, strong and good. Jake's smile always made her feel like there was hope, even when things seemed hopeless.

"So, are these new feelings for me? Or old ones?" he asked, teasing her gently. Jake saw her wrestling with his question. More than anything, he wanted Kai back—in all ways. In ways he'd dreamed of. But life had never allowed them that opportunity—until now.

"If you must know, they're old and new." Kai rubbed her chest. "When I fell in love with Ted Barnes I thought it was real. But when it came right down to it, he couldn't treat me as an equal." Her eyes flashed and her voice deepened. "And I was damned if I was going to end up like my mother, browbeaten by a man who thought women were second-class citizens. He helped me realize my mother was a victim. For that, I should thank him, but it was a damn painful lesson. I don't have to be like my mom, and that realization freed me a lot from my past with her, with the confusion I had about her as a child. I could never figure out why she didn't leave that alcoholic bastard she married. At least with Ted, I realized I could walk away. And I did."

Jake nodded. "That was a valuable lesson to learn, Kai...." He could see the pain in her eyes and hear the anguish in her softened tone. She was a proud woman, so very capable and able to stand on her own. Yet her feelings confused her and she was less sure of herself. Kai wasn't invincible and that made her that much more precious to Jake. "I know you had a lot of confusion about your mother. If Ted helped you clear that up, it was probably worth it to you, Kai." Jake gave her an understanding look. "We all need someone in our lives. None of us want to go through it alone." Opening his hand, he said, "I fell in love, too...or thought I did. Learned a lot of hard lessons along the way of what I did and didn't want." Casting a glance at Kai, he added, "And if it's any consolation to you, no one ever measured up to you, Kai."

Jake scratched the back of his head. "Maybe I was comparing these women to you, which sure wasn't fair to them. If I did, it was unconscious. You made a hell of an impression on me."

"It's not good to compare," Kai agreed, her heart warming as she realized again that he'd never forgotten about her or what they'd shared.

"Are you over Ted?"

Nodding, Kai said, "Almost. It took a year to get back to normal." She gave him a jaded look. "And just when I was swearing never to mix it up with any guy again, you rolled back into my life, Carter."

Chuckling, he said, "You know how bad pennies are. They just keep showing up whether you want them to or not."

Realizing he was teasing her, Kai laughed. Touching her vest where the mask lay, she continued in a more serious tone, "What I was feeling was all the good things we shared when we were kids, Jake. And now those feelings are being magnified in me times ten. I don't know whether it's the mask…you, me…or the combination of events we're living through right now."

"Then let's give ourselves the time to see," Jake counseled. "It's enough to know you still like me a little bit."

"You're incorrigible, Carter!" Like him a little bit! Kai shook her head and hid her smile from him. If Jake only knew the power of her feelings toward him, he'd probably crow with delight and strut around like a rooster who owned the barnyard, judging from the warmth dancing in his golden gaze.

"But lovable," Jake murmured. Seeing Kai flush, he knew he'd hit a nerve. Could she love him? Was that possible? As a boy, he had been so deeply in love with her. Puppy love, but what a love it had been. Jake wanted it all back. He wanted Kai. He wanted to share with her his love, but he knew he'd have to give her time and space to come to that conclusion herself.

Glancing ahead, Kai saw the rolling red desert before them, the thick clumps of spinifex grass, the proud desert oaks dotting the horizon and the endless blue sky that seemed to stretch forever around them. Kai wiped the sweat from her brow with her sleeve.

"Does the mask affect you constantly?" Jake asked.

He'd noticed that Kai was unusually pensive today as they rode across the desert. She looked as if she were somewhere else, not here. Did the crystal hold properties that would change her? Influence her to love him? Jake didn't know, but he hoped so. He had observed that Kai's mouth, usually pursed and thin, was relaxed and full.

How he ached to kiss that mouth! How he longed to share with Kai the feelings he'd carried since the day he'd met her long ago.

Kai laughed briefly. "No question about it."

"Then keep on wearing it. I like the woman I see now, because she reminds me of the little girl from so long ago...."

Chapter 15

Less than thirty minutes later, Booster pulled up lame. Jake found a nasty thorn embedded in the camel's thick pad and pulled it out with a pair of pliers. To avoid putting excess weight on the wound, Kai went to ride behind Jake on Rocket. Sitting in the rear saddle behind Rocket's hump, she held on to Booster by wrapping the rein to his nose peg around her hand. It was only three more hours at the most until they got back to the Mulga Camel Station. Rocket could easily bear their combined weight.

As she swung and swayed atop the tireless animal, she was very aware of Jake, who was less than a foot away from her on the other side of Rocket's hump. Kai felt the crazy sensation that the crystal was continuing to create emotionally within her. Touching the mask, which she carried in the pocket of the vest she wore over her white cotton shirt, Kai felt as if all her feelings, good and bad, were being amplified. First she would feel far more emotional than usual and then her emotions would recede, like a tide going in and out. She knew some of it had to do with Jake, sitting so close to her now on the camel's back. She recalled all the wonderful feelings she'd had for him when she was a child, and it left her feeling both vulnerable and secure with him.

"You comfy back there?" Jake asked, turning and glancing at her over his shoulder. Out of the corner of his eye he could see Kai's face glistening with perspiration. The temperature was easily a hundred and thirty degrees, the waves of heat undulating before them and making the red desert and sand ridges look as if they were moving mystically around them. To Jake it seemed almost as if they were between dimensional worlds as the landscape wavered in the heat.

"I'm fine. Just not used to being a copilot," Kai said, grinning briefly.

"Oh…yeah, that's right, you're used to piloting your own fighter jet."

"My own car, my own camel—you know how it goes."

"Yeah, the lady likes to be in control."

"One of my many quirks," Kai told him drolly. She heard Jake chuckle and it lifted her spirits. A second later, her attention was snagged by an unusual sound. Frowning, she automatically reached for the pistol at her side, unsnapping the leather strap across the butt of the weapon.

"Jake?"

"I hear it…." He pointed in the direction of Yulara, a good ten miles away. They couldn't see the small community behind the shimmering curtains of heat.

"I got a bad feeling on this one." Kai pulled out her pistol and flipped off the safety.

"Coober said there were a lot of helo flights near Uluru," he cautioned her. "It could just be a tourist flight, so let's not overreact." His gut said something different, however. Worriedly, Jake scanned the light blue, cloudless sky. The sun was hanging like a glaring yellow eye in the west.

Kai shook her head and compressed her lips, her gaze scanning the sky ahead of them. "I hope you're right, but I keep wondering if my dream is going to come true.... There, at ten o'clock." She pointed past his left shoulder into the sky.

Squinting his eyes, Jake saw a speck on the horizon. "Get the binoculars out."

"Already in my hands," Kai muttered, and she swung them up to her eyes. The slow swaying of the camel made it impossible for her to get a fix on the helo. "Stop Rocket. I can't focus on the aircraft while we're moving."

Jake pulled the camel to a stop, his heart starting to pound in his chest. While Kai searched the skies, he leaned over and unsnapped the thick leather guard across the Remington Safari rifle. Grimly, he straightened.

Kai waited, frustrated. She got the helicopter in her sights, but it was still too far away to make out the paint scheme. "I don't know.... I can't see the colors on the fuselage yet...."

"Take your time," Jake said, wiping his mouth with his hand. Looking around, he saw that there was no place to hide if they were fired upon. Somehow, he knew they would become targets. It sent a prickly, icy feeling up his back. Again Jake studied the land before them. There was a fifteen-foot-high sand ridge less than a quarter mile away.

The ridge ran for at least a mile before it slanted back down to the flat desert floor. To their left and right were other ridges. Anyway he decided to go, they'd have to climb a slope. Furthermore, Rocket had two riders, twice the weight as before. Jake knew camels could run fast, but he also knew that two passengers would not only slow the animal down, it would throw him off balance if they didn't synchronize their movements.

"I got it!" Kai said. "It's Marston's Huey! Those bastards are heading straight for us, at about five thousand feet by my estimate."

"Ditch the binoculars," he ordered Kai grimly. "And get ready to run." He jerked the long Safari rifle out of the sheath. "Here, take this."

Kai quickly put the binoculars away and then dropped Booster's rein so the camel could run free. As usual, he stayed very close to Rocket's flank. Kai took the gleaming mahogany rifle, though she said, "I've got my pistol, Carter."

"You think you can hit the rotor area above the blades with it?" Jake gave her a cutting smile. "No way. You're gonna need that elephant gun. Hold on, we're moving into overdrive with Rocket. Have you ever ridden a galloping camel?"

"Hell no, I haven't!" Kai's heart was pounding now. The helicopter was less than three miles away. There was no question they were in its sights, because it was losing altitude and flying directly toward them.

"Listen to me," Jake said, his voice urgent. "Whatever you do, ride *with* me, Kai. It's just like riding double on a horse, bareback. You know how to do that, right?"

"Sure I do." She grabbed the long bullets Jake handed her and jammed them into her pocket. The huge elephant gun had to be hand loaded for each round. That would be a helluva thing to accomplish on a running camel. Kai wished the damn rifle had a magazine on it so the bullets would automatically feed up into the breech to be fired.

"Okay, Kai, let's put the pedal to the metal. We've got a ridge to clear." Jake leaned forward, dug his heels into the camel's shaggy sides and took the riding crop, which he'd never used until now, into his hand. He snapped the whip solidly against Rocket's flank. Uttering a low, guttural sound, Rocket gave a start and then leaped forward, his long, spindly legs flying out in front of him.

Not expecting the camel to be able to surge into high gear so quickly, Kai was nearly jerked out of her saddle. If she hadn't grabbed hold of Jake's shirt, she'd have tumbled off. Cursing softly, she hauled herself upright and then leaned forward. The camel grunted, laid back his ears, stretched out his neck and ran. Kai had had no idea how fast a camel could go, but soon got used to the long, abbreviated seconds before his padded feet hit the desert floor, sending veils of sand flying up on either side of them.

Booster, who wasn't going to be left behind, followed on Rocket's heels. The rein flew along beside him, but it wasn't long enough to reach the ground, so couldn't tangle in his legs or get stepped on. Kai saw that the camel limped slightly, but otherwise didn't seem to be impeded by the injury to his footpad.

Her attention shifted upward, drawn by the whapping sounds of the approaching helo. The afternoon heat was heavy with unexpected humidity, and the bird's blades were slapping the air like paddles slammed flat on a lake's smooth surface. The reverberation went straight through Kai with each punctuating turn of the rotor. She felt buffeted, literally, by the violent pounding.

"They're coming in!" Jake yelled. "Get ready!"

Kai jammed the pistol back into the holster at her side. Jake was right: if she hoped to fire at Marston's men, the Remington rifle would be a lot more effective than her shorter-range pistol. But it was a helluva balancing act getting the rifle settled into the crook of her shoulder and ready to fire with Rocket lunging toward the sand ridge.

The helicopter approached swiftly, blades thudding as it circled like a wolf, tracking its quarry from above. Kai gulped. The wind tore past them, making her eyes water. She'd had no idea a camel could run so fast! Kai estimated Rocket was going at least twenty-five miles an hour. The animal was huge, his long legs flying beneath him in a blur of speed, sand from his hooves spraying past her in thin, sparkling veils in the sunlight. Booster, running at Rocket's side, was startled by the closeness of the helicopter. He suddenly veered off along the bottom of the ridge they were approaching, frightened by the beating sounds.

The helo turned, its nose pointing toward them threateningly. Kai cursed and twisted around in the saddle. It was impossible to turn completely because of the bobbling of the camel beneath her. She clamped her thighs to Rocket's sides, hearing the camel grunting with each long stride.

"Hold on!" Jake yelled.

Rocket groaned as they hit the slope of the ridge. Kai

felt her legs losing their grip around the camel. Reaching out with her free hand, she grabbed Jake's broad shoulder for support. Leaning forward as the camel began the steep, vertical climb, Kai found herself off balance. The rifle nearly slipped out of her sweaty hand. *Damn!* Gripping it hard, she devoted all her attention to staying on board Rocket during the dizzying climb.

"How fast can Rocket run?" she shouted, her words torn away in the wind.

"Very fast," Jake yelled over his shoulder. He focused his attention forward as they raced up the hill. At this speed, if Rocket didn't watch where he was going, he could hit a clump of spinifex grass and they'd all go flying through the air as the camel tripped and fell. If that happened they'd be dead meat, Jake knew. The men in that helicopter would pick them off like fish in a barrel. Again and again he slapped the crop against Rocket's flank. Camels weren't like horses in maintaining speed. The big desert animals would slow down the moment they could, so had to have the whip laid to their thick, shaggy side with rhythmic repetition.

They were almost at the top of the ridge! Jake was pleased that Rocket was as fast as he was. He might not be a racing camel, but for a single-humped dromedary, he was no slouch. He had certainly earned the name Rocket.

"Shit!" Kai yelled. One moment she was anticipating the camel's front feet hitting the slope, the next she found the animal and his two passengers flying through the air! Eyes huge, Kai saw the land blurring beneath them as the camel *jumped* the last six feet to the top of the ridge. They were sailing up and over it! Kai hadn't known it was possible for a camel to leap like that.

She could see Rocket's huge brown eyes rolling with fear at the roar of the helicopter, which probably gave him incentive to run like hell. Jake could barely control the animal with the threatening sound of the copter thundering down upon them.

"Hang on!" he yelled in warning. He automatically leaned far back to prepare for the approaching descent. Kai's hand was gripping his shoulder like a vise. She was hanging on with everything she had. Seated behind him, she couldn't see what lay ahead.

Rocket hit the downward slope with a huge grunt. Like a surfboard, his front pads skidded at least ten feet over the surface before sinking into the red sand. Unprepared as she was, Kai crashed into Jake's back, her head striking his. Stunned by the impact, she struggled to keep her seat, and above all, hang on to the rifle held tightly in her right hand. Sand exploded up around them as Rocket landed hard. Her skin stung as bits of grit and rock struck her hands and face.

Just then, Kai heard popping sounds. *Gunfire!* She couldn't look up but knew the helo was about a thousand feet above them. Kai had her hands full just staying in the saddle as the camel began to charge down the sand ridge at full throttle. The scenery became a blur again as they picked up more and more speed. She heard Jake yelling at Rocket, laying the whip to him as the animal lunged forward. She had just gotten the broken rhythm of the camel again when she heard more popping sounds.

It wasn't her imagination! Kai saw geysers of sand fly-

ing up all around them. Bullets were being fired, and ca-
reening damn close to them.

"They're shooting at us!" she screamed. The sound of
her voice was drowned out by the helicopter, which was
now stalking them in earnest. Kai hoisted the rifle, though
she knew it would be impossible to try and shoot at the helicopter as the camel ran down the ridge. Sprays of red sand
flew everywhere as Rocket continued to gain momentum
on the downward slope.

Kai twisted angrily from one side to the other. The helicopter was directly behind them, making it impossible for
her to lift the rifle to her shoulder and fire. *The bastards!*
More popping sounds reached her ears. Lips compressed,
she jerked her head forward. Jake was leaning far forward
over the camel's neck, urging Rocket on with every ounce
of strength he had. She saw the flat desert floor coming up
fast. Off to their left, she saw Booster hightailing it toward
them, red dust rising in his wake. The camel was running
hard to catch up to them.

This time, Kai was prepared for the leap. Grabbing
Jake's shoulder, she clamped her thighs hard against
Rocket's sides and leaned far back to take the punishing
slam as the camel hit the desert in long, reaching strides.

The jolt nearly unseated her, but she managed to swing
her body forward in rhythm with Rocket's strides. She clung
to Jake's shoulder until she had regained her balance. Looking ahead, Kai saw they had about half a mile of flat land
before the next ridge rose to challenge them once more.
Booster had nearly caught up to them, bawling continuously,
his mouth open, white foam flying out of either side of it.

The popping sounds were closer this time. Fountains of red spray blew up in front of them, and Rocket bawled, too. Jake shouted encouragingly in Arabic to the animal, which surged forward. Booster shied away as more bullets were fired.

Kai's rage turned cold and lethal. This was not so different from sitting in the cockpit of an F-14 to fire a rocket at an enemy below. She twisted around and brought the butt of the rifle up to her shoulder. She'd never fired an elephant gun before, but knew there was a sizable kick once the bullet went screaming toward its objective. As she raised the barrel and tried to sight, a nearly impossible feat, she saw how close the helicopter really was to them.

There were two men in the cockpit. One had the window open on the left side, firing off round after round with a pistol. The other was the pilot. She tried to see their faces, but with their baseball caps and dark glasses, it was impossible. The only good thing about the situation was that the helicopter was encountering strong and powerful updrafts from the desert thermals at this time of day. That meant the pilot had his hands full trying to keep the copter level and smooth, so that the gunman could draw a bead on them. As it was, the helo was bouncing all over the place.

Smiling savagely, Kai decided the odds were even. Lifting the rifle, she laid her perspiring cheek against the smooth, deep red mahogany stock and took aim. She held off firing until the split second that Rocket lifted off with his front legs, when Kai was level and could sight true. Timing was everything right now. She waited. Breath suspended, Kai caressed the trigger with her slippery index finger. The helicopter was no more than six or seven hundred feet away from them—an easy range for this size rifle. Squeezing the trigger, she fired the Remington. The butt of the rifle jammed savagely into her shoulder, nearly ripping her out of the saddle, and with a shout of surprise, she slammed into Jake's back.

Rocket jerked sideways at this latest terrifying disturbance. Jake had his hands full guiding him forward once more. He pounded his left heel into the camel's side and pulled the nose rein to the right to straighten the camel out. Rocket bawled again, long strands of foam flying from his mouth as he ran.

Gingerly, Kai twisted her head to see if her bullet had hit it mark. *Missed!* Sucking in a breath through parched lips she again hefted the rifle. This time, as she pressed her cheek against the stock, eyes narrowed, she vowed to time the shot even more closely. Bracing herself tensely, she heard Rocket grunt each time he hit the ground. Jake was urging him on in Arabic. Each time he did, Rocket surged forward and tried to run faster. The wind stung her eyes. The sounds of the whapping chopper blades punctured her ears and made them ache. Sand was being sucked up around them in a huge circle because of the force of the blades as the Huey approached dangerously close to them. The camel zigzagged from side to side, scared to death of the huge, hulking aircraft thumping and thundering just above them.

Kai saw the shooter pull his pistol inside the window, eject a magazine and slam another one into it. Eyes slitted, she growled, "Not this time, dude..." And she squeezed the trigger. The Remington's bark was earsplitting. The rifle bucked powerfully. Kai absorbed the brutal jerk, which bruised her shoulder.

Rocket veered to the left, bawling in fear and protest over the gun roaring off another round.

Kai saw the bullet pierce the cockpit windshield. Plexiglas exploded in all directions. *Good!*

"Hold on!" Jake shouted. He wrestled with Rocket once again, trying to get him back into a rhythmic gallop. Booster was coming alongside, and Jake was worried that the other camel might weave in front of them, causing an unexpected collision. He could see that Booster was scared witless by the frightening noise of the helo. His herd instinct made him want to run alongside Rocket, but the thumping noise of the copter coupled with the bull roar of the elephant gun had completely spooked him. Weaving in panic, not knowing where to go, Booster was a real danger to them at this point. "We've got another ridge coming up!"

Great! Kai turned and grabbed Jake's shoulder. She didn't have time to check what damage, if any, her shot had done to their enemy. One second Rocket was galloping across the smooth desert floor, the next she felt him shift all his energy to his hind legs. And then they were climbing upward. The moment his front legs struck the slope, he lunged his twenty-five hundred pound bulk forward. With a cry, Kai felt herself slamming into Jake. If not for his solid body in front of her, she knew she'd be flying off the camel. Rocket hit the slope at an awkward angle as Booster unexpectedly leaped in front of him. Rocket tried to dodge the coming crash with his twin brother, and in the process stumbled.

The jolt unseated Kai, though Jake remained solidly in the saddle. Hurriedly, Kai reseated herself, amazed that she'd stayed on the camel. As Booster flashed in front of them in a blur, Rocket righted himself, lifting his long front legs and fiercely attacking the slope with all the speed he could muster. Booster kept galloping at an angle to the top of the ridge, well out of their trajectory.

Kai finally jerked a look over her shoulder as the chopper. The rifle bullet had shattered the middle of the cockpit's Plexiglas. The Huey was pulling back and gaining altitude!

"They're backing off!" Kai cried. "I hit 'em! I got a shot into the cockpit!"

"Good!" Jake yelled, still flailing the riding crop against Rocket's side. The camel sensed they weren't running just for the pleasure of it. Did he realize those geysers of sand flying up around him were bullets meant to kill them? He must, Jake thought. He saw the spittle flying from the camel's open mouth, his nose flaps flared wide to drag huge draughts of air into his lungs. Booster flew over the top of the ridge, heading for his home, Mulga Station, in the distance.

As Kai regained her seat once more, she gripped Jake's shoulder and turned. Her eye widened when she saw black smoke pouring from the helicopter's engine.

"Smoke! Jake, I hit something! The chopper's going down! He's landing behind that last ridge we just crossed!"

Jake glanced back briefly. He saw the Huey floundering, the pilot barely able to keep it under control. Black smoke was pouring from the engine assembly above the cockpit. He could hear the whine from the motor. The blades were floundering awkwardly. Grinning, he said, "Good shot! They gotta land! They can't keep chasing us!"

Relief surged through Kai as she twisted around in the saddle. Rocket topped the ridge, and this time she was prepared for his leap. And when he started down the opposite slope, she leaned far back, her shoulders almost brushing the camel's rump as he raced downward. Once again sand exploded around them, and closing her eyes, Kai felt the sting of particles against her sweaty face. She shifted forward again as the camel lunged down the ridge at dizzying speeds. The landscape looked like light and dark green blurs all around Kai.

Once they hit the desert floor, there were no more ridges to cross. Off to the left, Booster was galloping ahead of them. He kept looking back, and started to slow down. With the helicopter nowhere around, he finally waited for his twin brother to catch up to him. Kai was amazed that Booster even remained in the vicinity. She guessed his herd instinct had kicked in yet again, and he wanted company in this frightening adventure. That was good, she thought, as Booster rapidly closed the distance, to run at Rocket's side once more. Still, his panicked behavior had almost caused them to crash on the ridge—too close for comfort for Kai. She couldn't even begin to envision such heavy animals, running at mach three, with their hair on fire, slamming into one another. For sure, she and Jake would have died in such a brutal collision.

Jake kept up the hard gallop until they reached the out-skirts of the station. Finally, he allowed Rocket to slow down. The camel was panting, his sides drenched in sweat, his flanks heaving. Pulling him to a halt, Jake turned back to scan the desert.

"You can't see them," Kai said, her voice hoarse. She leaned over and slipped the rifle into its sheath. "They've either crashed or had to land."

Grimly, Jake searched the horizon for a long moment, bringing the restive Rocket to a standstill. There was no sign of smoke on the horizon. "They musta got down safely. If they hadn't, we'd see a big black cloud of smoke where they crashed."

Kai nodded. She released Jake's shoulder, which she was sure was black and blue from her grip. "I agree."

"We need a change of plans, Kai."

"Oh?"

"We don't know if there are more of Marston's men waiting for us at the airport." They were to take a commercial flight directly from Yulara to Sydney upon re-turning from the desert. "If we try to board a jet at Yu-lara, they could have men there to take us down. We can't risk that."

Frowning, Kai wiped her sweaty face with the back of her arm. "You're right…. You got any bright ideas?"

"If they know who we are, they can check a commer-cial flight and find our names on the roster. They could have agents on board, or worse, agents waiting to grab us at the other end when we land in Sydney…."

Kai frowned. "I've got to start thinking ahead of the curve

on this. Could we rent a car, drive to Alice Springs and catch a jet from there? I know there are flights bound for Sydney."

Jake smiled a little. "Even better, that Bell Longranger helicopter was for rent. How about I fly us to Alice Springs? It's two hundred miles away, and in a chopper we can cover that distance in a helluva hurry. The sooner we get out of Dodge here, the less likely it is our friends can catch us. If we rent a car, they can trace us, and they'll have time to catch a flight to the coast to set up and nail us. Or we might end up with a nasty little welcoming committee when we drive into Alice Springs. With a helo, we'd have a major advantage of time and speed. We might catch a flight to Sydney and slip out of here, undetected by Marston's men."

Nodding, Kai said, "Good plan, Carter. You up for a little flight?"

His smile became wolfish as he turned Rocket back toward the station. "Oh, yeah…that's my bread and butter. Gimme a helo anytime."

Some of the fear that had been pounding through Kai's veins began to recede. She gave a shaky laugh. "Okay, let's go for it…."

Chapter 16

"Y̶ou ready?" Jake turned and looked at Kai, who sat in the copilot's seat of the Bell 206 Longranger. She had just strapped in and had put on a pair of headphones so they could communicate with one another. She looked grim and he could feel her tension.

"Yeah, let's get outta this place. I'm jumpy. I look at everyone around the airport and think they're bad guys." So far, they hadn't seen the Huey fly in, nor the two men who were in it. That didn't mean there weren't other Marston operatives present.

Jake went through the motions of starting the engines. Outside, off to their right side, a man was ready to take the chocks out from beneath the helo wheels once the blades were engaged. "You're used to knowing the bad guys by seeing them as a blip on the radar screen of your F-14. Not dressed in civilian clothes looking like the rest of us."

Adjusting her vest, which held the crystal mask, Kai swept a wary eye around the airport. "Yeah, you're right about that. I guess I have to get used to the two-legged variety." Yulara Airport was small, relatively speaking—a few aluminum Quonset hut hangars, the main control tower and the passenger lounge for tourists. There were two commercial airliners on the tarmac and crews running busily around them, servicing them for upcoming flights. Compressing her lips, Kai remembered that she and Jake were scheduled to be on one of those flights, if not for their change of plans. Were the bad guys still out there on the desert, walking back because she'd shot out the rotor cuff assembly? Were they standing next to their shot-up Huey with a cell phone, calling for help? She hoped so.

Putting on her aviator glasses, she looked over at Jake. He inspired confidence in her as he pushed buttons and flicked switches here and there on the control panel in front of him, as well as overhead. In his earphones and black aviator sunglasses, he looked utterly military to her. That was comforting under the circumstances. She felt naked without an F-14 strapped to her butt. Now she had to rely on Jake, who knew copters and seemed very much at ease, which helped bleed some of the tension away from her.

"So much is happening," Kai muttered, frowning. The sunlight lancing through the Plexiglas cockpit was making her sweat. She was relieved when Jake turned on the air-conditioning, for the blast of cool air felt heavenly against her hot, sweaty skin.

"It is," Jake murmured. "Just keep looking around. This is a commercial helo, which has no HUD—heads up display—to show air traffic that's friendly or not."

"You expect trouble?"

Shrugging, he settled his right hand on the collective and

wrapped his left hand around the cyclic between his legs. "I don't think we should get sloppy, Kai. We know who we're dealing with. That's *why* we're taking this route—to hopefully avoid the bad guys and get out of the country without another confrontation with them."

"Right," Kai agreed fervently. The shoot-out in the desert had left her shaky and nervous. It was one thing to ride a fighter jet in the skies and flip a couple of switches to release an arsenal of bombs, rockets or missiles. It was quite another to fight a ground-to-air battle as they just had—and survive it. And on a camel, of all things! Reaching down between the seats, Kai dragged up a bottle of water and drank deeply. She'd lost a lot of fluid on that run-and-gun across the desert on camel back. She noticed that despite their dangerous ride, Jake looked incredibly calm and unruffled by the experience. Kai admitted she was more shaken by this attack than he appeared to be.

"I'll give you something to do," Jake said. Pulling out a map of the area, he handed it to her. "I talked to the pilot at the desk where we rented this girl, and he said to just follow the highway out of Yulara eastward, then northward, and it will automatically lead us to the Alice Springs Airport. Want to confirm the route for me?"

Kai opened the air map, settled it across her thighs and smoothed it out. She was no stranger to air charts.

"That's right. Follow the highway. It's more or less a straight shot."

"Sounds good to me." Jake punched into the computer the radio tower codes he'd use to speak with ground and air control.

Adjusting the map again, Kai bent down and found their position. "Alice Springs is larger than this podunk place."

"I would imagine. Once we're airborne, give me the numbers for Alice Springs radio frequency?"

"Roger that."

Jake gave a half smile. "Engaging rotors…" They were working like the close team they were beginning to become. That made him feel good.

Kai lifted her head when she heard the low whine of the engines as it engaged the rotor assembly on the top of the helicopter behind them. Sluggishly, the blades began to turn. In minutes, the Bell Longranger was trembling around them. Kai knew that if they didn't have earphones on, the noise level from the engines would be too high for them to talk to one another. She saw the man on the tarmac bend down and remove the chocks from beneath the three wheels. Once he was clear, he gave them the takeoff signal with his hand.

Jake flipped a salute out of habit, then settled his hands around the collective and cyclic.

"Okay, ready to take this bird into the air?" He glanced over at Kai. She had the map laid out across her long, curved thighs, her hands resting over it. Some of the tension was leaving her face, but her eyes were still narrowed and watchful behind her aviator style sunglasses. Just the idea that Kai might have been killed out there made his heart contract with terror. Jake didn't know what to do with the chaotic feelings that avalanched down upon him at the thought.

"Let's get out of here…." she murmured.

"Roger." Jake engaged the helicopter and it slowly lifted off the tarmac. At a certain altitude, he eased it forward, following the strip of runway. Once beyond it, he climbed to three thousand feet.

It was early evening, the sun glaring balefully on the western horizon. Fortunately, the worst heat of the day was over, so the severe up- and downdrafts weren't as bad, but they were still present. The Longranger was a good helo, in Jake's opinion, and he liked piloting the bird. Below them, he saw the two-lane asphalt highway stretching away from Yulara as they headed east.

"Desert looks the same," he mused to Kai. It was dark red, and from this altitude the clumps of spinifex looked like green dots thrown across it.

"It's beautiful," Kai murmured, gazing around. The air space was empty. She didn't think there would be too many planes out here, since Uluru was literally in the middle of nowhere. In the distance, she saw a cattle station coming up on her right. The main house was surrounded by silver-barked eucalyptus. No wonder. With this kind of heat, that shade would be considered a godsend to any desert dweller. She'd have planted thousands of acres if she could. But then, rain wasn't plentiful out here, either.

"How are you doing?" Jake glanced over at Kai.

"I'm okay."

He smiled slightly. The helo bobbled as it hit another air pocket. Jake expertly smoothed it out with a slight touch of the controls. It felt good to fly. Being on a camel was one thing, but in the air, he felt confident and safe.

"You know, you used to tell me the same thing—'I'm

okay'—when I'd meet you at the old beech. But you weren't...."

Mouth pulling inward, Kai muttered, "Yeah. My nose bleeding, my eyes black and swollen.... I was okay because I'd survived, Jake. That's all I cared about."

"But you weren't really okay." *Far from it.* How many times had Jake held her when they were children, all the while inwardly shaking with helpless rage over what her father had done to her? Because they lived on the res, he knew that family abuse often went unreported. The tribal police came when they were called, but usually the woman never called no matter how badly beaten up she was. Even if she was in the res hospital, she wouldn't make out an official complaint against her husband and abuser. Jake shook his head. He didn't know why. If anyone had beaten him, he'd have gone running for help. As it was, Kai's grandmother had called the police many times, begging them to intercede, but when her daughter refused to press charges, nothing was done.

"No...I guess I wasn't. But there were no options at the time." Kai shifted restlessly in the seat, running her hands nervously across the map. Glancing around like the fighter pilot she'd been trained to be, searching the horizon for enemy aircraft, she tried to avoid the emotions Jake's softly spoken words had triggered. Usually, she could. But at the moment she couldn't.

Generally, Kai could tuck her feelings away so that she could think clearly. Right now, she knew she was having an adrenaline letdown after that attack out on the desert. They could have died. After looking at Jake from beneath her lashes for a second, Kai turned her head toward the window. Again, she felt a sharp pang of fear. And pain. What if Jake had been wounded? Killed?

Rubbing the center of the vest between her breasts, she muttered, "This crystal is driving me crazy."

"Oh?"

"Ever since I tucked it into the inside pocket of the vest this morning, my feelings have been doing crazy things. I thought it would stop, but it hasn't."

"Such as?" Jake looked around, automatically scanning the sky. The sun was just setting and he saw the inky cover of darkness stalking them on the eastern horizon. Below him, the elegant desert oaks and clumps of spinifex cast long, thin shadows across the red sand ridges and desert floor. The view reminded him of a Salvador Dali painting, where everything was elongated and distorted.

"I feel emotionally overwrought...." Kai began, her voice low and tentative. She felt her fingertips tingle as they rested on the crystal hidden in her vest. "I was a lot more scared than I should be out there on the camel when we were attacked. I had a helluva time keeping my feelings under control. Things that usually wouldn't touch me emotionally were hitting me like boulders." Kai gave him a wry look. "When you're in the hot seat of an F-14, with enemy fire coming in, you aren't touchy-feely. But you know that."

Chuckling, Jake said, "Yeah. We turn off our feelings to do what we do."

"Mine were turned on and up this afternoon."

"The crystal is lying near your heart," he observed. "Maybe proximity is causing this reaction in you?"

Shrugging, Kai allowed her hand to drop from her vest. "I don't know. I don't dare put it into my duffel bag. I want to carry it on my person until we get it home to Grams."

"You do have to keep it close to you," Jake agreed. "Did your mom or Gram ever talk to you about crystals having that kind of ability?"

Shaking her head, Kai muttered, "No. My mother had a small quartz crystal she used in healings, but nothing like this one. I remember her using it on some of the people who came to her for help, but I haven't a clue what she did."

"And Grams?"

"She knows a lot about crystal healing. But I never showed an interest in it. Go figure…" The helicopter bucked as it hit an updraft. Kai liked the motion of the bird; it made her feel safe. Being in the air always had, and maybe that's why she loved to fly so much—it helped her escape from the painful memories of the past that haunted her like a curse. Kai removed her dark glasses and pinched the ridge of her nose. Where the oxygen mask had sat when she flew the F-14, there were two small, permanent indents into her skin. It was a painful reminder of her past, of what had been stripped unfairly away from her. All pilots who flew combat jets had these indents on the bridge of their nose.

Smiling, Jake met her wide blue eyes for just a moment. He loved to look at Kai and absorb her into his heart. Into his soul. Her mouth was soft and full now, and he realized there was a remarkable difference in her. Maybe the crystal was helping her to relax. "Maybe your Gram didn't know about these other qualities of the mask. It wasn't her job to take care of it. Usually the family who guards the totem knows most about it."

"That's what Grams said. She told me what she could. I'm glad we got it. I needed some way to clear my family's name. I know what people of the res are thinking—that I'm no good, that our whole family is poisonous and—"

"The res is a place where gossip burns like living fire," Jake agreed sadly. "Anyone who knows you, though, knows you're a fine person, Kai. You have honor."

"Fat lot of good that does me now, with a court-martial and a BCD." Frowning, she scanned the sky again, out of habit. Kai never relied on her instruments alone to find an enemy plane. She saw the dark, curving mantle of night approaching, staining the sky on the eastern horizon. The day was dying, the light fading. Riveted by the deep indigo hue below, she was amazed once again by the many colors of the desert. Every moment, there were different nuances, new tones and subtle color changes. Nothing was ever the same for long here, she realized.

"I have to retrieve my honor, Jake. I want to take the stain off my family's name because of what happened to me." Kai said the words grimly, her voice laced with steel. "I know I'm not to find all the stolen totems for the clans. My dream showed there are two women who will find the others." Touching her vest, she said, "But retrieving the Paint Clan mask will make our people respect my family's name again, and that's good enough for me. I just want a clean bill of health with folks on the res, that's all."

Nodding, Jake saw the road to Alice Springs fading in the dusky light. "I'm sure everyone will respect what you've done." He took off his sunglasses and tucked them into the pocket of his short-sleeved white shirt. "By bringing back the crystal mask, you'll show them that you're a warrior of the first order. They'll respect that and respect you. Your Gram will be able to hold her head up with pride once more."

"That's what I hope will happen," Kai said in a whisper.

Mouth quirking, Jake said, "It will, don't worry. Hey, I don't know about you, but all I want right now is a cool shower, some hot food and sleep. I'm whipped."

"Makes two of us," Kai murmured, giving him a sympathetic look. Jake's beard had darkened and it gave him a dangerous look. When his full mouth curved upward, her heart beat a little faster. Seeing the care in his golden eyes, Kai almost said, *And I want you to hold me, like you did in the hut at Kalduke. Right now, I'm feeling terribly vulnerable and unsure....* But she didn't. Stunned how her feelings were flowing so easily to the surface, Kai knew the crystal was doing *something* to stimulate this overly emotional response. Ordinarily, Kai was never this needy. She hadn't been since she was a little girl....

"I feel like I'm going to live," Jake sighed, coming out of the bathroom, rubbing his wet hair with a towel.

Kai sat on the bed in a fresh set of clothes, combing her recently washed hair. Looking up, she saw Jake was wearing a white towel around his narrow hips, water droplets still clinging to the dark hair on his torso and arms. His chest was wide and well-sprung, and his shoulders, the same shoulders she had cried on when she was a child, were proud and strong-looking. Jake was in good shape, she realized again. There was nothing she could do to fight her response to his near nakedness. And Kai discovered she didn't want to fight it.

"Good," she murmured. "There's a restaurant attached to this hotel here in Alice Springs. Get dressed and let's go eat. I'm starving."

Wiping his face with another towel, Jake smiled. "I'll jump into some clean clothes and we'll boogie on down there in a heartbeat." Kai looked refreshed and pretty in a white silk camisole with a kelly-green blouse over it, and tan silk trousers. As she combed her hair, he decided it looked like a beautiful ebony cloak around her shoulders. His fingers ached to tunnel through that mass and caress it. Would it feel as silky as it had when he'd held Kai at the hut only a few days ago? Haunting memories flowed through Jake as he turned and padded back into the bathroom to get dressed. As he quietly closed the door, he wondered if it was a good idea for them to stay in one room together. Their fake identities said they were husband and wife. This hotel didn't have adjoining rooms available, so tonight they'd have to bunk together with no door separating them. Of course, they'd slept in the same brush hut at Kalduke, but that was different. Or had things changed?

He wasn't sure, but whatever Kai wanted, he'd go along with. Jake was in no hurry to press her for a personal relationship. She had a lot on her plate right now. No, the timing sucked, Jake knew. Still, he'd held her once. Kai had come to him. Would she do so tonight? He ached for that to happen, but he wasn't going to expect too much.

At the restaurant, Kai sat opposite Jake in a black leather booth toward the rear of the busy restaurant called Kangaroo Jack's. It was a family place, with lots of children of various ages sitting with their parents. The noise level was relatively low, all things considered, and Kai was grateful for that.

"Smart choice of where to sit," Jake exclaimed as he cut into his well-done prime rib steak.

"Sitting at the rear of the place, facing the door, is the only way to make sure we're not jumped," Kai said with a slight smile. Famished, she cut into her rare prime rib. The baked potato slathered with butter and sour cream smelled heavenly to her, too. They had already demolished their soup and salad. "I guess I picked up that little fact from my childhood. I always sat in the rear of the kitchen, waiting to see my father come staggering through the door. That way, I knew how drunk he was and what kind of mood he was in."

Jake lost some of his appetite. He knew Kai had the crystal mask in her shoulder bag. It sat next to her, tucked between her body and the wall of the booth, so that no one could snatch it away from her. "Maybe some of your ways of protecting yourself will help us now," he told her. Jake saw Kai's black, arched brows move downward for a moment. She, too, stopped eating momentarily.

"It's this crystal," Kai growled, giving the white leather purse beside her a disgruntled glare. She knew that was the reason the past kept coming up for her.

Giving her a tender look, Jake said gently, "Kai, maybe it isn't all that bad. You've got a lot of good and bad feelings tied up inside of you like knots. No one can carry them forever. They have to come out someday." His mouth hitched slightly. "Look at it this way—better they come out here, between us. We have history with one another. And I won't hurt you—ever. At least, not knowingly."

"I guess you're right...." With her heart expanding and opening, Kai rubbed her brow. Beneath the table, their feet touched. Ordinarily, Kai would have moved, but for some reason, she didn't. She wanted Jake's nearness as never before.

"Come on, eat up," he urged. "We have to check in with Mike at Medusa when we get back to our room. He needs an update on what's goin' down."

Kai finished giving Mike Houston a report on where they were and all that had happened. They'd had no time after returning the camels to Coober at the station to call Medusa. Unsure of how many of Marston's men were in Yulara, they had decided to call Mike after things quieted down. Sitting on the bed now, Kai crossed her legs and held the satellite phone to her ear. Jake sat nearby, but not close enough to make her uncomfortable. It always amazed Kai how he seemed to understand that she needed her personal space.

"I'll contact the authorities in Yulara," Mike told her grimly, "and we'll see what we can get on those two dudes who tried to take you out."

"What about Marston? What else did you find out about him?"

"He's definitely a global collector of what I'd call power objects. You know that every Native American nation has rattles, feathers, pipes, crystals and other things that are used for ceremony. Over time, these ceremonial objects collect a lot of power. The more they're used, the more powerful they become. I don't think it'll be a surprise to you that people like Marston want these things precisely because they do have power."

Nodding, Kai pinched the bridge of her nose. "Yes…my grandmother tried to tell me about people like Marston. We call them power stalkers—people who want to steal an object and use the power in a selfish way—a way that isn't necessarily good for the people."

"Correct. Now, I'm South American Indian, and my mother told me that within our tradition, if a sacred object was in the wrong hands, it could kill or make someone very sick. It's a lethal weapon of sorts. I don't know about your crystals. We believe Marston has put several men up to steal them for him. Are they like that?"

Shrugging, Kai said, "I'm not sure, Mike. I do know Grams said that the health and wealth of the clan depends upon that crystal mask, and without it, our clan will wither and die over time."

"Sounds like Marston might want these clan crystals because they could bring him more wealth. Whoever owns them, owns the energy and its expression."

"That's right," Kai murmured. "I didn't think of that."

Chuckling, Houston said, "We can't prove—yet—that Marston took the other totems, but he's a good lead with what you found in Rowland's wallet. Further, you said it was Marston's men who attacked you, so we're starting to build a case against him. If we can catch those two dudes that attacked you and have the police interrogate them, we *might* be able to finger Marston directly. But that's future stuff. Right now we need to get you out of Australia with that Paint Clan mask. What's your plan for tomorrow, Kai?"

"Jake and I talked it over and thought we'd get a commercial flight to Sydney from Alice Springs."

"And if these people know your names, they could have some way of hacking into the airline's computer system to see if you're taking that flight out tomorrow."

Frowning, Kai said, "What can we do, then, Mike? It's nearly a three-thousand-mile drive across Australia to Sydney by car. That's not a trip I want to make."

"What about flying the Bell Longranger? You can hop from one small, local airport to another down to the coast, probably to Adelaide, which is the nearest big city. From there, we can pick you up by Perseus jet and bring you home. Is that doable from your end?"

"Hold on, let me talk to Jake about this…." When Kai filled him in, Jake instantly smiled.

"Sure, I'd love to fly us to Adelaide. No problem. The helo has the range to do it. We can pick up fuel at little airports along the way without any problem."

"Okay," Kai told Mike, "that's what we'll do."

"We have a Perseus jet stationed in Auckland, New Zealand, at the moment. It will take you a day or two to reach Adelaide. I'll get on the horn to the merc pilots flying it and reroute them pronto."

"Sounds good," Kai murmured.

"Stay alert," Mike warned her.

"We will. And we'll contact you again once we reach Adelaide."

"Roger and out."

Setting the phone on the bed stand, Kai gave Jake a slight smile. "You're like a kid in the candy store, Carter."

Holding up his hands, he chuckled. "Hey, flight hands. What can I tell you? I miss flying my Apache. The air is my home."

"That's one thing we have in common," she said, standing up. Feeling a bit anxious, she looked around the large room. They had never had to sleep together like this and it made her nervous. Of course, they'd slept in the same hut in Kalduke, so why was she all of a sudden feeling panicky? Jake had held her in the hut, too.

"You take the bed," Jake told her, rising. Seeing the confusion and worry in Kai's eyes, he decided to stop hoping. It just wasn't the right time for an intimate relationship. He pulled off the bedspread and took one of the two king-size pillows. "I'll sleep on the floor over here."

Stunned, Kai turned. "Was I that obvious?" She watched as he laid out the spread near the wall.

"A little," he teased. "It's okay, Kai. We're in a dangerous situation. Maybe, if things were different, I might suggest otherwise, but not right now."

Hearing his gruff tone, Kai felt her heart expand. "Thanks for being sensitive about this…." She gestured helplessly. "I want to, Jake…but—"

"Wrong time, wrong place." He sat down and pushed off his tennis shoes. "And it's okay, Kai. It really is. I don't know that I'd be any more trusting if I'd come out of a family like yours. Trust isn't something you give easily." She'd given her trust to Ted, though, and Jake hoped that Kai would, in time, trust him. Unbuttoning his shirt, he removed it. Kai was standing on the other side of the bed with a watchful look on her face. He wasn't going to strip down to his boxers until she was in bed and the lights were out. Kai was stressed enough.

"Okay…" She turned away to get her silk nightgown, which she'd hung on the bathroom door.

"I'll have the lights off when you come out," he told her.

"Thanks…." She shut the door.

Releasing a long, shaky sigh, Kai decided she was the consummate coward when it came to men. She didn't trust them worth a damn since Ted. Still, the thought of Jake's arms around her… Kai waffled about asking him to lie in the bed with her. That would be stupid. What if he kissed her? Or she kissed him? Could they stop? Would she want him to? Groaning, Kai shook her head. Emotionally, she just wasn't ready for that kind of commitment.

Unbuttoning her blouse, she shrugged it off and placed it on a hook on the door. Her heart was crying out with yearning for Jake. Kai was sure, now, it was due to the influence of the crystal upon her. The powerful medicine object was digging out all her fears for her to contend with—and all her dreams. Scowling, Kai slipped out of her clothes and donned her lavender silk nightgown, which came to her knees. The bodice was cut low, with delicate white Bemberg lace decorating the front.

Everything in her life was being thrown upside down and turned inside out. Kai came to that conclusion as she shut off the light and opened the door. Good at his word, Jake had made sure the entire room was drenched in darkness. A bit of light was peeking out around the wall-to-wall drapes, so Kai was able to find her way to the king-size bed. Relief trickled through her as she lay down and drew the sheet up over her hips. The pillow was made of goose down, and she sank deeply into it. The crystal was wrapped in red cotton cloth and hidden in the drawer of the bed stand next to where she lay.

"Good night, Jake."

"Sweet dreams, Kai."

As she closed her eyes, the only thing Kai wanted was a deep, long sleep without any dreams at all. She'd had her fill of them and then some. Spiraling down into the folds of darkness, feeling her body begin to release its tension one muscle at a time, Kai found her last conscious thought was to wonder if they would get safely to Adelaide without any other problems. As sleep enclosed her like a pair of owl wings, she felt danger would stalk them again—a matter of life and death.

But it had to be her imagination....

Chapter 17

"Red storm rising," Jake warned, pointing to his right out the Plexiglas window of the Bell Longranger he was piloting.

"What?" Kai looked up from the air map she was studying. They were flying at five thousand feet, a good two hours south of Alice Springs. It was nearly 0800, the morning air smooth and the sky cloudy.

"Sandstorm," Jake warned. "Again." He frowned and looked at the wall of red dust rising well over ten thousand feet—and coming toward them.

"Dude, that is some serious dust in the air," Kai muttered, her gaze narrowing. She hadn't forgotten about the sandstorm at the canyon. "The meteorologist at the weather desk didn't say anything about this…." She dug under a bunch of papers resting on her lap to reread the weather forecast for the Alice Springs–Adelaide flight route.

"Listen," Jake said, giving her a glance, "when I was stationed over in Saudi Arabia, these sandstorms could blow up out of nowhere. There's no way, usually, to forecast them on any given day. They kick up when a cold front's coming through, and we'll be flying through a low later today. That sandstorm is the front of the weather change."

"Rotten," Kai muttered, staring out the window. To her left, the sky was a light blue, with long, gray strands of alto-stratus clouds below. Her gaze settled on Jake for a moment. His profile was so strong and masculine. He was handsome, not matter how much she tried to ignore that fact. This morning he wore a short-sleeved, white cotton shirt and a pair of dark blue chinos. His chin was nicked from shaving and she felt an urge to touch the small wound in a soothing gesture, but squelched that unexpected response. It wasn't much of a cut, but for whatever reason, Jake suffering any kind of pain bothered Kai.

"What do you do in a sandstorm if you're piloting a helo?" Kai asked him. "I know what I'd do if I was in an F-14—avoid it."

Grimly, Jake studied the threatening wall of sand. It stretched from northeast to southwest like a huge, impenetrable red barrier slowly advancing upon them. "That's right. Avoid at all costs. These storms follow the line of the cold front that can be hundreds of miles in length and there's no way for a helicopter to get above it or fly around it. Usually you land and wait it out. The grit can get in the rotors and cause a lot of problems."

"Aren't Aussie helos somehow prepared for this?" Kai waved at the curtain of sand. It was a good thirty miles away from them, but given the direction they were heading, it would eventually overtake them.

"Probably are," Jake said. "For example, the Apache I

fly has titanium-edged blades. Even when I was flying in Saudi Arabia on top secret missions, we'd have to replace those blades about once a week, because the sand is silica, and penetrates any metal over time. Then you have pitted blades and you're going to have in-flight problems with stability, for starters. It goes downhill from there real fast."

"Oh…" Kai frowned. She picked up the thermos of coffee stowed in a net pocket beside her seat. Their flight was smooth this morning, nothing like yesterday, during the heat of the afternoon. She could pour a cup of coffee now without spilling a drop.

"Want some?" she offered.

"No…" Jake's attention was on the wall of the storm. It was a deep red color, the colder air scooping downward and lifting the crimson sand off the floor of the desert, then whipping it upward on a fast, rising thermal of super cooled air. The front of the wall looked like the endless curve of a wave that was continuing to ascend and was finally going to come down and crash upon the beach, only it never would. The crest would churn endlessly high in the air, slowly rotating ahead of the major wall of the storm. The winds in that frontal crest were rough, and dangerous to all aircraft.

Kai sipped her coffee after she'd stowed the thermos back in the side pocket of her seat. "Have you flown in a sandstorm before?"

"Yeah…once. We were on a mission to protect an Army Special Forces A team of ten men who were hunting down terrorists. They were pinned down and needed air support in the middle of this sandstorm, and we had to fly even though we shouldn't have."

Looking at the grim set to his square-jawed face, Kai realized the memory was a brutal one. "Pretty rugged?"

Giving a sharp bark of laughter, Jake said, "*Rugged* is a good word. We were able to supply them the firepower they needed to break free of the jam they were in. They made it by foot to a mountain, where they lost the enemy, then they hunkered down to wait out the rest of the sandstorm. After it rolled by, a Blackhawk went in and extracted them."

"What happened to your helo?"

"The blades were so badly pitted from us flying thirty miles into that storm and out of it that it was rough getting away alive. I wasn't sure we'd make it back to base. The controls were loose and I thought we would crash, but we made it back to the base okay. They removed all those blades immediately. When we looked at them in the hangar later, they were so pitted that I didn't know how they'd held that bird up."

Eyeing the sandstorm, Kai said, "Then we need to set down." She began searching the map for the nearest airport.

"Yeah, that's the long and short of it," Jake said, glancing over as she ran her long, slender fingers across the map. How beautiful Kai looked this morning. He hadn't slept much on the bed he'd made on the floor, and not because the carpet was hard or uncomfortable. Just being in the same room with Kai was an aching torture for him.

He'd tossed and turned all night. The air-conditioning had been on and it had muted the sounds of his restlessness. Knowing Kai lay sleeping in the bed about five feet away ate at him. Jake wanted to be up on that bed with her, beside her, holding her…just holding her, as he had so long ago. As he'd done just a few days ago. He had gotten up at last and quietly taken a shower, then dressed and left the room. But not before looking down at Kai, who was sleeping the sleep of an angel.

He would never forget what he'd seen this morning. The image was branded forever on his heart. Kai had worn a pale lavender nightgown and she'd been lying on her back, one hand near her head, her fingers slightly curled. Black and loose, her hair had formed a beautiful halo about her head and shoulders, emphasizing her coppery skin, her softly parted lips and high cheekbones. Jake had stood there absorbing her beauty into his heart like a thief. He'd felt guilty standing there, slobbering like a rabid wolf, but couldn't help himself. He had been rooted to the spot, hands just itching to reach out and caress her thick, silky hair, to softly touch her smooth cheek once more.

Kai lay there like an innocent, the covers down to her hips, exposing the ripe curves of her breasts, which rose and fell slowly with her breathing. In that moment, Jake saw the real Kai Alseoun. Not the embattled survivor who had clawed and scratched her way out of her dangerous childhood. Not the combat warrior who had, until very recently, rode and tamed the most powerful fighter jet in the world. No, he saw the woman herself. The person who was open and vulnerable, with no walls erected to keep her tender emotions protected. Oh! How he'd wanted to simply step forward, sit on the bed and tell her what a fantastic woman she was, how much he admired, respected and loved her.

Swallowing hard, Jake looked away from Kai as she studied the map. Love. Yeah, well, that's what it was. She was the first love of his life. And when she'd been wrenched unexpectedly out of it, Jake had thought he'd die of grief, his love for her had been so deep and true. Now, so many years later, he was finding that the love he'd held then had matured, grown and was now so powerful he couldn't ignore it. Jake didn't know what to do with that realization. It was the wrong time. The wrong place. Wrong everything.

"Jake…"

He heard the tension in Kai's tone. Looking in her direction, he saw her staring out at the cloudy sky. "What?"

"I see a helo coming at us—fast. They're on our six."

That was bad news. The "six" position was the tail of their copter, a place where enemies could sneak up to get a shot at them without them shooting back. That wasn't a good sign. "Get the binoculars. Check it out." His mind spun with questions—and options. There was no way Marston's men could fix a Huey overnight and get it airworthy. Or could they? And how could they follow them? Of course, Jake knew that the Longranger was the only other helo there at Yulara, and anyone could walk in and see that they'd filed a flight plan for Alice Springs. That had been a mistake, Jake realized now. He should have lied about their destination. *Damn.* There was nothing they could do about it now. Lesson learned, Jake told himself. He watched as Kai drew the binoculars from the case that sat between their seats. Dreading what she might see, he glanced over at the approaching wall of red sand. It was much closer. Threatening.

"Damn!" Kai rasped. "It's *them*, Jake!"

"Are you *sure?* Same color scheme? The *same* Huey?"

"Yeah, I'm positive." Kai watched as the helicopter continued toward them at a rapid rate. "Blue-and-yellow paint scheme. The same bastards."

"What about the tail numbers?"

Kai searched, and as the Huey turned slightly, she read them off to Jake. Pulling the binoculars away, she said, "It's the same damn helo. How'd they get it fixed so fast?"

"I don't know. It doesn't matter. What matters is they're stalking us and we're helpless in the arms department. I wish we had an Apache. We'd have seen those dudes stalking us a long time ago. We'd have rockets and a chain gun to blow them out of the air. Right now, we have next to nothing."

Kai stowed the binoculars. She quickly grabbed her pistol from the canvas bag that sat behind her seat. "Well, we know what he's going to do. He's going to get close enough to start firing at us. And I'm not going to sit here and let that happen." She slammed a clip into the butt of her pistol. Placing a bullet in the chamber, she turned and studied the door on her side of the aircraft.

"Did you see rocket launchers on the Huey?" Jake asked. His gaze moved across the dials in front of him. They had half a tank of fuel left.

"No...nothing outwardly that I could see." Grimly, Kai watched the chopper, which was a thousand feet above them and hurtling down toward them. Her pulse leaped. "They may have an elephant gun this time. I sure wish we had that Remington right now. My pistol is only effective at close range. If they have a rifle, they have a much longer reach and we're dead meat. I'll never be able to hit them with a bullet, but they'll sure as hell hit us...."

"Yeah, I know," Jake said worriedly. "Get on the satellite phone. Call Mike. Tell him we're under attack again. Give him the details. If we go down, he's got to know our coordinates so they can send a team from Adelaide to search the wreckage...."

"That's no consolation," Kai muttered. She eyed the storm, which was less than five miles away from them. Grabbing the phone, she dialed in the number.

Jake divided his attention between the Huey, which was now diving directly at them, and the wall of sand. They were bracketed between two evils and had nowhere to escape to. What should he do? If he flew into that sandstorm, they could be in real jeopardy. What if sand got into the rotor area? The silica could jam up the oiled mechanism and cause all kinds of problems. Furthermore, he had no sophisticated instruments that could fly him successfully through a sandstorm. He would for all purposes be flying blind. Worse, vertigo could occur, and he would have no sense of up or down, right or left. He had to rely on his instruments, and the ones aboard the Longranger weren't fine enough for the job.

Hearing Kai get off the phone, he saw her tuck it into her canvas bag.

"Mike's on it. He's calling the Royal Australian Air Force base in Adelaide to get us help."

"Too little, too late," Jake muttered, perspiration popping out on his brow. Glancing from the approaching Huey to the wall of the storm again, he growled. "By the time they get here, it will be all over, Kai. Those jets scrambling from Adelaide have got at least thirty minutes of air time before they reach us."

"You're right." Fingering the side of the fuselage, Kai found there was a small window that could be pushed open and closed. Large enough for her to shoot through? "What are your options?"

"We've got to duke it out with them. I can't go into that storm, Kai. We could crash."

"That's what I thought," she muttered. The Huey was coming down fast. "Okay, do what you gotta do. Want me to call out his position to you?" She knew Jake would need another set of eyes to help him avoid any gunfire. He had no instruments to help him locate their stalking enemy. Looking over at him, gripping the pistol in her hand, she saw that his face was set, his golden eyes dark and filled with frustration. About now she'd like to be in the seat of an F-14 Tomcat with her RIO—radar information officer—calling out the coordinates to put a lock on this bastard and blow him out of the air.

"Yeah, let me know where he is. I'm going to try maneuvering first. A Huey's a lot more nimble than a commercial helicopter, though, so I don't know how far that will get us."

"I'm more interested in the weapons they have on board. If they've got a rifle, we're in *real* trouble."

"Yeah, I know that, too."

"Okay, here he comes. He's about one mile out, eleven o'clock on your port...."

In that instant, Kai heard a pinging sound behind them. "He's firing at us!" she yelled.

Instantly, Jake took the copter into a steep, sliding bank to the right. He had no idea how well or poorly the Longranger could handle air to air combat. It certainly wasn't designed for it! Gripping the collective and cyclic, he felt the harness straps bite into his shoulders and hips as the helo groaned and banked.

Cursing, Kai called, "He's following us down! And I can see a rifle sticking out the window. He's got a rifle!"

"Hang on," Jake yelled. He kicked the Longranger out of the sliding bank. They'd lost two thousand feet of altitude, and the wall of the storm was nearly upon them. Not wanting to lose much more altitude, he saw the Huey flash past them. It had built up too much diving speed to bank as quickly as he'd just done. *Good!*

Heart pounding, Jake felt rivulets of sweat leaking beneath his arms and trickling down his rib cage. His breathing was raspy as he forced the copter higher. If he didn't get air between him and the Huey, Marston's men could pounce on them and fire from above. Not wanting to give them that opportunity, Jake shoved the throttle to the firewall. The Longranger shrieked and he felt the entire airframe shudder as the blades spun, clawing upward through the sky,

Kai was thrown around by the maneuver, but in the process she saw the Huey below them. "He's down a thousand, about four o'clock on your starboard. And he's going to try and make up the altitude."

"Yeah, he'll do it, too," Jake muttered. Gaze glued to the

altimeter, he wished this commercial helicopter could climb as an Apache could. His combat helo could leap through the sky like a cougar running full tilt. But this copter wasn't created for combat; it was an excellent commercial aircraft, but not made for this kind of jockeying around in the sky. Jake didn't know the limits of the airframe or what kind of punishment this Bell could take—but they were going to find out fast.

"He's coming around on you!" Kai shouted, rising up out of her seat to keep a bead on the blue-and-yellow Huey. "Less than five hundred feet…"

Ping, ping, ping.

Gunshots riddled the cabin.

Ping, ping, ping, ping.

Glass exploded around Kai. She gave a yell and threw up her left hand to protect her eyes. The window on her side of the helo was blown out. Bullets tore through the cabin. Wind roared in, whipping the map off her knees and sucking it out the window. Anything that wasn't stowed was flying around in the cockpit.

"Damn!" Kai yelled. Instantly, she felt the Longranger lurch to the left. Straps bit into her shoulders and, disoriented for a moment, she gasped. The Huey flashed past them, barely out of the rotor range.

Kai's heart pounded and rage tunneled through her. "Get close to them!" she snapped at Jake. The door was riddled with bullet holes. When the Longranger jerked upward, the engines screaming in protest, her door was suddenly sheared from its hinge, torn off by the maneuver and wind speed.

When Kai saw the door snap off the airframe, she gasped. She now hung by her harness alone, over nothing but air and the ground far below. Scrambling, she slapped her left hand against the frame and pushed herself back into her seat as Jake banked the aircraft once more. The wind was ferocious. Although she wore aviator glasses, which protected her to a degree from the roaring blast circling within the cabin, her eyes still watered badly. Jerking her head up, she frantically searched for the Huey.

"There! Jake, get close enough for me to fire at them, dammit! I'm not going down without a fight! They're a thousand feet above us, at ten o'clock, to port."

The Longranger groaned. The blades grabbed for air and thumped hard, each rotation causing a thick shudder to ripple through the aircraft. It was vibrating like a wounded beast as it moved closer and closer to the Huey.

Kai unsnapped her harness and shoved it away.

"What are you doing?" Jake yelled. "Get that harness back on!"

"Screw it." Kai situated herself in the door frame. Four thousand feet below her was the desert, a red blur. Her gaze was pinned on the approaching Huey. Jamming her left boot against the copter frame, she pressed her back against the opposite side. Bracing with her right foot, she effectively jammed herself into the space where the door had been. The good news was she had a clear shot at the approaching Huey. The bad news—she had nothing to hang on to when Jake maneuvered the Ranger. Kai knew she could be torn out into space and fall to her death.

Breathing hard, she yelled, "Closer! Dammit, get closer!

I *want* this son of a bitch!" Air slapped and pummeled her, tearing remorselessly at her eyes. The Huey was coming directly at them. She saw the two men in the cockpit—the same bastards as before.

Raising her pistol, she gripped it in both hands to steady it. This was a game of sky chicken. Kai recognized it for what it was.

"He's coming right at us! Ten o'clock. You have to jump him, Jake! On my word, I want you to bank *toward* him! It'll give me the shot I need!"

That was an insane maneuver! Jake didn't say that, though. Instead he split his attention between flying the Longranger and watching the approaching Huey. Scared to death that Kai would get yanked out the door by his sudden maneuvers, or that a bullet would find her, he clenched his teeth. No! Kai couldn't be killed! She just couldn't be! His heart ached with a fierce refusal to allow anything to happen to her. All he could think about was going after the Huey and knocking it off balance. But Kai was right. If he followed her advice and suddenly lurched *toward* the Huey, it would spook the pilot and he'd bank in the opposite direction. When he did that, Kai could get a clean, close shot at them.

Gripping the cyclic and collective so hard his knuckles whitened, he yelled, "Tell me *when!*"

Seconds flew by. The wind was punching at Kai's body like a boxer, and she had to use all the strength in her legs to keep herself jammed tightly into the door frame. She saw the Huey coming at them like a shark ready to eat them alive. Her hands gripped the pistol tighter. Raising the barrel, she sighted on the red-haired copilot, who had his rifle sticking out the window—pointed directly at them.

The distance closed swiftly. Two thousand feet. Fifteen hundred. A thousand. Kai's mouth grew dry as the Huey's nose loomed closer. The wind shrieked around her. The Longranger was screaming with the strain of climbing upward to meet the assault.

Five hundred feet.

"Now!"

Kai felt the Longranger lurch. Gravity pulled at her with invisible hands, trying to jerk her out the door to her death. Wind slammed at her as the helicopter arced and moved directly into the Huey's face.

Kai saw both men's jaws fall open at the unexpected maneuver. She saw the pilot react, his mouth stretched in a scream. Taking aim, she waited for a split second as the Huey came closer and closer.

Kai felt the sickening shudder of the Longranger. Air punched and grabbed at her repeatedly, making it difficult to breathe. Hands sweating, she gripped the pistol with all her strength. Train the barrel…train the barrel… She followed the cockpit of the Huey as it suddenly changed position.

In that instant, Kai squeezed the trigger. They were so close! She saw the black blades of the Huey rotating closer and closer. The Longranger was moving drunkenly, like a wounded dragon. The smell of burning oil filled her flared nostrils as she squeezed off round after round.

When the Huey banked sharply, Jake followed it down with his own banking maneuver. He knew they were close, within each other's rotor circumference, and that there was a real possibility of their blades colliding. He heard the *pop, pop, pop* of Kai firing her pistol. *Great Spirit, let her be accurate!* Gravity tore at him. The straps of his harness bit savagely into his shoulders as he followed the Huey downward.

The two helos were now plummeting like rocks, the copter below them. Grim satisfaction soared through Jake for a second as he heard Kai give a cry of triumph. He couldn't see the Huey, or even look at Kai—he had to fly this bird for all it was worth. He felt the strain on the engine; they could vibrate apart at this speed, no question. He knew the Bell wasn't built for combat maneuvers like this. The blades were pounding, pounding, pounding, the reverberations thumping like fists through his body. Unable to breathe, he gritted his teeth and held the bird on course.

Kai kept firing. She emptied one clip into the Huey and, with a cry of triumph, saw the bullets land with deadly accuracy. The Plexiglas on the pilot's side exploded inward. She saw blood splattering the cockpit glass on the copilot's side.

Suddenly, the Huey lurched and began an uncontrolled free fall. Kai leaned out to watch, the wind pulling mercilessly at her. She threw her pistol back into the cabin and held on with both hands to the airframe overhead.

"He's going down!" she cried. "He's going to crash!" She watched as the Huey began to turn in wide, wobbling circles. She'd hit the pilot with one or more bullets. He was the only one who could fly, apparently; the gunman in the copilot's seat was just that—not a pilot, just a murderer.

"Die, you sons of bitches!" she shrieked. Hands gripping the airframe, Kai leaned out to see the Huey explode beneath them. Then the Longranger lurched upward and she was thrown back into the cockpit. Landing in her seat, she flailed momentarily until she managed to grab the armrest and hang on until Jake leveled out the chopper and put it in hover mode.

Gasping for breath, she scrambled upright and, with shaking hands, fastened the harness across her shoulders and lap once more. Glancing over, she saw Jake looking out of his window at the explosions below. Grinning, she said, "We nailed them!"

Adrenaline was pumping through Jake as he watched the Huey burn below them. Wrenching his gaze away, he looked at Kai. Her hair was torn out of her braid, tendrils curling around her glistening face. Her blue eyes were narrowed with St. Elmo's fire, a kind of lightning that would dance around a ship's mast during a thunderstorm. She was a warrior through and through just then, her eyes fierce, her mouth curved ruthlessly in a smile of triumph.

Shakily, he asked, "You okay?" Those bullets flying through the cabin could have gotten either one of them.

"Yeah, I'm fine...and you?" Kai looked at Jake. If she'd ever had doubts that he was a combat pilot, those doubts were gone now. His face was sweaty, his golden eyes slitted like those of a hunter after his prey, his tensed body flushed with adrenaline.

"Yeah, I'm good. But we've got problems. I think we took a bullet in the fuel tank. We're losing too many pounds of fuel too fast...."

"I lost the map," Kai said, "but I know that thirty miles

from here there's a dirt strip near a cattle station that had fuel. We could set down there…."

"Yeah." Jake looked at the approaching sandstorm. It was a few miles away, coming on like a relentless freight train that threatened to run them over. "I think we can make that. Do you recall the coordinates?"

Grinning, Kai pushed loose strands of hair off her damp face and away from her eyes. "You bet I do." She rattled them off, then, heart pounding, reached back and gripped her pistol. From her pocket, she pulled another clip of ammunition and slammed it into the butt of the firearm. Looking around the sky, she muttered, "I wonder if there's more of them?"

"No way of telling…." Jake concentrated on getting them to that cattle station before they ran out of fuel. "But we need to stay alert."

"I'll call Mike." Kai leaned back and picked up the satellite phone out of her bag. The wind was still whipping through the cabin. There was nothing they could do about it now that the door was gone. Punching in the numbers, Kai waited. When Mike came on, she practically had to shout over the shriek of the wind. Reassuring him that they were all right, she gave him the coordinates of where they were hoping to land the Longranger. Once he got the info, Kai knew he'd cancel the military jets out of Adelaide, put a new mission into motion to pick them up, plus contract Australian aviation authorities about the Huey crashing. Mike would have to do a lot of interfacing with not only the aviation department, but the police, as well. Maybe, if there was anything left of the two men, they could find some sort of identification on them—fingerprints or otherwise—that might give a clue as to who the hell they were.

Jake was never so glad to see a silver-green grove of eucalyptus appear on the horizon, indicating the main house of the cattle station was nearby. Below, they saw thousands upon thousands of cattle foraging across the desert, as well as drovers on horseback here and there. Aiming the Longranger toward the small dirt strip on one side of the complex, Jake set the helo down—just in time. He pointed to the fuel gauge before shutting the engine down. "We had fifty pounds of fuel left."

"That's not much," Kai said tensely, looking at the indicator. She'd never been so glad to be on the ground, if only to stop that buffeting wind. Looking through the cockpit Plexiglas, she saw several men on horseback riding toward them at high speed. "Well, I'm sure they weren't expecting us to drop in."

Jake grinned sourly and flipped off the engines. "No, but I think they'll be glad to help us." The blades slowed; the shaking and vibration began to ease off. Wiping his sweaty brow with the back of his hand, he watched the men galloping toward them. Within the next ten minutes, he knew, the sandstorm was going to hit.

Pulling the vest that held the crystal mask a little tighter around her, Kai climbed out of the helo. Jake opened the door on his side and got out in turn. The first of the four riders was a large man with a gray beard and a floppy, sweat-stained brown bush hat. He was riding a big, rangy bay gelding at least sixteen hands high.

Moving around the front of the helo, Kai joined Jake. "What kind of story are you going to tell them about the missing door?"

He turned and grinned at her. "They're going to see bullet holes in the fuselage, too. But we'll tell them as little as possible."

"Mike said he'd be getting a Perseus flight crew out of Adelaide to come for us as soon as the sandstorm passes by. They'll be flying a Blackhawk helicopter."

"Sounds good to me. Well, let's go meet our station folks. I know they'll give us food, water and shelter." Looking up at the wall of the red storm approaching, Jake added, "This is a helluva way to spend a morning...."

Chapter 18

"This...this is just so wonderful," Ivy said softly to Kai and Jake as she sat at her rough-hewn kitchen table with them. The morning was young, the sun barely having risen. Heat from the roaring fire took the chill off the room where they sat, cups of steaming coffee in front of them. Patting the black leather pouch that she'd made specially for the return of the Paint Clan crystal mask, Ivy lifted her hand and wiped her damp eyes. "We have the first of the three stolen totems back for our people. I think my heart is gonna explode with joy." She glanced fondly at Kai, her voice wobbly.

Touched, Kai reached out and patted her grandmother's work-worn hand. "I'm just glad we could get it back." She tugged at the dark blue, mock turtleneck she wore, then rubbed her sweaty palm against her black corduroy pants. It was turning out to be a very cold autumn. Upon their return to the Great Smoky Mountains, Kai had borrowed a pair of Jake's thick black socks to wear with her boots to keep her feet warm. She found it a shock to go from a burning Australian desert to a cool autumn in North America. It had snowed lightly the night before, but Kai was sure that, here in North Carolina, the snow would melt soon. It wasn't lost on her that the extremes of weather mirrored her life.

"We made a good team, Grams," Jake murmured. He took a sip of his coffee. This was the first time he'd been back to the Quallah Reservation since he'd left so long ago. It was a bittersweet journey to this beautiful place nestled deep in the Great Smoky Mountains. Gazing out the frosty cabin window above the sink, he could see the early morning "smoke" that the mountains were named for. The fog reached halfway up the mountain at the end of the valley where the cabin sat, surrounded by snow-dusted evergreens.

"I thought I could do it alone, Grams, but I was wrong." Kai gave Jake a warm, proud look.

Ivy's dark brown eyes sparkled. "It's good that you young'uns have peace in your lives now." She looked down at the pouch holding the crystal mask, and stroked it gently, as a mother might a baby. "Our family will be spoken of with respect and honor from now on. You've done much, Kai, to rescue our good name. I'm proud of you, child."

Kai looked across the table at Jake. He wore a blue plaid, long-sleeved flannel shirt, jeans and a pair of boots. His golden eyes were filled with humor, and his mouth curved upward.

Kai felt heat in her cheeks as her grandmother looked at her with a glint in her eyes. "Thanks, Grams. It means a lot to me to clear our family name. At least I've done something right, for once."

"You've done a lot right, child. Just don't let your experience with the Navy stain your life any longer. The Great Spirit moves in mysterious ways. Maybe you were needed here to bring this totem home to us more than the Navy needed you. Have you ever thought of that?"

She hadn't. Kai shook her head. "I loved my life in the Navy, Grams. I'm a warrior, and I'm good at defending people. Helping out that way makes my heart sing."

"I know, child, but you were all those things on this quest for the mask, too. I'm sure another door will open to you soon. The Navy is in your past. You've got to look forward now."

"I know...." Kai whispered, her throat aching with unshed tears. The Navy had been her life, the one good thing she could point to that had come out right.

"The world needs warriors like you," Jake told her gently. "Your skills won't be wasted, Kai."

"She certainly hasn't wasted them so far!" Grams said, holding up the pouch. "She had a vision and look what happened! Now, we wait to see what woman will be contacted in the dream state to get the second totem back to us."

"I've told Mike Houston about that," Kai said. "I keep wondering if I'll get another vision, or how it will unfold...."

"Tut, tut, child." Grams reached out and patted her hands, which were resting on the table. "Don't fret about this. The Great Spirit showed you the whole thing. Don't you think that, at the right time, you will be contacted again? Dreams are our connection to one another through spirit. Have faith."

Kai had more faith than she'd started out with. "Just

having my dreams about Ooranye come true blew me away, Grams." Kai touched her head. "I thought I was crazy, maybe. But I know there are medicine people who have dreams like this all the time."

"Yes, and those people help others through their dreams, too—" she smiled kindly at Kai "—just as yours brought the first totem back to us. You'll have another vision. You'll see the woman, just as you saw Ooranye. You'll be led to her, and who knows? She may well have a dream about it at the same time you do! Among medicine people, it's a common occurrence to dream the same dream, at the same time." She grinned at both of them. "That's one way we communicate. A secret one."

Jake smiled. He knew his mother was a lucid dreamer, someone who could move in and out of that state with ease. He recalled how she'd often dreamed of a certain herb or ceremony to help someone, and then did just that. "I can confirm that, Grams," he told her, giving Kai a reassuring look.

"That's right, your mother was very famous for her dreams, often finding just the right herb to help someone. And she certainly wasn't crazy."

Holding up her hands, Kai murmured ruefully, "Okay, time out. I hear both of you. I'll stop gnashing my teeth, worrying about having another dream to help find the next totem."

"You're always too hard on yourself," Jake murmured.

Kai sighed and held his gaze. "I was a little hard on you from time to time on this mission, too."

Shrugging good-naturedly, he answered, "You were just testing me, was all. I tried to be a good sport about it."

Ivy studied him for a long moment. "Jake Stands Alone, you have always been different from any little boy I knew on this res when you were growin' up. You're still different, and I don't know why. But I like your heart. Kai's lucky to have had you on this mission." She held the crystal mask, which she had wrapped gently in rabbit fur and placed in the roomy leather pouch in her left hand.

Feeling heat stealing into his face at Grams's words, Jake moved the cup gently between his hands. "Not different, Grams, just being myself is all."

Kai saw her grandmother's face grow solemn. Grams could see auras, and Kai knew she was looking at Jake's. This morning, Grams wore an old yellow robe made of fluffy polyester. It made her look like a fuzzy yellow duck, or maybe Big Bird. This picture of her grandmother, with her steel-gray hair in two thick, long braids hanging down the front of her yellow robe, was one Kai wanted to impress into her heart's memory forever. She loved Grams fiercely, for all she had done for her throughout her life.

"I remember your daddy saying you were different, too," Grams murmured, giving Jake a sly look as she sipped her coffee.

Chuckling, Jake said, "Oh, that… Well, I was pretty rebellious in my younger years. I'm sure that's what he was referring to."

"Maybe…maybe," Grams murmured. She smiled, reaching out and patting Jake's arm. "You're a good man. I like what you've grown into." She glanced down at the pouch again. "I'm going to take this over to the medicine people of the Paint Clan later on this afternoon. I know there will be a celebration ceremony planned for the whole nation because of its return." She looked at Kai. "You said someone was stalking you? That there's a white man involved in stealing our totems?"

"Yeah," Kai muttered, "the latest we heard from Mike Houston, who helped us get over to Australia to find the mask, was that a multimillionaire named Robert Marston is probably behind the theft of all three objects. And he sent us a photo of him and it's the same man I saw in my dreams. We can't prove anything yet, legally, though. I'll let you know when we find out more, though."

"Hmm. Marston? That is the man I suspected. I talked to Mabel Red Fox over at the Cherokee Museum about the thefts when they occurred last year. You remember her, don't you? She's taken care of that place forever and done a right good job of it."

Frowning, Kai searched her memory. "Mabel...yeah, I think I do. She's real old now, isn't she?"

Chuckling, Grams raised her steel-gray brows. "She's the same age as me, child."

"Oh...sorry."

Grinning, Ivy said, "Mabel is the curator of the museum, in case you forgot. She's steeped in Eastern Cherokee history and lore. I went to her right after the theft and I remember her saying that there was a list of rich men around the world who want our sacred ceremonial objects. I just betcha Marston's on that list." Grams frowned. "He's well known to all the Indian nations. He pays medicine people big sums of money to get artifacts and sacred things for his collection, from what Mabel told me. You know, there are a number of people in the world that hunger for power objects, and we have our fair share of such things." Her hand caressed the pouch that held the crystal. "It looks like this Marston fella set it all up."

"Sounds like a good probability," Jake murmured. He looked over at Kai. Today, she'd left her hair hanging free. Kai had a natural beauty that few women could match.

"Yes…I think I'll get Mike on the phone and give him this info. I'll also give him Mabel's name."

"Child, even if it was Marston who carried this off, how could he do this? Try to kill the two of you?"

"We can't be naive about this," Jake said quietly. "I've heard about rich folks who have the money to buy anything they want—and all they want is power. Who knows? This guy has hired a bunch of goons to go after us, with orders to do whatever was necessary to get the crystal totem, would be my guess."

"Great Spirit, help us," Grams whispered. "If this mask, or any of the other clan totems, falls into the wrong hands, there could be *real* trouble." She frowned and studied the pouch. "Each one of these totems is so very powerful. If someone knew the ceremony, which we keep secret, they could use this crystal to do whatever they wanted. If this Marston fella got his hands on the totem, he could use it to kill someone."

"Wow!" Jake said quietly. "I didn't know it could do that."

"Well, it depends upon who is handling these things, Jake, as to how they respond." Grams gently touched the pouch. "A medicine person with a good heart can ask the spirit of the crystal to do good things for others. A man like

Marston…well, he might use it to harm someone if he was angry at them."

"I didn't know the crystal had that kind of power," Kai murmured, staring at the pouch in utter surprise.

"The information is known only among medicine people, child. But weasels like Marston have gotten inside information. He must have. Otherwise, why would he try so hard to steal our clan totems?"

"Could he have paid off a medicine person to tell him about the ceremony and other information?" Jake wondered.

"Humph! It hurts to think that he might have been able to do that, but you know, two days after the theft, John Otter, who was a trained medicine man, suddenly ended up dead."

Kai raised her brows. "Oh? I remember Otter. He was a drunk just like my old man was."

"I'm afraid so, child." Shaking her head, Grams said, "I just don't want to believe that John would sell out his nation's sacred totems to Marston for money."

Jake reached out and patted Grams's arm. "People with that kind of addiction would sell their souls for another drink. Otter might have found himself desperate enough to give Marston the information."

"Yeah," Kai said, "He might have told Marston exactly where the Ark of Crystals was kept. Marston is rich enough to hire anyone to come and take them. They knew where to look. Who to go to."

Rubbing his chin thoughtfully, Jake looked up at the ceiling of the log cabin. "And if Otter did sell out, it would make sense that Marston had him killed. Why have a drunk raving about it?" Jake looked over at Grams. "Was any cause of death determined?"

Shrugging, she said, "He was found dead on a back road. The res police said it was a hit-and-run. They never found out who did it. There were no witnesses."

Kai gave Jake a worried look. "You think Marston had Otter murdered?"

"Sure, why not? It would make sense to keep him quiet. A drunk never keeps a secret. You know that." Jake gave Kai an apologetic look. Seeing the momentary pain flit across her eyes, he placed his hand on her arm and gave it a slight squeeze. When she nodded her head, Jake withdrew his hand even though he didn't want to.

"What's even more troubling," Grams murmured, "is that John may have given Marston the ceremony for these totems. I just now thought of that."

Frowning, Kai asked, "Would Otter have known those ceremonies?"

"Of course he would." Tapping her chin, Ivy sighed. "Oh, if he did give that secret away, that means we're in a heap of trouble. If Marston gets his hands on any one of the totems, he can wreak havoc on earth."

"What did Mike find out, Kai?" Jake asked as he sat with her the next morning at the Blue Heron Hotel restaurant, plates of scrambled eggs, bacon and grits before them. They'd taken two rooms under assumed names just outside the res. Yesterday she'd given the info about Marston to Houston, and they'd chosen this restaurant, which wasn't busy, so they could talk without others overhearing their conversation.

"Just after you came down here to order breakfast, Mike called." She picked up her utensils and began to cut into the fluffy scrambled eggs mixed with parsley, cheddar cheese and bits of ham. "He said Marston is our enemy as far as he's concerned. There's lots of peripheral evidence that makes Mike fear he's the culprit. The dude is well known as an amateur archeologist, and he's got a world-class collection of sacred objects that most museum curators would die to have."

Spearing a piece of bacon, Jake said, "Is there any proof he hired those men in Australia to nail our hides?"

"Mike's still working on that angle," Kai picked up her coffee and sipped it. "They've taken DNA samples from the two dudes found in the Huey crash. So far, the Aussie police didn't find any identification on them that they could use. The helo was pretty well burned up."

"Yeah, but what about their names on the manifest at the Yulara airport?"

Shrugging, Kai murmured, "They didn't file a flight plan, Jake. There are no names. No trail to follow. The Huey was owned by Marston Enterprises—that much is a fact. Mike's now getting the Aussie police to contact the company. He thinks it's a front, and so do I, for running stolen objects for Marston when he wants them sent to his Hong Kong home."

Kai wore a pink mohair vest with a bright red long-sleeved shirt beneath it. Instead of her Rail Riders, she had put on a trim-looking pair of tan wool slacks. Jake noticed that she wore small coral and sterling silver earrings to complement her outfit. Today she looked highly feminine, and he wondered why the change. Not that he didn't like it. He'd never seen Kai in a dress or skirt, but her life on a Navy carrier would discourage her wearing anything but a flight suit.

Stopping himself from devouring her with his gaze, Jake decided he'd better concentrate on eating his breakfast. "Well, we know someone wants the totems."

"That's right…." Kai studied Jake across the table. Despite the lingering questions, she was enjoying their time together in the small hotel. It was an old Victorian that the owner had lovingly restored and brought back to life. She liked the soft classical music playing in the restaurant, the many green plants in decorative pots that graced the small dining area. It was like bringing nature indoors, and Kai appreciated the gesture.

Finishing his breakfast, Jake sipped his orange juice, watching Kai butter her toast and slather grape jelly across each piece. Smiling to himself, he recalled Kai's love of grape jelly and peanut butter sandwiches as a child.

"Remember how I used to steal jars of grape jelly and peanut butter from my home and bring them out to the beech tree for you?"

Lifting her head, Kai drowned in his warm golden eyes. Her heart responded to the tender smile pulling at Jake's well-shaped mouth. There was nothing to dislike about him. This morning he wore a simple fisherman's cream-colored sweater with a light blue cotton shirt beneath it, the collar visible above the crew neck. The pair of stone-washed blue jeans he wore emphasized his long, hard thighs. As always, he wore a pair of dark brown leather boots. In this weather, with below-freezing temperatures at night, it would be foolish to wear street shoes.

Kai smiled wryly. "Yeah... You knew that was my favorite sandwich, and you always had those jars tucked away in a box behind the beech."

Warm feelings threaded through his heart as he saw her blue eyes soften at that shared memory. "We've got a lot of past history with one another."

"I know...."

Fear stabbed at Jake. He took another sip of juice and set his glass and plate aside. Folding his hands on the table, he murmured, "You thought about what you're going to do now that you've retrieved the crystal mask, Kai?"

Nodding, she wiped her mouth with the white linen napkin and dropped her hands in her lap. "I've been thinking a lot about what Grams said the other day, about looking ahead." Her heart beat a little harder. "I need to get a job. But it has to be something I love to do."

"You have any ideas about that?" Jake held his breath. Kai always kept her cards close to her chest. She wasn't one to confide in anyone; she'd learned not to in childhood.

Rubbing her brow, she set her own plate aside, picked up her coffee cup and rested her elbows on the table. Staring at Jake, she saw worry in his darkening gold gaze. His mouth, usually so quick to show that little-boy smile of his, was pursed.

"I did...and I'd like to discuss it in a minute with you. Right now, I'd rather tell you that I had another dream last night," she said in a low voice.

"Like the original vision you had?" Jake remembered

Grams saying that Kai would be given another dream, about the woman who would be responsible for finding the next clan totem.

Quirking her lips, Kai held the cup between her hands. "It was about the totems. I saw her, Jake. I saw the seven-pointed star crystal appear, and then I saw her face—the woman who's supposed to find it. She's got straight dark brown hair that barely brushes her shoulders. Her face is oval, and she has high cheekbones and green eyes." She saw Jake studying her intently. "This is all so crazy to me…"

Pursing her lips, she went on. "She was standing on a gold sand beach and I could see a city in the background. And then I saw this black snake crawling around her feet, and I heard hissing."

"Okay," Jake murmured, "so far so good. At least you know what she looks like. Did you get a city name? Her name?"

Shrugging, Kai muttered. "I heard Lima. I guess that's Lima, Peru. But what would our clan totem be doing down *there?*" She threw up her hands in frustration. "This dream doesn't make sense to me! I'm afraid I'm making it up, because I feel pressure to produce something for Grams, so our nation can find the other two totems. I don't know…."

"Listen to me," Jake whispered, gently placing his hand over hers, "you're *not* making this up, Kai. Whatever you dreamed is solid. We've seen it before. You were told where Ooranye lived, shown things you needed to know. What else did you see or hear?" Jake could see Kai fighting the dream and its meaning. She was a no-nonsense combat warrior having mystical experiences, and she still wasn't entirely used to it.

"I saw an Apache helicopter," she muttered, lowering her eyes. "And you fly one. So that's why I think I'm making this all up. I must be—"

His fingers tightened around her hand. "What else did they show you?"

"She was wearing a black uniform of some kind with a mandarin collar. I could only see her head and shoulders...."

"What color was the Apache?"

"Black."

Jake patted her hand, then released it. "Then it belongs to a black ops outfit, Kai. The ones I know of are camouflaged either in jungle or desert color schemes. I know some are painted black, but I don't know where they're stationed." He smiled as he saw her perk up a little. "This is something we can talk to Mike Houston about. Perseus is part of the inner circle of secret squadrons around the world. He'd know who has black Apache helicopters, I bet."

"Okay... I still think it's a wild-goose chase."

"I don't. You still look bothered by something. Care to share?" Jake liked the intimacy that was developing between them. He craved more of it. Seeing Kai give him a sheepish look, he smiled more broadly. "Remember? I'm the one whose shoulder you always cried on? How many times did we sit and talk about what was bothering you?" Jake was glad he had been there for Kai. He wondered what she would have done if she hadn't had someone to lean on. Would she have turned to drugs? Been so rebellious that she broke the law and got sent to juvy court? None of the possibilities were good.

"It concerns you—and me." Kai felt her heart pounding with dread. "And I'm afraid. Me, of all people! I can with no problem stare down a SAM missile trying to knock me out of the sky, but when it comes to confronting myself and how I feel about you, I'm scared to the point of losing my voice." Kai gave him a twisted smile and set her coffee down as the waitress came over and took their dishes away. When they were alone again, Kai devoted all her attention to Jake, who was sitting relaxed, eyes curious.

"I'm going to take Mike Houston up on his offer to work for Perseus." She waved her hand in a helpless gesture. "I'm cut out for combat, Jake. I hate the idea of not being in the military, and yet no one will have me now with a BCD."

"That's good news," Jake murmured. "So why are you looking like your best friend died?" His mouth quirked slightly. Jake felt Kai searching for words. She was nervous, shifting her feet repeatedly beneath the table and occasionally bumping his boots. She got that way when something really serious was bothering her.

"Well…dammit, Jake, this isn't easy…." Her nostrils flared as she looked at him.

"Can I help you?"

"No…this is mine to say." Taking a huge gulp of air, Kai held his warm gaze and said, "I didn't think I was ready for another relationship after Ted. I was really burned, Jake. And then you dropped into my life. I never thought I'd see you again, but here you are…."

"I hope I haven't always been a pain in the ass, Kai. I know you didn't want me along on this mission at first."

Jake held her troubled blue gaze. She was gnawing her lower lip now, a sure sign of agitation. In fact, Kai looked as if she was going to burst if she didn't get out what was eating her. Jake had no way to help her because he didn't know what she was trying to say. Instead, he slid his hand over hers. "In the past, I was your best friend, Kai. You can look back on our history and know that I care, that I'll listen to whatever's bothering you—"

"That's just it," Kai whispered, her voice strangled. She gripped Jake's hand. "I guess I changed my mind about you—about us. Don't ask me when it happened. Maybe it was in the hut, when I crawled into your arms." Shaking her head, she muttered, "I had forgotten what it was like to be held by someone who cared for me. How could I have forgotten that, Jake?"

"Time and life events have a funny way of doing things like that," he murmured.

"Maybe you're right." She took a deep breath. "Okay, here goes. I know Perseus demands a man-woman team on missions. I got to thinking that, since I'm joining, maybe you would think about it, too. That way, we'd be together…" Kai looked at him through her lashes, fear washing through her as she saw his surprise. "Mike told me before we left that your contract with the military is up in a couple of months, and that it would be time to re-up…or quit."

"Would you want me as a partner?" He was afraid of her answer and saw cloudiness come to her blue eyes.

"Yes, I would."

Watching Kai brush her hair away from her brow, Jake said, "I'd like to think that I contributed positively on this last mission." Opening his hand, he added earnestly, "We're a good team, Kai. We work well together. What one of us didn't have, the other one did and vice versa."

Nodding, Kai scowled down at her tightly clenched hands. "I know…. I already talked to Mike Houston about that aspect and…us…."

Jake's heart thudded once to underscore the moment. Oh, he would miss flying his combat helo, no doubt about it, but on a scale of one to ten, he'd much rather be with Kai. Besides, there was danger connected to many Perseus missions, and the last thing he wanted to do was leave Kai open to attack. He simply couldn't fathom losing her now that he'd rediscovered her.

"Well…" Kai muttered, "you have a decision to make." She forced herself to look at Jake, whose face wore a serious scowl. Taking a deep breath, she said, "I owe you an apology of sorts…and I'm as close as I ever come to making one…."

Jake sat back in surprise. "Apology? For what?" He saw a real struggle on Kai's face, the way her lips thinned, her eyes narrowed as she pulled her gaze away from him and looked up at the ceiling.

"I was wrong and Mike was right. I did need a partner on this mission. I didn't see the danger coming. I really didn't think I'd find the crystal mask, much less encounter someone willing to kill us to get it." Licking her lips, Kai shifted her gaze back to Jake, who was looking stunned in the aftermath of her admission. "I'm a proud person, Jake. Maybe too proud. I've been on my own so long that I thought I didn't need anybody for anything. I could and did make it solo." She waved her hand in a frustrated motion. "The Navy torpedoed me with their prejudices against a good woman combat pilot, but that's the past and I gotta get beyond it." Kai pushed her fingers through her hair in a nervous motion. "Mike really nailed my hide to the wall this morning in that phone call. He told me that if it hadn't been for your skills as a helicopter pilot, I'd be dead meat right now and that crystal mask wouldn't be home safe, but in the hands of someone who wanted it for the wrong reasons."

Jake saw Kai struggling mightily to own up to her mistakes. His heart beat a little harder. She wanted him as a partner on future missions. Jake wanted to be a part of her life.

Kai muttered, "Damn, this is hard…" She blew a shaky breath of air between her taut lips. "Would you consider coming to work at Perseus—with me? Please?"

Jake waited. He was scared in so many ways. Funny, how he'd ached to hear her say that she needed him, and now that the words were spoken, his heart hammered violently in his chest. Did dreams really come true? Was this all a fantasy of his?

"Okay," Kai muttered defiantly, "here's the bottom line, Jake. Mike asked me who I wanted as a partner when I joined Perseus." She gave him a flat stare across the table. "I told him I wanted you."

Jake could hear the growl in her tone. He saw the struggle in her eyes. "You could have chosen someone else."

"Yeah, I could have…but no one has the background you have. Between you and Ooranye, I learned so much out there about our Native American cultural legacy. Growing up, you learned a lot from your mother, a practicing medicine woman, and you remember a lot of things that helped that mission in Australia move forward. Without your knowledge, I'd have been dead in the water."

"Thank you...."

"Don't sit there looking so pleased, Carter. This is a tough thing for me to admit...."

Jake said, "I appreciate your honesty, Kai. It becomes you, and it makes me feel like I wasn't just dead wood on that mission."

Eyes wide, she stared at him, her mouth dropping open for a moment. "Dead wood? You? Hell, Jake, we'd have been toast several times over if you hadn't been there. I didn't know a thing about camels, or rock climbing, or helicopters...."

Chuckling, Jake said, "Some of that was pure coincidence, Kai."

"Maybe," she muttered defiantly, giving him a stern look. Seeing the little-boy smile lurking at the corners of his mouth sent her heart skittering as it always did.

"I know I'm asking a lot of you, out of the blue. Is it too much? Are you set on doing twenty years in the Army? Maybe you don't...want to be around me again...." That hurt to say, but Kai had to be ruthlessly honest. She was asking Jake to leave his way of life for hers. Holding her breath, she waited.

Jake's face thawed of all the tension he'd been holding. He squeezed her fingers gently. "Somewhere along the way, Kai, I lost the dream I had for us. When we were kids...well, all I did was hope that someday we'd be together." He shook his head and held her gaze. "When you were ripped out of my life, the dream cracked and shattered. So did my heart. You were the other half of me. It took me ten years to get over feeling like I was only partly there. Like I was missing half of myself." He lifted her hand to his lips and kissed her skin. "And now I can't imagine life without you again. Yes, I'll finish off my two months with the Army. I'll come to work for Perseus, to be your partner on other missions."

Warmth flooded her. Jake really wanted to be with her! "I'm cranky sometimes, Jake," she warned.

"We all have our moments," he told her mildly.

"And I don't trust very much…. I know it's a weakness in me."

"I'll work hard to gain your trust, Kai."

She muttered, "You make it so easy, Jake. You did when I was a kid. You're doing it now."

He got up and pulled her to her feet. "Come on," he urged her quietly, "let's go to one of our rooms and finish this talk."

Kai nodded, so Jake paid the bill and they left. The day was cold and breezy, the last of the leaves blowing off the trees surrounding the hotel. Heart beating with joy and fear, she unlocked her room and they went in together.

Putting the key on the dresser, Kai turned and saw Jake shut the door behind him. Looking into his eyes, she watched him walk toward her. Swallowing hard, she felt some of her fear and trepidation dissolving with each step he took. This was the little boy who had given her a haven so long ago. This was the man who loved her.

Kai realized it was true. Jake had never stopped loving her. Had she ever not loved him?

Jake halted in front of her and placed his hands on her proud shoulders. Giving him a quizzical look, she whispered, "You love me, don't you?"

Smiling, Jake gazed into her wide blue eyes. "I never stopped loving you, Kai."

"What a fool I've been," she muttered, and slid her arms around his neck.

"You're still raw, Kai. I can see it in your eyes. I hear it in your voice." Lifting one hand, Jake brushed her cheek with his fingers. Her lashes closed partially in reaction, her lips parting slightly. "I don't want to rush you. If you want a partner to work with, then I'm the man for you. I don't mix and match here. You said you wanted a partner for missions." How close she was. How proud and beautiful and strong. Jake ached to take her, to love her. His body was hard and screaming. He was old enough to know not to get selfish with her because of his own needs right now. If he did, Kai would retreat. Possibly walk out of his life—for good. That threat was enough to make him walk a fine line. She had to want *him,* not just the other way around. It wouldn't work if she didn't come to him first—just as she had crawled into his arms that day in Australia. That had been the sweetest moment he'd experienced since she'd been taken from him.

"I'm scared, Jake. Scared and happy. I feel like yelling at the world and jumping up and down for joy at the same time. I also feel like this is a dream and I'll get ripped out of it at any moment."

As he slid his fingers across her cheek, she pressed against his open palm and closed her eyes. Such trust. Yes, she was trusting him. "I feel the same way. We're reacting to what happened when we were young, Kai. But we've grown up. We're adults now, and in control of our own lives." A smile hitched one corner of his mouth as she opened her eyes, turned her head and pressed her lips into his palm. His flesh tingled wildly. His heart began hammering.

"You're right," she murmured, burning beneath his hooded look. Jake wanted her. Kai felt her entire body, every single cell, respond to his scalding gaze.

Jake stood there, frozen. She had kissed his palm. Kai was such a surprise. He'd never thought she'd do that. Feeling overwhelmed, yet not wanting to let her go, he leaned his head forward and whispered, "Kai, I want to kiss you in the worst damn way…but this has to be mutual…."

Laughing softly, Kai lifted her head and melted beneath his gaze. "Then kiss me, Jake Stands Alone Carter. Kiss me and join our past with our present…." And she stepped forward and pressed her body against his.

Closing her eyes, Kai relaxed fully against Jake as his arms folded tightly around her. The breath exploded from her as she melted into him. Turning her head slightly, she met his descending mouth, her world coming to a halt.

As his mouth slid across her smiling lips, Kai moaned with desire. She moved her arms around his neck, holding him as tightly as she could, drinking and sipping from his strong male lips. As she did, she had a flash of memory— of that one shy kiss he'd shared with her once beneath the old beech tree. Now he was a man, strong, capable and filled with incredible confidence.

Lips parting, she moved her tongue in a slow, delicious

arc against his. Jake groaned. His arms tightened around her. So many flashes of the past arced through her mind's eye as his mouth kissed hers with tenderness, coaxing, then a fierce intensity. Her mind was turning to mush, her thoughts shorting out. Kai was aware of his hand cradling her head, his fingers tangled in the strands of her hair. His other arm held her close, a willing captive who wanted more and more of him.

Their breathing became chaotic, their mouths wet as they slid against one another, taking and giving. Kai felt an insatiable hunger for Jake, so powerful that it caught her completely off guard. Breaking contact with his mouth, she breathed heavily. The need she felt was dizzying. It scared the living hell out of her.

Jake eased away. Kai's eyes were a soft blue now, the pupils huge and black as she stared wordlessly at him. Giving her a boyish smile, he said, "That was some kiss! It almost makes up for all the ones we never got before this…."

Giving him a rueful look, Kai reached up and slid her hand against his cheek. "One kiss…" He'd shaved recently and she could feel the sandpapery quality of his beard beneath her fingertips.

Jake closed his eyes and absorbed Kai's touch. His heart was pounding so hard he thought it might explode out of his body. Aching to take her, but knowing it wasn't the right time, he opened his eyes and stared into hers. "I can see you're shaken, Kai."

"Yeah…a lot…" She felt heat flood her face as she eased a few inches away from him. Jake's arms settled around her waist, and she was glad that he'd given her that freedom. "I don't know what it is about you, but you always seem to read my mind about what I need and when I need it."

Jake shrugged. "Just lucky, I guess." He saw that she didn't believe him, and gave her a rueful smile. "Maybe it's because I love you, Kai. When you love someone it's easy to read them, to know where they're at, what their needs are."

Nodding, Kai whispered, "I know you love me…."

Jake knew she wasn't ready to say that to him. "It's a love that's been there from the day we met, Kai. It never went away. It's always been in me."

"You're the most patient person in the world, Carter. Either that or a glutton for punishment, wanting to love someone like me."

He understood why she'd said that. It came out of her haunting past, when her father had told her she was ugly and would never amount to anything. Threading his fingers through her hair, Jake said, "Listen, you're easy to love. But you need to believe it, Kai. I could tell you forever, but until you realize it, what I tell you will fall on deaf ears."

"Are you okay with our relationship as it is? I need time…."

"You've got all the time in the world, Kai." Jake released her and touched his heart. "I've waited this long. Waiting some more with you at my side isn't going to be a stress, believe me."

Kai smiled tremulously. "Okay…then we need to tell Mike our decision. I know he'll offer you a job."

"I'm sure he will," Jake told her. He walked Kai over to the sofa in their suite. Sitting down with her, he opened the cell phone he'd taken from his pocket.

"I'm still in charge of our team," she said, a warning in her voice.

"Of course you are. I'll be your shadow, Kai. I'll be there when you need me, and when you don't, I'll stand back. Listen to me, will you?" Jake leaned forward, his voice rough with emotion. "Remember, we're a matriarchal nation, and my mother raised me to know that women were just as strong—even more so, in some respects—as men. She never made me feel less than worthy, either. We just bring different skills and abilities to the table, that's all. I really respect what you have and I want to support you any way I can."

His impassioned words moved through her and touched her heart as nothing else could have done. Leaning back on the couch, her hands resting in her lap, Kai asked, "Do you always say the right thing, Carter?"

"On some days, I get lucky." And Jake chuckled as he saw her mouth curve into a smile.

* * * * *

Be sure to pick up Lindsay McKenna's next
Silhouette Bombshell title
SISTER OF FORTUNE,
in December 2004.

Also available from Lindsay McKenna

MORGAN'S LEGACY
February 2004

MORGAN'S HONOR
April 2004

FIRSTBORN
June 2004

DAUGHTER OF DESTINY
July 2004

And coming in December 2004,
book two of SISTER OF FORTUNE,
only from Silhouette Bombshell.

ATHENA FORCE

Chosen for their talents.
Trained to be the best.

Expected to change the world.

The women of Athena Academy
share an unforgettable experience
and an unbreakable bond—until
one of their own is murdered.

The adventure begins with these six books:

PROOF by Justine Davis, July 2004

ALIAS by Amy J. Fetzer, August 2004

EXPOSED by Katherine Garbera,
September 2004

DOUBLE-CROSS by Meredith Fletcher,
October 2004

PURSUED by Catherine Mann, November 2004

JUSTICE by Debra Webb, December 2004

**And look for six more Athena Force stories
January to June 2005.**

Available at your favorite retail outlet.

www.SilhouetteBombshell.com   SBAF04

and *USA TODAY* bestselling author

JULIE BEARD

bring you

**Twenty-second century crime fighter
Angel Baker in her first adventure**

KISS
OF THE BLUE
DRAGON

An Angel Baker Novel.

Angel Baker's goal is to rid the
world of crime—and have a life.
But her mother's kidnapping forces
Angel to come to terms with powers
she didn't know she possessed.
When the trail leads her into
Chicago's dark criminal underworld,
she must call on new reserves of
strength and determination—and
work around one very stubborn
detective. It's all in a day's work....

Available at your favorite retail outlet.

www.SilhouetteBombshell.com   SBABN1

HARLEQUIN®
INTRIGUE®

No cover charge.
No I.D. required.
Secrecy guaranteed.

CLUB UNDERCOVER

You're on
the guest list
for the hottest
romantic-suspense
series from

PATRICIA ROSEMOOR

A team of outcast specialists with their own dark secrets has banded together at Chicago's hottest nightclub to defend the innocent...and find love and redemption along the way.

 VELVET ROPES
July 2004

 ON THE LIST
August 2004

Look for them wherever Harlequin books are sold!

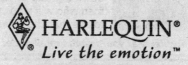

HARLEQUIN®
Live the emotion™

www.eHarlequin.com

HICU04

Silhouette®
BOMBSHELL

introduces a richly imaginative miniseries
from veteran author

EVELYN VAUGHN

**The Grail Keepers—Going for the grail
with the goddess on their side**

Don't miss modern-day goddess Maggie Sanger's
first appearance in

A.K.A. GODDESS

August 2004

Is Maggie Sanger's special
calling a gift or a curse?
The ability to find mysterious
and ancient grails and protect
them from destruction is in
her blood. But when her
research is stolen and
suspicion falls on her
ex-lover, Maggie must
uncover the truth about
her birthright and face
down a group of powerful
men who will stop at nothing
to see that she fails....

Available at your favorite retail outlet.

www.SilhouetteBombshell.com   SBGK1

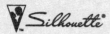

Silhouette®

INTIMATE MOMENTS™

From *New York Times* Bestselling Author

HEATHER GRAHAM

IN THE DARK

(Silhouette Intimate Moments #1309)

After she'd stumbled onto the body of a dead woman, Alexandra McCord's working paradise had turned into a nightmare. With a hurricane raging, Alex was stranded with her ex-husband, David Denham—the man she'd never forgotten. And even though his sudden return cast doubt on his motives, Alex had no choice but to trust in the safety of his embrace. Because a murderer was walking among them and no matter what, she knew her heart—or her life—would be forfeit.

Available at your favorite retail outlet.

Visit Silhouette Books at www.eHarlequin.com

SIMIT

Silhouette
BOMBSHELL

COMING NEXT MONTH

#5 KISS OF THE BLUE DRAGON—Julie Beard

Angel Baker wasn't your typical twenty-second-century girl—she was trying to rid the world of crime and have a life. Then her mother was kidnapped and Angel was forced to rely on powers she didn't know she possessed, and was drawn to the one sexy detective she shouldn't be....

#6 ALIAS—Amy J. Fetzer

An Athena Force Adventure

Darcy Steele was once the kind of woman friends counted on, until her bad marriage forced her to live in hiding. But when a killer threatened the lives of her former schoolmates, she had to help, even if it meant risking her life—and her heart—again.

#7 A.K.A. GODDESS—Evelyn Vaughan

The Grail Keepers

Modern-day grail keeper Maggie Sanger was on a quest, charged with recovering the lost chalices of female power. But when her research was stolen and suspicion fell on her ex-lover, Maggie was challenged to uncover the truth about the legacy she'd been born into—and the man she once loved.

#8 URBAN LEGEND—Erica Orloff

Tessa Van Doren owned the hottest nightclub in all of Manhattan, but rumors swirled around that she was a vampire. Little did anyone know this creature of the night had a cause to down the criminals who had killed her lover. Not even rugged cop Tony Flynn, who stalked her night after night....

SBCNM0704